WITH A KISS DUET
BOOK TWO

# SINS
## *of*
# BLISS

## A.R. ROSE

# OTHER TITLES BY A.R. ROSE

**Ridgewood Series**
Between the Flames
Wicked Games We Play
Marked By Cain

**Standalones**
Wreck Me
Only One Night

**Twisted Heroes**
Siren

**With a Kiss**
Sins of Sorrow
The Sinners

Deny thy father and refuse thy name, Or if thou wilt
not, be but sworn my love, And I'll no longer be a
Capulet.

-*William Shakespeare*

*To my amazing readers - I promised I'd mend your heart in this book, but I never promised to do it quickly. Just remember as you hate me, I love you.*

# Sins of Bliss Playlist

Not Afraid Anymore - Halsey
War of Hearts - Ruelle
What a Time - Julia Michaels, Niall Horan
Unsteady - X Ambassadors
Lose Control - Teddy Swims
Mercy - Shawn Mendes
Silence - Marshmallow, Khalid
I Walk The Line - Halsey
Are You With Me - nilu
Lie - Halsey, Quavo
But Daddy I Love Him - Taylor Swift

# A Note from A.R. Rose

Sins of Bliss is a contemporary romance novel created for adults. This story depicts dark adult scenes and situations. This book cannot be read as standalone.

Reader discretion is advised. Sins of Bliss contains content that may be triggering for some.

Your mental health matters. For a full list of content warnings please visit www.authorarrose.com/content-warnings.

For those of you ready to begin, I hope you enjoy.

# Previously in Sins of Sorrow

## Vinnie - Bonus Chapter

*The Day Sly Left*

My head throbs as my eyes fight to open. There's a heaviness behind them, a desperate need to stay closed. I don't understand. Confusion swirls as I struggle to open my eyes. The slivers of light make the pain in my head worse.

The slamming of a door sounds from inside the apartment, and I groan as my head rolls to the side to see who it is. There's a searing ache at my hairline, and as carefully as possible, I reach up to touch it, feeling the spot wet and sticky.

Whimpering from the way it stings, I hold my hand up to see my fingertips covered in blood.

"Vinnie?" Lia's voice calls out as her footsteps draw near.

A silent tear slips from my eyes and rolls down my cheek.

"I'm in here," I croak, my throat dry and hoarse.

Cecilia pushes open my bedroom door, and the moment she sees me on the floor, she falls to her knees at my side.

"Oh, my gosh! Vinnie! What happened? Are you okay?" She's frantic. Her hands are all over me, pushing my hair from my face, cradling my neck with the back of her hand as she assesses the spot at my hairline. "I'm calling 9-1-1."

"No," I croak again, my lips darting out to wet my lips. "I'm okay. Call Dr. Yang."

"O–okay," she stammers. Then, with confidence, as though she's flipped a switch and turned her fear off, she nods. "Okay." Pulling her phone out, she calls my primary doctor.

Dr. Yang has been my doctor since I moved out of my parents' house and left the family doctor. I wanted her to call *him*, knowing he will make a house call and save me a trip to the hospital, along with the unnecessary paperwork, *and* the press.

"He's on his way," she tells me after a brief conversation with him. "I want to move you to the bed, then I'm going to get you a wet compress for your head and try to clean you up a little. It looks like the bleeding has stopped already, though, so that's a good sign."

As she slides her hand out from under my neck, I wince a little again. My neck and shoulders are sore.

"Vinnie, *what happened?*"

For a moment, everything is a blur, but then the memory returns crystal clear.

August, entering my home and my room. The file. The photos. The threats.

And then the assault.

*Sly.*

I was supposed to meet Sly.

I'm late!

Pressing my palms into the floorboards, I try to sit up. "What time is it?"

My head feels light, and my vision swims. I can feel my body sway, and Lia wraps her arms around me. "Hey, I've got you. You're okay, Vin."

"What time is it?" I repeat, closing my eyes to try and keep myself from crying.

"Around one-thirty," she tells me, and as the words leave her lips, my heart falls.

"I've got to go." My hands claw at my bed, trying to grab onto it to help myself up, but my limbs feel like they weigh a thousand pounds. The more elevation I get, the more intensely my head throbs, and the woozy feeling settles in.

My stomach rolls, nausea reaching all the way in my throat.

"You look green," Cecilia says as she helps me stand.

My body falls forward, my palms landing flat and sticking to the glossy photos scattered across my duvet. "I think I'm going to be sick."

Lia keeps one hand on my back as she picks up a pile of photos with the other. "What is all of this?"

Letting them drop, she pushes as many as she can out of the way so I have a place to lay.

"August—he did this. He found out about me and Sly and had us followed." I take a deep breath, still trying to inflate my lungs and steady my heart. "I was about to leave to meet Sly to tell him I want to tell our families about us when August showed up. He let himself in somehow, then showed me all this. I thought he was bluffing, Lia. Just trying to scare me into submission. Then he hit me, and I guess I hit my head as I fell."

Her grip on my hand tightens when I told her August hit me. "We should call the police."

"No," I say with conviction. "We can't. He's already threatening to kill Sly, Cecilia. I won't let August hurt him."

"It's not your battle to fight, Vinnie. If we report him to the police, they can handle this."

"The police won't protect him. August and my brother have most of them in their pockets. The only one who can protect Sly is *me*, and I'll do that in whatever way I have to. August won't hurt him, Cecilia. I won't let him."

"Even at the cost of your own happiness?"

"Sly *is* my happiness, and what August wants is me. If that's the price to pay to keep Sly safe, then so be it."

Cecilia blows out a shaky breath. "Sly is a big boy. His family is just as powerful as yours is—and August's. Why don't you let him handle it?"

I pick up a handful of photos that I can reach and

shake them in between us. "*This* is why. Sly is meticulous. He is street smart and knows the good and the bad sides of people. If he didn't suspect August was having us followed, even on the most secluded of dates, it means August is more conniving than we thought. I *can't* tell Sly until I have a better idea of what I'm dealing with."

She nods several times, taking in everything I'm saying. Her eyes squeeze shut for a moment, and she blows out another breath. "Okay. We'll figure it out. I'm here for you, always. You know that. You're not in this alone, and we *will* figure it out. Together."

"Thank you." I squeeze her hand.

"The doctor will be here any minute. Let me go get that washcloth really quick."

"Could you hand me my phone first? I have to call Sly. I'm supposed to be there." My voice cracks, and a fresh round of tears streams down my face. It makes my jaw clench, which only pulsates my headache further.

My face must show my pain, because Cecilia brushes her fingers across my temple, pushing a little at the spot as she rubs it to try and relieve some of the ache.

"I think you have a concussion," she tells me as she hands me my phone. "I'll just be a second. *Don't* fall asleep."

"Okay."

As much as I don't want to lie to Sly, I'll just tell him I slipped and fell, and that I'm waiting for the doctor to be evaluated. It's not too far from the truth, although he might be upset that I didn't call him first, since he's a doctor. I'll just tell him Cecilia called before I had the chance to.

The lie makes me nauseous all over again, but it's what I have to do to keep him safe.

My fingers dance across the screen as I type in my code and pull up my call log, pressing Sly's name as I pray to God he answers and gives me the chance to explain.

But his phone is off. Instead of ringing, the immediate sound of it clicking over to a generic voice mailbox that says it's full sounds through the speakers.

I hang up and try again, only for it to go straight to voicemail.

Refusing to accept it, I try again.

And again.

And again.

I try until the phone slips from my fingers as Lia takes it from me, the tears a constant river flowing down my cheeks and pooling at my collarbone.

*I'm too late.*

He probably thinks I purposely didn't show.

I'm too late.

*The voice mailbox is full and cannot accept any messages at this time.*

*Goodbye.*

*Beep.*

*Beep.*

*Beep.*

"But come what sorrow may, it can't offset
the joy I receive from one minute of being
in her sight.

*Act 2, Scene 6 - Romeo & Juliet*
*William Shakespeare*

# Prologue

## Vinnie

***Eight Months Ago***

"What's this?" I ask as August drops a manila file on the table in front of me, and I eye it skeptically.

I thought sneaking up to my parents' rooftop terrace after brunch, despite knowing I'd be out in the bitter cold, would grant me some alone time.

I should have known better.

Before reaching for the file, I pull my coat tighter around me. The air feels like snow is imminent, despite it being a little too early in the winter. But with the way the sky looks, I wouldn't be shocked to see little flurries come with the rain.

My eyes meet August's as my fingertips graze the folder. I shouldn't give him the satisfaction of even engaging in this conversation, but he somehow knows what buttons of mine to push.

His cocky smirk infuriates me, and I glare at him before returning to the file.

It's ordinary—the exact type he brought to my apartment when he turned my life upside down. My heart rate accelerates as I hesitate to see what's inside.

Finally, I flip the cover back. My breath hitches when I'm met with photos of Sly.

Forget the snow—a flurry spins in my stomach. Icy little butterflies come back to life as I look at his face, scattering the pictures to see them all, then pick up the one on top to study it closer.

Sly is crossing the street in a city I don't recognize, with a cigarette dangling from between his fingers. It's strange to see—smoking is not a habit I knew him to have.

Maybe it's new.

Setting the picture down, I pick up another while fighting back tears.

Sly's walking out of a building, but it's hard to distinguish where he may be from the way the photographer obviously zoomed in on his target. In the window to his left, a neon sign that reads *'too'* is visible.

My brows scrunch as my eyes trace over every inch of his body—searching for any sign, any clue. They catch on something wrapped around his upper arm, sticking out from his t-shirt.

Is that…plastic wrap?

Placing the picture down, I continue looking through the pile, sliding them around so they're all visible.

Looking up at August, I hold his gaze, hoping to distract him long enough to carry out a crazy, impulsive thought.

"Where is he?" I seethe, my voice surprisingly steady as I continue rifling through the photos, though this time it's for show.

When his gaze is locked on mine, his overly confident smile pinned on his face, I act.

As inconspicuously as possible, I push one of the pictures into the sleeve of my jacket. The air in my lungs constricts under August's heavy gaze and the fear of getting caught, but his eyes never dip to the movement of my fingertips.

When I'm sure the picture is safely tucked away, pushed deep into my sleeve, I drop my focus back to the table.

For a moment, I consider that August is lying. That these pictures are somehow fake, or old.

But my gut says they're recent.

*August knows where he is.*

It's been two weeks since Sly left.

Two weeks since I lost a piece of myself and signed my life over to the devil.

*It's to keep him safe,* I remind myself. *Everything is worth it as long as he's safe.*

But I haven't stopped loving him. I haven't stopped thinking about him every second of every day, keeping him with me in my heart.

August chuckles and plucks the photo from between my fingers, placing it back in the folder. He pushes the rest of the photos back in and closes the cover. Resting his palm on top of it, he looms over me, trying to make me feel small as he does.

"Oh, my lovely *fiancée*. Do you think I'm idiotic enough to tell you where your *boyfriend* is?" August sneers, tsking as he picks up the folder. Waving it in between us, his smile gleams. "This right here is my insurance policy. You *will* obey me, Vinnie. You will be a doting fiancée and wife, and in return, I'll let him live."

"Why are you doing this, August? You still haven't explained."

"And I don't need to, but if you must know, you're the picture-perfect bride, and I want you on my arm. Plus, you have something else I want."

"Which is?"

His smile widens. "You'll find out in due time, sweetheart. All you have to do is keep being the perfect little wife and everyone wins."

Emotion lodges in my throat, but I force it down, refusing to let August see the pain he's causing me. "And how can I be sure you'll uphold your end of the deal? I marry you, and Sly won't be harmed, or so you say. How will I know he's alive?"

August crosses his arms over his chest, clutching the file in his hand still. "I thought you might ask. It's a pity you have a brain inside that pretty little skull of yours. How do monthly photos sound? Proof of life, and whatnot."

"Bi-weekly," I counter immediately. The only way

I'll get through this is if I *know* he's out there living his life.

Narrowing his eyes, August thinks about it for a moment—I'm sure just to see me squirm. "Okay. Bi-weekly," he finally agrees.

A rush of air leaves my lungs in relief.

"We have dinner scheduled with the mayor on Thursday night, and the *New York Times* has been calling, wanting to interview us, so I'll be in touch," he taunts as he walks away. "Now, where's your smile, *wife*? Oh, and put your ring back on."

"I'm not your wife yet," I mutter, more to myself than him because he's already across the rooftop.

The door slams shut behind him, and once again, I'm alone.

But now, instead of finding solace in the quiet, my mind is filled with worry and regret.

Instinctively, I look around and make sure I truly am alone before I pull out the photograph still safely hiding in my sleeve, and stare down at it.

My fingertips trace Sly's face as a lone tear falls from my eye onto the image.

I'm overtaken with emotion as a single Shakespeare quote pops into my head—one from Romeo and Juliet, the play that holds uncanny parallels to my reality. The quote brings me little comfort, if any, still I repeat it in my head again, as I so often do.

*"Good night, good night! Parting is such sweet sorrow. That I shall say good night till it be morrow." William Shakespeare.*

But there's nothing sweet about our parting, only

sorrow. The only thing I can hope for, though it may not be tomorrow, is that I'll get to see Sly Lucchetti again one day, and hopefully, when that day comes, he will be happy, safe, and living his life as fully as he can.

That's the only thing that will make this hell I'm willingly marrying into worth it.

# Chapter 1

## *Vinnie*

***Now***

The sun's glare is blinding as it reflects off the edges of the silver platter on the table in front of me. It's filled to the brim with cheese, crackers, meats, and grapes that have been sitting out in the sun for far too long. No one, aside from me, seems to notice or care.

Obnoxious laughter floats through the air, full of fake enthusiasm and cattiness.

Another day, another rooftop luncheon.

I never used to mind coming to these events—in fact, I used to enjoy them. But that was months ago, before I became a shell of the woman I once was.

Grief will do that to a person. Make them hate the things they used to enjoy. Make them see darkness instead of light.

The first few months after Sly left were bearable.

Normal, even. Painful, but I kept a smile painted on my face as I pushed through my responsibilities and acted as though nothing was amiss.

I should have known better than to think I could continue through the motions. Somewhere around month four was when August *insisted* we move in together.

We're getting married, after all.

With my refusal to cohabitate came another attack. This time, he was more careful—only leaving bruises where they couldn't be seen. Wouldn't want to draw suspicion that New York's most loved man is actually a monster.

I knew moving in with him would be dangerous to my safety, but I feared what he would do if I refused again. Would he lift his hand to me? Kick me while I was on the ground? Knock me unconscious?

These were all things he's done to me—just the lovely side of August the world doesn't get to see, but when I rile him up, or even when I don't, he shows me his true colors.

The only thing stopping me from running, hiding, and refusing to live with him, is the looming threat that he'll turn his anger toward the one person I'm trying to protect.

It isn't worth finding out if he'll make good on that threat.

So, I packed up my daily belongings and moved in with my fiancè, leaving the solitude of my apartment in the hands of Cecilia, who begged me not to go.

But I had to. I had no choice.

Every two weeks, August brings me new photos of Sly. Evidence that he's still breathing and living his life. Those snapshots are my only reason to keep going—they keep me focused. Reminding me the only thing standing between Sly and the threat August placed on his head is my compliance.

Still, every photo of him ignites an ache in my heart that takes another two weeks to dissipate, only for the wound to reopen when August drops more pictures in my lap.

He's dangling the bait, and I take it every time.

Seeing the images of Sly hurts even more because I now know where he is. August started leaving the pictures for me to keep a few months ago, and after weeks of piecing together buildings and road signs, I was able to reverse image search on the internet and figure out Sly is in a place called Ridgewood, California, a small city a little outside of San Francisco.

I have no idea why he ended up there, but knowing where he is brings me a little peace.

It's a blessing and a curse, getting these bi-weekly reminders, but I know once August and I are legally wed, it will stop. Once I'm no longer a flight risk, and everything August and Joseph want is finally obtained, the threat to Sly's life will end.

"Oh my gosh, Vinnie! How is wedding planning going?" Hera Whitney and her friend, Norah, take the open seats across from me. Hera is a hotel heiress who thinks she's God's gift to New York. She immediately dialed up her fakeness level with me once my engagement to August St. Jean became the talk of the town.

"I still haven't seen your ring in person," Norah comments, reaching her hand across the table, clamping her fingers open and closed to signal for me to give her my hand.

I don't.

"It's going great," I say simply before popping a grape into my mouth. I have no interest in speaking to either of them, let alone filling them in on wedding plans.

The truth is, my mother has taken the reins on those tasks, spearheading the event with grace and precision. Every detail has been thought of, no expense spared. The only decisions I've made are my dress and the flowers. Not that I care about any of it, but if I have to marry the worst man ever, these two elements of the wedding day will be exactly how I want them.

They'll be the only glimmer of happiness on what is supposed to be the best day of my life.

Instead, it will be the worst.

"Tell us everything!" Norah insists, not getting the hint.

Lifting my gaze, I find her leaning forward with her chin balanced on the top of her hand, waiting to hang on my every word.

"Spare no details," Hera adds, and when my eyes slide over to her, she's seated the same as Norah.

These women are staring at me as though I've stepped into the nickname the press gave me—the

Paladino *Princess*. Eight months ago, they couldn't have cared less about my life, and now they're begging me for details.

Unbelievable.

Shaking my head, I abruptly stand, and the chair groans against the floor as it's pushed out. Something inside of me snaps, and I become overwhelmed with emotion.

Anger.

Sadness.

Irritation.

As desperately as I want to give them the cold shoulder, manners and upbringing force me to excuse myself. "Ladies, I'm sorry. I'm not feeling well. Please excuse me."

My heart hammers in my chest as I walk away, ignoring the curious glances as I weave past the round tables.

I wish Raina was here with me, but she woke up sick and had to cancel. She would have calmed me down— she's become exceptionally good at grounding me when the world feels like it's caving in.

Reaching to open the door, my eyes catch on the glittering diamond situated on my left ring finger, and the nausea I felt earlier when I put it on hits me all over again. I take a deep breath and push through the door, letting it close behind me with a loud thud as I rush down the staircase.

The Townsend's two-story brownstone is familiar, having grown up with both their son and daughter, so I continue on down the second staircase until I reach their main floor. My back presses against the wall, and I work to steady myself, taking controlled breaths as I place my hand on my chest, giving myself a mental pep talk that everything is okay.

But everything's *not* okay. I miss him. Every day, it feels like he's slipping further and further away.

The depth of my love hasn't diminished, but the hope of there someday being an us again gets smaller and smaller.

Tears prick my eyes as I think about him, my back still pressed against the wall.

I'm right outside the kitchen and can hear the clattering of dishes and cookware, and the laughter of those inside. The scent of rosemary and butter wafts from the room—lunch must be close to being served.

Footsteps near, and I hear soft feminine voices speaking while they work. One is murmuring something I can hardly decipher, but then her voice raises enough for me to hear.

"Wait, which Lucchetti?" the other woman asks. The sound of a spoon hitting the side of a cup almost drowns out her voice.

I know I shouldn't eavesdrop, but hearing Sly's last name has me frozen in place.

"The runaway one!"

*Sly.*

I take a step to the side so that I'm closer to the edge of the wall and able to hear them better.

"He was shot? How do you know?"

My eyes widen, my hand flying to my mouth to stifle a whimper.

"My friend Misha is their housekeeper and called me right after she heard. Apparently, they got a call from the hospital this morning that he was admitted with a gunshot wound to the chest. Misha was the one who answered the phone. She watched Mrs. Lucchetti fall to her knees and sob. Said it was heartbreaking."

"But he's alive?" the woman presses.

I'm holding my breath, tears streaming silently down my cheeks as I lean in toward the open threshold, hanging on every word and praying to God that Sly is alive.

"Yeah. He's alive, but from what it sounds like, he's in pretty bad shape."

I can't listen anymore.

My stomach roils aggressively, practically forcing me to double over. Bile rises in my throat, and I don't think, I just move, running out of the house and onto the sidewalk, where I try to breathe.

Tears blur my vision as I pull my phone from the clutch I've held under my arm and text my driver, telling him to pick me up as soon as possible.

I begin to pace on the sidewalk as I pull up my phone's web browser and search for plane tickets for flights out of LaGuardia. The soonest flight to Ridgewood leaves in just under three hours, and I don't hesitate to input my credit card information and purchase a seat.

Ten minutes later, Ross, my driver, pulls alongside

the curb. I don't wait for him to get out before I throw open the door and climb inside.

Through the reflection of the rearview mirror, I see him quirk his brow at my quick entrance.

"Where to, Miss Paladino?" Ross asks tentatively, obviously gauging my mood.

I click my seatbelt into place. "Home. *My* apartment. And stay in the car because I need you to take me to the airport immediately."

He pulls out into traffic, his eyes bouncing between the road and me through the mirror. "The airport?"

"Yes, and Ross, it's imperative that this stays between us. You didn't take me to the airport. You dropped me off at my apartment, and that's the last time you saw me. Understand?"

Ross has never betrayed me, still, I feel the need to stress the importance of his discretion.

But right now, if I'm being honest, that's the least of my concerns.

A fresh wave of tears slides down my cheeks. Through the mirror, I see Ross' eyes soften as he nods once.

"I understand, Miss Paladino. Mum's the word."

I spend the drive to my apartment holding back a sob, consumed with thoughts of Sly and trying to figure out how I can get to him as fast as possible.

I need to see him. Touch him.

*Make sure he's breathing.*

It never occurred to me that while I was here,

making sure he stayed alive, there could be outside factors that would risk his life, too.

He can't die.

He can't.

I love him too much. *Need* him too much. I'll do anything to keep him alive.

But as we pull into the underground parking structure of my building, I realize it's not up to me. I can't control this.

It's out of my hands.

*Do you hear me, God? You can't let him die.*

# Chapter 2

## *Sly*

**B**efore my eyes even open, I sense the brightness of light behind them. My upper body hums with a dull ache as the unmistakable sounds of machines beep and drone all around me.

My eyes fight to open, the heaviness of them protesting the movement. When they finally begin to show me my surroundings, my vision is blurred. Beyond the unfocused haze is the shape of a woman with dark brown hair.

*Vincenza?*

Of course, she's the first thing I think of when I wake—she's the first thing I think of every single day and every night before I go to sleep.

For months, I've tried to stop loving her. Begged myself in the darkness of the night as I lay awake, to let her go. So badly, I've wanted to move on from the the hurt inside and the love I still cling to, but I can't.

Telling myself not to love her is like telling myself to stop breathing.

Impossible.

*Unfathomable.*

"Ah, it's good to see you waking up," the figure says, her voice sweet like honey, but not the soft sound I long to hear.

Blinking a few times, she comes into view, her warm smile greeting me as I get my bearings.

She reaches forward and grabs the remote attached to my bed, lifting it so that I am seated more upright.

"Try not to move around too much. You might be in some pain. My name is Nurse Franklin. You're at Ridgewood General, safe and in fantastic hands. I'm going to ask you a couple of questions, and I'd like you to answer to the best of your ability." She moves to the machines, reading the figures, before returning her attention back to me. "Can you tell me your name?"

"Sylvester Lucchetti," I croak, my voice hoarse.

"Good. Wonderful. Can you tell me why you're here?"

"There was a shooting. I was shot."

"You were. You came in with a gunshot wound to the chest. The doctor will go over everything with you —he should be in shortly. Can I get you anything in the meantime?"

My mind is racing, memories flooding back from the shooting. The roar of engines from incoming motorcycles. The gunfire ringing out into the middle of the barbecue I attended.

"Is Rosie okay?" I ask, my voice cracking as I say her name.

Shortly after my arrival in Ridgewood, California, I joined a motorcycle club. The Sinners Warlord became my unexpected salvation. The group of men was the city's very own vigilante group, taking it upon themselves to assist the local police department with keeping horrible people off the streets. Protecting Ridgewood's women and children was the main priority of The Sinners.

Joining them and helping to protect the new place I call home seemed like a natural choice for me.

I left everything behind in New York.

*Everything.*

My family. My profession.

My love.

The Sinners became my family when I so desperately longed for mine. Without even knowing it, they helped me through some of the darkest weeks of my life. They gave me a purpose.

A reason to continue *living*.

And then there was Rosie.

When I joined The Sinners, the bar that they resided above was for sale, and within a matter of weeks, a new owner came in. A clause within the sale was that The Sinners' rental agreement was to be carried out for the full five-year term.

Which didn't pose a problem until the new owner realized our club's prez was her ex's brother. The same man who just so happened to break her heart.

She and I had parallel pain. I understood the heartache she faced when she looked at him, as it was a similar pain to what I felt simply thinking of Vincenza.

And Cain didn't make it easy on her to continue her healing process. He didn't want her to close the door on him. He wanted a second chance.

Rosie took me by surprise by slipping into the role of my best friend, filling the void left by not speaking to Sully and Enzo. She was firey, independent, and head-strong. I admired her and her strength.

Our friendship naturally progressed one evening when we both desperately craved an escape from the emotional turmoil we faced. I could not be with amore mio, and she was determined to push hers as far away from her as possible, but through each other, we were able to find friendship, comfort, and release.

She became my lover, and while our physical connection was there, as was our friendship, there was no further emotional connection. Neither of us wanted to pursue a relationship. We were content in our physical arrangement and used each other as such.

There were no expectations or hopes.

And while I was able to find release when I had sex with Rosie, the hunger to seek pleasure in my dominant side *with* Rosie was lacking.

Almost as though that side of me was completely reserved for the one person I couldn't share it with.

*I almost died.*

The thought comes rushing back to me, reality

sinking in further. By jumping in front of that bullet, I saved Rosie.

But *did* I save her?

"Mr. Lucchetti?" the kind nurse prods, her eyes sweeping over me with concern as I retreat back to the present from the recesses of my mind.

I attempt to clear my throat as I meet her gaze. "Rosie Adler. Is Rosie alive?"

"Mr. Lucchetti—"

"I need to know she is safe."

My nurse sighs deeply, setting the clipboard she's holding down on the edge of my bed to scroll through the tablet she's holding easier. "I will do my best to find out what I can about Miss Adler."

I read between the lines, knowing there are legal guidelines for what she can and cannot tell me. "Please. I would like to see her and Cain Michaels. I need to know they're safe."

"I'll do my best to reach them, Mr. Lucchetti. Now, can I get you anything in the meantime?"

"Water. Please."

She nods. "I'll be right back."

Turning, she scurries from the room quickly, and I'm left alone with my thoughts.

Anguish pushes through the forefront of my emotions.

More memories of the barbecue come rushing back to me as I lay in the hospital bed and wait for the nurse or the doctor. The sickening crack of Rosie's skull as it hit the pavement reverberates through my mind. Then, at the same moment, monumental pain erupted in my body. Everything fades after that—I must have gone unconscious.

My visions turn to images of my loved ones— Mamma, Papà, my brothers, Enzo, Sullivan, and Vincenza. I could have left this earth without seeing them again. Without *speaking* to them again. The thought causes a sharp pain in my chest.

*Vincenza.*

What I wouldn't give to hold her in my arms and feel the softness of her skin against mine. To smell her sweet, cherry blossom scent.

My hand reaches to touch the cherry blossoms tattooed into my skin, and I hiss, the movement causing a searing pain from the trauma to my chest.

But it's nothing compared to the gaping wound that the thought of leaving this world without seeing Vinnie one last time has reopened in my heart.

A knock sounds from the outside of my hospital room and seconds later, a doctor is pushing through the door, staring down at my chart. He's a younger man, not much older than I am, if at all.

"Mr. Lucchetti. I'm Doctor Roan. How are you feeling?" he asks, looking me over, then looking at the machines I'm hooked up to.

"I've been better. What is the damage, amico?"

"Straight to the point," he states. "I can respect that. The injuries you sustained weren't as bad as they could have been. You're very lucky. We were able to bring you in for surgery immediately upon your arrival and tend to the gunshot wound. You suffered a tension pneumothorax caused by fragments from the bullet, but they weren't severe enough to need intervention—your lung should be healed on its own within the next week or two."

As the doctor speaks, I drone out his voice. Easily, I could read my charts myself and understand exactly what my body has gone through and know what my recovery will entail, but I give the man the respect he deserves and appear to listen.

Truthfully, my thoughts are in two places at once. Here, in Ridgewood, wondering about the status of mia preferita, Rosie, and the man I now call my friend, her boyfriend, Cain. But they're also across the country, in New York, with lingering memories of amore mio.

A weaker man would have broken down and contacted her by now, and perhaps I should allow myself to take on that title for the amount of times I've longed to reach out to her—the number of times I've looked up her name in the search engine of the web browser. Still, I've resisted.

Now I've almost lost my life, while a new beginning for hers looms closer.

Within a few weeks, Vincenza will become Mrs. St. Jean.

And that hurts worse than any gunshot wound ever could.

"Do you have any questions, Mr. Lucchetti?" the doctor asks, pulling me from my thoughts.

Slowly, I reach up and adjust the nasal cannula

resting in my nose. "How long until I can take this off? And the IVs."

I already know the answer, but the doctor doesn't know my background. No one in Ridgewood does. To the people I've crossed paths with during my time here, I've never confessed my knowledge of medicine. To them, I am just a man from New York, running to escape the pain of losing his love to another man.

"Let's just take things day by day for now and see how you're feeling. Your nurse will be back in shortly. Should anything emergent arise, I'll be back. Otherwise, I'll check in with you tomorrow."

I nod, laying my head against the pillow. Before I close my eyes, I say, "Thank you, Doctor."

The soft click of the door upon his exit tells me I'm alone again, and this time, as I listen to the sounds of the machines and glue my eyes shut, I let myself experience all the pain—both physical and mental—knowing that it's been too long since I've allowed myself to.

# Chapter 3

## *Sly*

My nap is cut short when another nurse enters my room with a tray of food. Her smile is friendly, and as she places it down in front of me, she asks how I am feeling. At this point, I am irritable. No one has answered me as to whether Rosie and Cain are okay, and I am beginning to wonder if I am getting the runaround.

"Do you happen to know if there is a Rosie Adler or a Cain Michaels admitted here?" I ask, picking up the Jell-O cup from my tray. It looks disgusting, but I rip the foiled top from the container and pick up a spoon, regardless.

"I know Miss Adler is no longer a patient, sir. But aside from that, I don't have any information for you."

Relief rushes through me. "Please, I need to reach her."

"I'll see what I can do," she assures me as she turns to leave the room.

She barely passes through the threshold when footsteps sound in the hallway, and my assigned nurse glides through the open door and over to me, checking my machines. But it's who's behind her that stops me in my tracks.

"Mia preferita," I breathe. My relief is mirrored on her face as she hurries toward me. I reach my hand out for her to grab, and she takes it without hesitation. "I'm so relieved to see you in front of me. I was worried when I woke—it took two nurses before I learned you'd been discharged. Are you feeling okay?"

"I'm okay," she reassures. "Minor injuries compared to yours. Are *you* okay, Sly? How are you feeling?

"I feel stiff, but other than that, I am still here and cannot complain, bella. I'm just so happy to see you and Cain."

At the mention of his name, Cain steps closer, and Rosie moves my hand to his. I squeeze it reassuringly and smile at him.

"Good to see you, brother," Cain says, his voice thick with emotion. It makes me realize exactly how terrifying this situation was for all of us.

Setting my hand down, he walks back to Rosie and rubs his hands along her shoulders. "You saved my girl, Sly. I'll never be able to repay you for that."

Rosie and Cain look at each other, speaking loudly through unspoken words. Their love has bloomed so much in these last few months, and I am so happy Rosie was able to let her walls down and allow him to show her the man he is today.

"I would give my life for either one of you if it meant you two continued to have each other. But I didn't save her, mio amico. If anything, I caused her injury." My brows come together as fractured memories of the shooting play in my mind. "Rosie, I watched your head slam into the pavement with unwavering force. I am so sorry, bella. I never wanted you to get hurt."

Rosie opens her mouth to say something, but Cain cuts her off, shaking his head animatedly.

"Had you not pushed her, the bullet you took would have hit her. You saved her. There is no point in trying to change the narrative because whichever way you try to spin it, it will always end the same: you saved Rose's life. Don't bother arguing."

I've learned over my months in Ridgewood that arguing with Cain, the president of The Sinners Warlord, is a waste of time. Instead, I nod and look back at Rosie.

"I'm just grateful we are both still here," I tell her as I swallow the lump that's formed in my throat. I can feel tears prick the back of my eyes, an overwhelming sense of gratitude weighing upon me.

"It's more than some can say," she murmurs. My eyes instantly snap to Cain.

"Who?" I demand, knowing immediately we weren't all so lucky during this attack.

"Preston," Cain tells me soberly, and my heart instantly aches for my friend Nixon.

Nixon is the one who found me in a tattoo parlor

back when I first arrived, drowning my sorrows in ink. Had I not met Nixon, I wouldn't have been initiated into the Sinners and found this family.

Preston, the man we lost, was Nixon's cousin. He was young. Too young.

"And the rest of the Sinners?" I ask. Cain dives into updating me on the conditions of the rest of the members, all of whom are fine or sustained very minor injuries.

It appears Preston and I took the worst hits, followed by Rosie's injuries.

"What is the plan, mio amico? Will we retaliate?"

The Reapers Wings, a neighboring town's motorcycle gang, were the ones who did this. Unlike us, their club wasn't formed to help its city's citizens. The Reapers were bad news and held a grudge against Cain for ending the life of one of their members.

The words hardly leave my lips before Rosie is yelling, her head turning from me to Cain. "NO, you guys will not. That's reckless and dangerous. They already pulled their 'eye for an eye' bullshit, and if you clap back, they'll come at you again harder."

Cain wraps his arms around her, pulling her in close. She presses her face against his chest as he attempts to calm her, running his hand down the back of her head repetitively. She's so upset, she's shaking.

"Please, Cain," she murmurs. "No one else needs to get hurt."

"I know, baby, I know," he assures her. "King and I

are meeting tomorrow to discuss our next steps. Until then, everyone is lying low."

From above her head, my eyes meet Cain's, and it's as though I can read his thoughts.

He wants to call church to discuss this without Rosie's presence. And I can't say I disagree.

Later, after we've all eaten a real dinner—one that Cain went to pick up for us—a nurse comes to let Rosie and Cain know that visiting hours are over, but Rosie refuses to leave.

Chuckling, I watch the nurse and Rosie go toe-to-toe as both Cain and I keep our mouths closed.

"Visiting hours are long past over. You guys are welcome to come back tomorrow, but Mr. Lucchetti needs some rest, and frankly, Ms. Adler, you look like you could use some, too."

"Then bring me a cot because we're not leaving."

"Ms. Adler—"

"No," she says with finality. "Look, either I'm sleeping on this chair, or I'm sleeping on a cot you provide, but I'm not leaving. And honestly, I'd prefer a cot. Sharing a chair with that giant man over there doesn't seem like the most comfortable option when I'm still dealing with a concussion." She points her thumb toward Cain, and the nurse rolls her eyes, letting out a frustrated sigh.

"If I get in trouble for this, I'm sending my bosses to you," she promises when she comes back with a small, folded cot on wheels and linens over her arm.

She shoves the linens into Cain's arms. Laughing, he

takes the offerings, sets them down, and begins to help her make it up. "Sounds fair."

As she leaves the room with a huff, she shuts the lights off and tells us all to get some rest. I can't help but chuckle to myself, shaking my head with my eyes closed.

Now more than ever, I appreciate the fire that lives inside Rosie and am grateful to the two people in this room who care enough to not leave me alone.

The room is dark, only a faint glow from where the fluorescents in the hallway shine through the small square window on my hospital door.

Noise from the hallway wakes me, and from the shine of the eyes across the room, I can see they woke Rosie too.

My room is close to the nurse's station, perhaps one or two doors down, and the sound of whatever altercation happening in the hallway carries.

"Where is he?" a familiar, feminine voice shouts.

For a moment, I think my mind is playing tricks on me.

Cain grunts as he's jostled awake, presumably by the sound of the woman's voice outside.

Situating myself as upright as I can in my bed, I turn my full attention to the door, listening closely. For a brief moment, my eyes meet Rosie's, and she smiles, but I find myself unable to return it.

Inside, my heart is hammering. Recognition kicks my senses into high gear.

I know that voice.

*But it can't be.*

The nurse clears her throat. "Miss, it's past midnight. Visiting hours are between eleven and eight tomorrow if you'd like to come back then, but it's too—"

"I don't care what time it is! I need to see him."

"Vincenza?" I mutter, my brows creasing together as I use the remote to fully right myself, staring at the door and wishing I wasn't hooked up to all these machines so I could go see for myself.

*She's not here. Vinnie is in New York, tucked safely at home, in bed, probably next to her fiancè.*

"Miss, please, if you just come back tomorr—"

"I've been on a plane for six hours. *Please.* Just for a few minutes, at the very least. Just to know he's okay."

*It is her. I would recognize her voice anywhere.*

# Chapter 4

## *Vinnie*

Six hours. It took me six hours to fly here. Over nine, if you count the rest of the travel time on either end of the flight.

Yet it takes less than six minutes to get shot down by an irritated nurse, telling me I have to wait until morning to see the love of my life.

I'm exhausted and hungry. My feet ache in my ballet flats, and I'm feeling too warm in my peacoat for the California weather, but can't find it in me to take it off. My patience level drops to the point where I want to reach over the nurse's station and shake the woman, but I know I can't do that. I can feel myself about to snap at her, even though she's just doing her job.

Visiting hours have ended, I understand that, but what *she* doesn't understand is that I don't care. I refuse to wait until morning to see Sly.

The need to touch him and hear his voice, to know he's okay, overpowers my instinct to remain polite.

I've been worried sick for hours, my heart lodged in my throat, suffocating me as I choked back tears the entire flight here.

The look on the nurse's face can only be described as pity—but I don't want her pity. I want her to let me see him.

Exasperated, I throw my hands into the air. "If you won't tell me where he is, I'll find him myself."

Every hospital room has a small window, and I'll look through every single one if necessary.

"Miss, you can't," the nurse pleads as I begin walking to the first door, but she doesn't make a move to stop me, and I ignore her warnings.

Glancing through the first room, I see an elderly woman asleep in her bed. Quickly, I make my way across the hall, only to find another woman asleep.

The next window I peer through, I'm a little startled to find a woman sitting upright on a cot, watching me. I'm about to turn to head to the next door when my eyes sweep over to the hospital bed and collide with the stunning shade of hazel I've been praying to see. Even though his room is dark, the lights from the hallway illuminate his features perfectly, and my heart flip-flops at the sight of him.

"Sly!" I cry as I throw open the door and rush inside his room.

"Vinnie?"

I don't slow, or think of anything other than feeling his skin against mine as I crash into him.

Instantly, his hand tangles in my mess of wavy curls as he pulls me closer.

"Vinnie," he breathes against my hair, nuzzling his face against my cheek. "What are you doing here, amore mio?"

Pulling back, his hands encircle my face, brushing the hair away as he looks deep into my eyes.

Tears spike my vision. I'm so overwhelmed right now, I can't even distinguish which emotions I'm feeling. I can't stop the tears from flowing over the edge of my lashes, and he wipes them away with his thumbs.

"You honestly think I wouldn't hear about you being in the hospital, Sly? As soon as I heard, I got on a plane."

His eyes search mine, and a look I don't recognize flashes across his face. "Vincenza, your family. Do they know you've come?"

Pulling out of his grasp, I settle on the edge of his bed. Sly shifts his lower body slightly, giving me more room, but I don't need it.

Resting my hand on his chest, I shake my head softly. "If they haven't figured it out already, it won't take long now."

His eyes drop to my hand, and I know he's looking at the diamond I forgot to remove from my finger before I left. It makes my stomach roll, knowing that he thinks I chose August.

Assuming that is what he thinks. I can't be sure since we haven't spoken, but I am well aware of what it looks like.

An intense need to begin explaining myself and begging for his forgiveness overpowers my thoughts, but I push them aside.

*Everything I'm doing is to keep him safe.*

"Do you know the risk you've taken to be here?" he asks, reaching to pull me toward him again.

He has no idea of the actual risk I've taken. And I know the consequences.

Resting my head on his chest, more tears escape. "You've always been worth any risk, Sly."

It's the truth, and I should have been more forthcoming with that truth before it was too late.

He hugs me tighter, his mouth coming to rest against my head as he presses his lips to me in a long kiss. Neither of us makes any move to part, but a few moments later, the soft click of the door closing catches my attention.

Opening my eyes, I see that the man and woman who were in the room are now gone.

"Who were they?" I ask softly, wondering about the people he has obviously grown close to since he's been living here.

They looked like they were a couple, but there was also a look of something more in the eyes of the woman as she watched me come into the room.

I recognized her look. It was a look of possession. Of protectiveness. I can't help but wonder if she cares for Sly in the way that I do.

A deep sigh elevates his chest. "There are many

things we must discuss, piccola ladra. But first, it is important to me to know why you are here."

I rear back and look at him, feeling as though he's slapped me. So many thoughts collide in my mind—has he been with her? Moved on? Does he hate me?

Closing my eyes, I remind myself he thinks I didn't show up that day. He thinks I didn't care about him— that I *don't* care about him. He has no idea what's been going on.

But the words escape me, and the best I can manage is, "I couldn't *not* be here, Sly. You were shot."

With a clipped tone, he says, "How did you even hear about it?"

I've never felt more distant from him than I do now. Even through the time we've been apart, I've held onto the glimmer of hope that one day, things could be different.

Although, the way he's guarding himself right now makes me think maybe that ship has sailed.

"The housekeepers talk." My voice cracks, barely above a whisper, as my eyes fill with tears once again. "Of course I'd be here."

Looking down at my hands, I gently pick at my cuticles as I wait for him to say something. I'm not able to look him in the eye, suddenly feeling like he is about to reject me being here.

He'd have every right to after thinking for so long that I don't love him.

What am I supposed to say? How do I tell him that

the reason I've stayed away is because of the threat August holds over his head?

So I say the only thing I can say. The one thing I hope he'll believe when he looks into my eyes and hopefully sees the truth. "I don't love him, Sly."

His eyes darken with my words, his hand curling into a fist on his lap. The movement makes me flinch. Thoughts of August flicker in my mind—of him using his fists on me, but only in places that are easily hidden.

Sly sees my reaction and narrows his eyes, brows furrowing in confusion as he lets his hands go slack.

I shouldn't have reacted. If anyone can see through my mask of perfection, it's Sly.

"Then why is his ring on your finger?"

"It's complicated, Sly. My family—"

"You are a grown woman, piccola ladra. Free to make your own choices. Your family does not own you."

*No, but August does.*

"I know," I whisper.

"Then tell me what holds you back. You are the last person I expected to walk through that hospital door, yet here you are. When you did not show up at the park that day, it broke my heart. Yet, you show up here, months later, just to ensure I am alive. Explain it to me, Vincenza, because I feel there is a part of the story I'm missing."

Standing, I walk to the window. Sly's room overlooks the hospital's parking lot, which is quiet for this hour. We're both silent as I stare ahead, focused on one of the lights.

I'm caught between the truth and a lie. So desperately, I long to tell him the truth, but with the truth comes the danger and, no doubt, the retaliation he'd want to act upon. With the lie comes further heartbreak when I walk away.

This could very well be the end of us.

The decision is made in my mind before I truly realize it is. I have to continue to lie, as much as it breaks my heart to do so.

They say the truth will set you free, but *this* truth will only threaten to break our wings. I cannot let the man I love seek retribution for my actions, which I know Sly would gladly take.

My heart is heavy, slowly sinking to the pit of my stomach as my eyes fill up with tears again. When I found out Sly was in the hospital, I didn't stop to think. I just reacted and did what I could to get here. I hadn't thought about this conversation, or the way it would make either of us feel. I acted purely on emotion, and now I fear I might have made a mistake in coming here.

Trembling, I close my eyes and will myself to make the most of the time I'm here for, knowing it may be the last time I see him. My fingers reach up to my neck, and play with the necklace I'm wearing.

A locket.

One I purchased right after Sly left. I had the jeweler engrave a simple S on the back of the gold heart-shape. The locket hangs around my neck, pictureless.

*Empty.*

It feels symbolic of how I feel, somehow.

I hardly recognize my own voice when the lie slips from my lips and a lone tear falls over the rim of my lashes. "There's nothing to explain. Sometimes things just don't work out like we hope."

And just like that, I feel the glimmer of hope completely extinguish.

# Chapter 5

## *Sly*

Time stands still, my heart galloping against my rib cage like a wild stallion set loose for the first time.

Vinnie stares out the window, pretending to be more interested in what's outside than our conversation, but I know her tells. I know when she wants me to *see* her, and when she doesn't.

"Look at me," I command, my voice unwavering despite the fear settling into my heart.

The rumble of the hospital room's air conditioning unit stirs as I wait for her to turn, clashing against her silence.

Something about her behavior isn't settling right within me. It's so unlike the woman I grew to know, and though we've had months between us, a person doesn't change their core values and personality without reason.

The woman in front of me is not the Vincenza I asked to run away with me.

Alarm bells ring in my head, and I study her as I wait for her to turn to me as I requested. When it's clear she isn't going to, I push again. "*Vinnie.*"

This time, as I say her name, her eyes squeeze shut.

*What is going on in my piccola ladra's mind?*

Unease sends a shock wave through my system, a frigid blast akin to that of cold water. My fingers tingle, my entire body fighting a jolt at the upsetting realization that something is extremely off with her.

Finally, Vinnie faces me. I take in her appearance. The slight rosy tint on the apples of her cheeks, the tip of her nose. The faint stain of makeup tracked down her cheeks.

She's been crying. This entire time she's refused to look at me, my piccola ladra has been fighting silent demons and weeping quiet tears.

The pain on her face speaks volumes, ricocheting from her heart to mine.

Sadness overpowers the unease and all I can feel is the need to hold her in my arms.

"Come here," I rasp, pushing down my own emotion.

This time, she doesn't hesitate and crosses the room to me. As she does, I pull the blanket from my body, holding it open. "Get in."

Her eyes sweep over me. "You're hooked up to several machines, Sly. I don't want to hurt you."

*It's too late for that, piccola ladra.*

I almost say the words out loud. Instead, I say, "You won't."

She gives me a brisk nod before toeing off her shoes and climbing into the bed with me. Its plastic base groans from the extra body, but we both ignore it as I cover us with the blanket and press a kiss to the side of her head.

Her body hugs mine, curved tightly into my side. Her hand rests loosely on my bare stomach, head in the crook of my arm.

It feels as natural as breathing. As comforting as laying in the sun on a warm summer day.

"You don't have to explain," I murmur, though I wish she would.

Perhaps when I am healed, I will return to New York. It's clear *something* is amiss, and if I am in the city, at least I can be nearby if she needs me.

*She won't need you, you fool. She's about to be a married woman.*

But she isn't married *yet*, and although I do not condone cheating, the desire to feel close to her in every way possible, one last time, overtakes me—August be damned.

He's not a man I hold any respect for, anyway.

"What happened?" Vinnie asks, trying to keep a steady voice, but I can hear the unease in it.

Sighing, I know it is time to tell her the truth. Adjusting the blanket around her hips, my eyes catch on the simple gold heart necklace she wears, and I can't help but to wonder if August gave that to her too. Pushing it from my head, I rest my hands on her thigh and attempt to adjust my upper body so it is easier to look down at her as I speak.

"When I arrived in Ridgewood, I met a man who introduced me to the president of the local motor-cycle club." Vinnie's eyes widen, and I give her thigh a gentle squeeze. "They are not dangerous, piccola ladra. The Sinners Warlord is a vigilante club. They are passionate about the women and children of Ridgewood, and we work hard to keep them safe. The man who was here earlier—that's Cain Michaels. The president. And the woman? His love, Rosie."

At the mention of Rosie's name, her eyes narrow the smallest amount. Anyone else may not have noticed the slight shift, but I would have been able to spot it a mile away. I can imagine the thoughts raging through her mind, and it sits like a weight in my stomach, knowing I will have to tell her about my relationship with her.

"She seemed protective of you," Vinnie says hesitantly. "When I came into the room, she watched my every move. Her concern rolled off her in waves."

"Sì, Vincenza. I will not lie to you, or try to hide my recent past. When you didn't arrive at our meeting place, I left my heart laying on the gravel path amongst the dirt and the rocks. I boarded a plane and forced myself to leave everything I loved in New York. You chose August, and when I told you I would respect your choice, I meant it."

Dipping my head for a moment to gather myself, I

clear my throat. The words I am about to say taste like bile and betrayal despite me doing nothing wrong. "Rosie is my best friend in Ridgewood. She and I shared a mutual pain. I had just lost you, and she was fighting her own relationship demons. Through each other, we sought comfort, and an arrangement formed. It did nothing to diminish my love for you, but it helped dull the heartache. Once she found her way back to the man she is meant to spend this lifetime with, our relationship ceased immediately—prior to, actually. But I cannot deny that we did have a relationship, no matter how unemotional it may have been."

Vinnie's eyes shine with tears, and a few escape from the corners from my admission.

Reaching to her face, I use my thumb to wipe them away. "I love you, Vincenza. Nothing in the world can ever change the way I feel about you, which is why I needed to leave. I needed to give myself the opportunity to heal from the pain of losing you."

Her eyes drop and she nods. Her voice is quiet as she lets out a deep breath and says, "I understand."

She doesn't say anything more, nor does she lift her head to meet my gaze. It makes me feel like there's more I should say, but I no longer want to speak about my time with Rosie. Instead, I continue on with how I came to be in this hospital bed.

"With the weather warming, The Sinners held a barbecue outside of the bar Rosie owns. We'd recently put a stop to a man who had been drugging and raping women in Ridgewood and neighboring towns."

Vinnie's gaze snaps to mine. "I thought you sa——"

"That it was not dangerous," I finish for her. "Sì, I know, and typically it is not. But this particular man slipped something into Rosie's drink, which Cain witnessed. He did not take lightly to that and reacted before any of us could stop him. Not to say the man would not have met the same ending, but it would have been handled differently."

The way she gazes at me, so intensely listening to my words, makes me stop to stroke the side of her cheek with my knuckles.

"It turns out the man was involved with a neighboring city's motorcycle club, and unfortunately, unlike the Sinners, that gang is a violent one. They began to target the club, then sought their revenge by retaliating against us the day of our barbeque. I was hit by gunfire when I shoved Rosie out of the way to protect her from being hit."

"You saved her," she breathes, giving me a tight-lipped smile as she tries to hold back her tears.

"Sì, piccola ladra, I did. I am lucky, and grateful, to be alive. I escaped with only a tension pneumothorax caused by fragments from the bullet. My collapsed lung should heal within the next week or two. The only true worry is allowing the bullet wound to heal without infection."

"I don't know what I would have done if you had died, Sly. Hearing you were shot nearly broke me. I can't...I can't..." she sobs through the tears that flow freely down her cheeks.

Grabbing her face, I can no longer hold myself back and coax her to move so I can reach her lips. Kissing her slowly, I convey with my body what I'm unable to with my words. With our mouths connected, all the love I've never stopped feeling comes rushing to the surface, unlocked by the simple touch of her lips to mine.

Immediately, they begin their familiar dance. Long strokes of our tongues and nibbles to the lips. The exploration of hands.

I can't bring myself to console her, to continue whispering words of adoration and declaring my undying love for her, when my subconscious screams at me that she's *still* engaged. So I let my actions speak for me.

The kiss begins tender as we allow her tears to slow, but as soon as I can feel her breathing even out, I deepen it. I feel myself grow stiff beneath her again, and with a small moan from her lips, I know she feels it, too.

Desperately, I need to be inside her. The need is carnal and raw—the desire to simply unite our bodies, even if it does not end in release. I just need to feel her.

As I pull back to gaze at her, there's a look I don't recognize in her eyes, but also, one I do.

*Desire.*

"Vinnie," I breathe, lowering my face to meet hers as she tilts her head upward.

"*Please*," she begs, her features coated with sorrow and need.

I don't ask for clarification, nor do I wait for her to change her mind.

She's careful not to go near my chest and the bandage that covers it, but her fingers play against my lower abdomen, and my muscles constrict from her tender touch.

From within the loose-fitting pajama pants I am wearing, my length hardens, pushing the fabric upward as it tents it.

Our kiss continues, neither of us pulling away to catch a breath of air. It's slow, passionate, and full of unspoken words and longing. Regardless of her behavior since her arrival, and our lack of contact over these last several months, it is clear she has missed me as much as I've missed her.

It confuses me—the actions of her body differ so drastically from her words. Still, I try to push it from my thoughts and live in the moment with her.

What matters is she's in my arms—and in my bed—right now. Regardless of how long it may be for.

Unable to maneuver too much due to the pain, I slide my hand from under her body and up into her shirt, stroking the soft skin of her lower back.

As our mouths continue to reacquaint, I find her jeans are stretchy enough for me to push my hand into them and grip her backside. A soft moan floats from her lips to mine, and her hand drifts down to my cock. She palms it through the fabric, and it's been so long since I've felt her touch that my eyes roll back into my head.

"Take off your pants, piccola ladra." I tug at the waistband of her jeans for emphasis. "I need to feel your skin against mine."

"Sly," she groans, but the sound is less a protest and more a blissful approval.

Reaching to the button, I unhook it, then push her zipper down. Carefully, she pushes her jeans from her hips and past her thighs. When they reach her ankles, she sits up to finish removing them, and I hear them drop to the floor.

My thumb hooks through the lace of her panties, and I snap them softly against her skin. "These as well."

When her eyes meet mine, I can see the hesitation. "You're injured, Sly. We can't—"

It is not lost on me that her hesitation is because of my wound, not her fiànce. "I need to feel you." My words are practically a growl, my control hanging on by a thread, about to snap.

This woman drives me wild. We've spent more time apart than we spent together, yet, now, being back in her presence, it's like we've never missed a day.

"Okay," Vinnie whispers, pushing the scrap of fabric down her legs. As soon as she kicks them off, my hands are on her hips and I'm pulling her onto my body.

I suck a sharp intake of air between my clenched teeth, fighting through the singe of pain the movement sends through my chest as it stretches my stitches.

Concern floods her features and I nod my head slightly—I am okay.

Allowing me to guide her movements, she kicks a leg over and lowers herself so she's straddling me. When our bodies are flush together, I can feel how wanton she is—her wetness seeping through the thin fabric of my pajama bottoms.

Vinnie's fingers curl around my bicep—around the cherry blossoms encircling my skin—and with her other hand she traces the outline of the bandage on my chest with a touch so featherlight I'm not entirely positive she's actually touching me.

"I hate seeing you like this," she tells me as she moves her fingers from the edge of the bandage and dusts them down toward my waistband.

"I have endured much worse pain, though perhaps not physically. I will be fine, piccola ladra."

"It hurts me too," she says, but before I can question it, her hand palms me through my pants and I am caught off guard by her touch.

"Vinnie," I groan, and it's as though she reads my thoughts as she pushes the elastic of my waistband down and frees my length, taking it in her palm.

Bracing on her knees, she aligns us and sinks down until I fill her completely. Her walls clench around me, and simultaneously, our bodies shudder.

Being inside her feels like coming home. It's a comfort and a privilege. Something that I've missed and craved.

I pull her face to me again, resuming our kiss as it was earlier—slow and full of passion. Neither of us moves or begins our lovemaking. Being connected is enough, the contact more fulfilling than any orgasm could be when our hearts were in such a precarious place.

Time passes, but we stay in the moment.

"Can you forgive me?" Vinnie asks some time later once our kisses slow. I'm still hard, fully seated inside her as she straddles my hips, her upper body twisting slightly so her head can lay against my shoulder, opposite of where the bandage is.

"I already have, piccola ladra. My heart is yours to do with as you please, including breaking it. You own it completely. You own me, even if I cannot be with you. I long for things to be different, Vincenza, but I respect your decision and I won't try to fight it. Just please give me tonight. Allow me to pretend you are still mine."

"I *am* still yours," she whispers, but we both know it's a lie, even if she wishes it were true. It ignites a frustration deep inside me, one that hurts deeply. A simple glance at the ring on her finger reminds me her words and her actions do not align.

Expelling a deep breath, I say nothing, but she must sense my exasperation. Shifting upright, she leans forward to kiss me, and begins slowly rolling her hips as she presses her palm onto the part of my chest where her head just was.

My hands gravitate to her hips, and I begin helping her move up and down my shaft. She pauses each time I fill her completely, then together we're moving again. She's careful not to touch my chest, but the increased movement sends a jolt of pain through me.

Wincing through it, I push the uncomfortable feeling away and open myself up to the pleasure. Her wetness coats me, allowing her to slide easily along my length. Small moans tumble from her lips with every slow movement we make together.

The air is heavy with sentiments—thick with passion, and pleasure…and pain.

Instead of a reunion, it feels like the goodbye we were never given.

An onset of emotions slams into me and I find myself overwhelmed with the urge to cry. It's a feeling I'm not accustomed to, and it takes me by surprise.

Grabbing her by the face again, I kiss her.

I kiss her like it may be the last time. I kiss her as I thrust my hips upward and move inside her, memorizing the way she tastes and feels. I kiss her like there's not a ring on her finger, and she's still *mine*.

My body screams at me to stop—the movement sending the pain through me like a cataclysmic earthquake, threatening to rip my skin in two. But I ignore it as tears spring from the corners of my eyes and I can't decipher if they're from the pain in my heart or in my body.

Wordlessly, I bring my hand between Vinnie's legs and stroke her clit, rubbing it in precisely the way I know brings her pleasure.

It takes mere seconds before I spot the signs of her body allowing the orgasm to crest. Her body begins to hum in a way that tells me she will detonate soon. Pride blooms in my chest as I watch her face contort, knowing I'm the man unraveling her in the same way she has the power to unravel me.

It's a beautiful thing to watch her release overtake

her body, and as she cries out, she cups her hand over her mouth to muffle the noise.

If we had the time, I would continue to draw the pleasure from her over and over, but this is not the place, nor am I in the condition to keep pushing my body. Instead, I give myself over to the pleasure, allowing my own orgasm to flow from me as I follow her over the blissful edge of release.

Once I've stilled inside her, Vinnie leans her forehead against mine as we catch our breath. It takes everything inside me not to tell her I love her. I want to tell her how beautiful she is, and how much she means to me, but the words gather as a lump in my throat and I bite my tongue, refusing to say as much.

No matter how beautiful this moment just was, she isn't mine.

As though the spell is broken, Vinnie climbs off me as gently as she can, bending to pick up her clothes that are discarded on the floor.

"I should go," she mutters, not making eye contact with me. "I have an early flight."

I look across the room at the clock on the wall, surprised to see it is nearly three in the morning. We spent hours lost in each other, and I'm even more surprised to realize a nurse did not disturb us even once.

Concerned about the hour she's leaving at, I look at the cot across the room that Rosie occupied earlier. "Stay, Vincenza. It is the middle of the night. Get a couple hours of sleep and then catch your flight."

She buttons her jeans, glancing up at me with a

melancholy gaze. "I shouldn't, Sly. It'll just make leaving harder."

*I wish you wouldn't leave at all.*

"I understand," I tell her, forcing myself to keep all emotion from my voice. "I appreciate you coming here."

She steps closer, reaching for my hand. I allow her to take it, and I bring the back of hers to my lips and kiss it gently.

With my lips still pressed against her skin, I whisper, "Ti auguro di essere felice, anche se non posso essere io a portarti la felicità." *I wish you to be happy, even if I cannot be the one who brings you happiness.*

"What did you say?" she asks, her breath hitching, tears shining once again.

Shaking my head, I release her hand and tell her, "Be happy."

Leaning down, she places a gentle kiss to my lips, righting herself quickly before I have time to react. She gently squeezes my thigh before crossing the room.

As she reaches for the doorknob, I hear her soft words, "You too," even though her back is to me.

Then she's gone.

Quiet envelops me. The only sound projecting through the room is that of the machines I'm hooked to. Internally, I hear my own pounding heartbeat.

Seconds pass into minutes and I'm left wondering if perhaps that was all a fever-dream. A medication induced, beautiful conjuring my mind created. I wouldn't believe it was real if it weren't for the lingering scent of cherry blossoms and the phantom feel of her skin against mine.

And then suddenly, as though all of my guarded walls have shattered, the emotional pain sets in and I mourn the loss of the woman I love, knowing this time, it is goodbye.

# Chapter 6

## *Vinnie*

"Miss? We're preparing for landing and the captain is about to put the seatbelt sign on. Is there anything you'd like before we land?"

A sweet stewardess named Brittany has been attentive since I sat down in her section of first class, seeing the tear-soaked rivers on my cheeks and the redness in my eyes. I know I look a mess—I had stepped into the ladies' room prior to boarding and saw it myself, but I couldn't bring myself to care or try to fix my face before getting onto the plane.

I feel like a ghost. Soulless and alone, an emptier shell than I was when I landed in San Francisco less than sixteen hours ago.

Going to Ridgewood had been a mistake. Seeing Sly—having those final moments with him—I'll never forget. But I'm afraid I'll never recover from the heartbreak of having to look him in the eye and be dishonest. Making him think I actually want to marry August makes me physically ill. I've been nauseous since I left his hospital room.

Where I should feel some peace with my decision, or at least like I'm doing the right thing by not telling him everything, I feel worse than ever.

Looking up at the stewardess through blurred, teary eyes, I give her a tight-lipped smile. "No. Thank you, Brittany, you've been wonderful."

"It's been my pleasure. We'll be on the ground in twenty minutes, miss."

She turns to face the passenger across from me, and I return my gaze to the open window. New York is coming into view, the skyscrapers sitting within a layer of white fluffy clouds, cutting into the vibrant blue sky.

It's never felt less like home.

Having no luggage, I disembark the plane and move through LaGuardia with ease, bypassing baggage claim and making my way to arrivals. I sent a text to Ross earlier to let him know my landing time, so I'm unsurprised to see my black town car idling by the curb when I approach the automatic doors.

As I step out of the airport, I'm welcomed by warmth. It's nothing like California, but still, the sun-kissed air settles against my skin and brings me a tiny sliver of comfort.

There's a crossing guard standing next to the driver's window, gesturing with frustration at the curb, and I know Ross hasn't seen me yet.

"I'm here! Sorry!" I say to the angry worker as sweetly as I can, and he makes eye contact with me as I reach for the back passenger door. "We'll be out of your way right now, don't mind us!"

"It's a no parking zo—"

The shutting of my door cuts him off, but as soon as I'm tucked inside the car, I wish I was back out on the curb.

"Hello, Vinnie," August greets. His body's positioned so he's turned toward me with his leg propped on the bench seat. With his elbow resting on the back of it, he looks like he has no care in the world. "Took a quick trip, I see?"

My blood runs cold, his unspoken connotation slithering through me, invoking dread and fear.

Through the rearview mirror, I lock eyes with Ross and I can see the apology shining through them. I hope he can see the fury in mine.

"What are you doing here, August?"

He picks up a lock of my hair between his fingers, stroking the ends with his thumb. "Picking my future missus up from the airport, of course. When you didn't come home last night, I figured you and that maid of yours had an impromptu sleepover, but when I came to the penthouse this morning, you were nowhere to be found. What perfect timing I found your driver about to leave to pick you up. He refused to tell me where he was heading, but seeing as though I was already in the car, it was only a matter of time before I figured it out."

My gaze cuts to Ross again, but he neither confirms nor denies what August is saying.

"How's he doing then?" August prods, not bothering to hide the annoyance in his voice.

Turning back to him, I play dumb. "How is who doing?"

Dropping my hair, his hand falls to his lap, fingers flexing.

I've made him mad. The anger inside him is boiling, the rage within reflecting in his mud-brown eyes.

He pulls out his phone and his thumb dances over the screen before he turns it in my direction, showing me a photo of a closed door with a single window and the number eight-forty-seven—Sly's hospital room.

"One call, Vinnie. It would take just *one* phone call and your boyfriend won't make it out of the hospital. I should have already made it since you've taken it upon yourself to play me like a fool. You're lucky the press didn't find out about your little trip. How did you figure out where he was, anyway?"

"Don't you *dare*," I seethe through clenched teeth. "I came back, didn't I? The only person who knew I was gone was Ross. No one else."

His hand grips mine, pulling it from my lap and squeezing it so tightly I wonder if he's trying to break bones. Dropping his voice to a low, deadly tone, he says, "Had anyone else found out, my dear fiancée, I would have killed him while you laid by his side in his hospital bed."

He leans forward, his hand cupping around the side of my neck as he brings his lips to my ear so only I can hear his words. "Tell me, Vinnie. Did you fuck him like the slut I know you are? Did you suck his dick one last time? Because you'll *never* see him again. I've kept him alive to keep you complacent, but I'm done appeasing you."

Releasing me, he looks at me so darkly I fear he will act out even with Ross as an audience. But August is smart and conniving. He wouldn't dare.

Rebuttals swirl through my mind, but I know anything I say will fuel his fire, so I force myself to keep quiet. Regret is at the forefront of my mind. I should have told Sly. I could have come clean to him about everything that's happened with August and *why*, but I chose to keep my silence and now I may come to regret that.

I've never feared August like I fear him right now.

Several times, he's lashed out at me physically, but I've never seen the hellish look in his eye like what's shining through at this very moment.

And with our wedding in less than two weeks, I wonder if I've only just begun to see the *real* him.

Relaxing back into his seat, August rests his ankle on his knee and looks toward the front of the car. "Ross, take us back to *our* penthouse, please. My fiancée and I have a lot to catch up on."

With my broken heart sinking to the depths of my stomach, I turn to look out my window, watching the familiar Manhattan streets pass by in a blur, and I know *exactly* why it no longer feels like home.

The elevator up to August's penthouse is silent, but I can feel his eyes on me as I stare up at the floor indicator as the numbers ascend. My heart races, palms sweating from the anticipation of the unknown.

August has proven himself to be unpredictable with his outbursts. There've been times where I'd anger him and he wouldn't lash out for hours, even days, only to come at me out of nowhere to punish me for things he thought I deserved retribution for. Other times, he sprung on me the second we were behind closed doors.

Today, it's the moment the elevator dings.

"I should take you for a spin, too, Vinnie. Fuck you like the whore you are," he spits, wrapping a tight fist in my hair. He uses it to pull me inside the penthouse, tugging me next to him roughly until we reach the middle of the entry space.

Jerking me forward, he releases me with a firm jolt, knocking me to the ground.

"*No*," I cry out, the thought of August inside me roiling my stomach painfully, though I know his words are idle. He has yet to try to sleep with me, instead holding the threat over my head, using it alongside Sly's life to keep me compliant.

"Don't worry, I wouldn't stick my dick in you if you begged me to. Not after I know *his* was just there."

He delivers his first kick to my ribs as I'm attempting to scramble to my feet.

The second kick comes when I'm down.

"You thought you could just fly to California and I

wouldn't find out?" He kicks me again, this time landing his foot in my gut.

"You are *my* fiancée, and in less than two weeks you will be my wife."

My body contorts into the fetal position. I hug myself tightly as tears stream down my face. *"August,"* I whimper. *"Please."*

*"August, please,"* he mocks, kicking me again. This time, a searing pain radiates as his loafer connects with my rib cage.

Crying out, my hand flies to where the pain ricochets from, and a fresh wave of tears fall. From my peripheral, I see August crouch down next to me. He reaches to brush the hair away from my face, and I flinch at his touch.

His knuckles drag down my cheek, and for a moment I think he's going to hit me in the face, despite knowing he wouldn't leave visible marks. My eyes clench closed, and for several long seconds his knuckles hover just above my cheekbone.

Scoffing, he stands.

As he walks away, he raises his voice, laughing manically as his voice echoes off the white walls. "Betray me again, Vinnie. See what happens."

Then he walks away, leaving me crying in a crumpled, broken ball on the floor.

# Chapter 7

## *Sly*

"No, no. There is no reason for you to come down here, mia preferita. You have a lot to help Nixon with. They are discharging me tomorrow, and I will come to the bar as soon as I am out."

"You will *not*," Rosie squeals through the phone, at the same time Cain, who is also talking to me through speakerphone, barks, "Would you quit referring to my girl as your favorite? Find your own woman."

"Oh, don't go all caveman, Cainy-boo. I *am* Sly's favorite," Rosie quips, and I can practically see the glare Cain gives her.

Chuckling, I pull the pillow from behind my back and slowly turn my body so I can stand. "Apologies, mio amico. Old habits. She is not wrong though—she may be yours, but she is still my best friend in Ridgewood."

"I'm telling Nixon you said that," Cain grumbles, and I laugh again.

Rosie's stern voice overpowers Cain's muttering

complaints. "If you're not up for visitors today, you have to promise me the first thing you do tomorrow will *not* be coming to the bar."

"But my room is above the bar, bella," I argue.

Her deep sigh sends static through the speakers, and I know she is relenting. She needs to accept that I will be going there tomorrow—I live there. At least for the time being.

"We'll see you tomorrow. Rest up, brother."

"Sounds good, amico." More static sounds through the speakers, Rosie's protests overpowering the noise.

"Hey, I wasn't done tal—"

The call disconnects and I chuckle again, setting my phone down next to me on the bed. Gripping the edge, I give myself a gentle push and stand.

My wounds are healing nicely, but I know better than to overexert myself.

The time spent with Vinnie was enough to set me back the next day and I spent it in more pain than I had post surgery.

Walking to the window, I watch the sunset. Glorious oranges and pinks stand bright against the contrasting darkness that has begun to settle.

After a few moments, a sharp rap against my door has me turning, just as a nurse comes into my room with a dinner tray in hand. "How are you feeling, Mr. Lucchetti?"

"Better," I say with a warm smile as she places the tray on the small table by my bed.

"I hear you're leaving tomorrow! I'm sure it'll be lovely to go home."

"Sì. Thank you for bringing my dinner."

"Of course, Mr. Lucchetti. Page the nurses' station if you need anything else."

Nodding, I walk back to the bed and sit. On the plate is a hamburger with sweet potato fries and a pudding cup for dessert. It looks unappetizing, and if my stomach wasn't already growling, I would order food from the app on my phone.

Picking up the burger, I sink my teeth into it, biting off a large portion. It tastes as bland as it looks.

Next to me, my phone catches my eye again, taunting me through the darkened screen. I know what I must do, though it sends dread through me. It shouldn't—contacting my family should be joyous, but I know my parents are probably angry with me. And Enzo…well, I'm not ready to speak with Enzo yet.

My jaw clenches as I peer down at my phone. Finally, I pick it up before I change my mind. Inputting the numbers I've had memorized for most of my life, I listen to the ring resound in my ears.

"Pronto," Mamma's beautiful voice singsongs into the receiver. My heart soars from hearing her after so long, a reaction that catches me off guard.

My emotions are heavy, and I feel tears prick the back of my eyes—something that I'm finding is happening more and more frequently as of late.

"Mamma," I croak in greeting, my voice cracking.

"Sylvester? Sly! ANTONIO—SLY IS ON THE

PHONE. Sly, il mio dolce ragazzo! Are you okay? Where are you?" The words flow from her in a long slur, her mind working overtime to ask me all the questions I've denied her of over the last several months.

"Mamma, sì. I am alright. I'm so sor—"

"Come osi interrompermi, Sylvester Lucchetti. Mi avevi giurato che non l'avresti fatto, poi ti giri e fai esattamente quello! Allora, devo sapere al telefono da un medico che ti hanno sparato! Cosa diavolo ti è successo?" *How dare you cut me off, Sylvester Lucchetti! You swore to me you wouldn't, then you turn around and do exactly that! Then, I have to find out from a doctor over the phone that you've been shot! What on earth happened to you?*

Her native language is so thick with fury, even I have trouble distinguishing some of the words as she berates me through the phone. She's right though, and as I listen to Mamma, I hang my head in shame.

"Mamma, I am sor—"

But she cuts me off again, clearly not ready to hear my apology. "Ero preoccupatissimo per te. Sai quante notti sono rimasto sveglio chiedendomi dove fossi? Per qualche tempo ho temuto la tua morte, ma non la sentivo nel mio cuore, quindi mi sono costretta ad allontanare i pensieri. Mi hai spaventato, ragazzo mio. Più di quanto tu mi abbia mai spaventato prima." *I have been worried sick about you. Do you know how many nights I laid awake wondering where you were? For some time, I feared your death, but I did not feel it in my heart, so I forced myself to push the thoughts away. You have scared me, my boy. More than you have ever scared me before.*

This time, as she finishes her thought, I don't allow her to continue and tell her to listen. "Mamma! Ascoltare!"

She sighs dramatically, and I hear heavy footsteps through the speaker.

"Sylvester?" Papà's voice questions.

"Sì," Mamma confirms.

"Ciao, Papà."

"When are you returning to New York?" is all he asks, his voice gruff. He is angry. I can hear it.

"Soon, Papà. I am being discharged from the hospital tomorrow and I have some loose ends to tie up here in California, then I will return."

"Your healing?"

"It's fine. No infection, and my lung is repairing itself. I must take things slowly for some time, but I am mending."

He grunts, then I hear his footsteps again, presumably walking away.

"You scared us, mio figlio. Your papà is not happy with you, and neither am I. Do you have any idea how worried we have been? And for you to tell us not to come..." her voice cracks, and I hear her suck in a breath.

"I know, Mamma. I am sorry." There is so much more to say, but it doesn't feel like the time. My heart and my body ache, my mind heavy with thoughts of helping Nixon plan Preston's funeral, and making my arrangements to go back to New York.

"Is this because of the girl?"

My heart skips a beat. *Does Mamma know of Vinnie?*

"What girl?" I ask tentatively.

"The girl you met. I know my son well enough to know when he has met someone whom he truly cares about. It was written all over your features, despite you not saying any words. You had met someone shortly before you left."

A shuddering breath blows past my lips, and I scrub my face with my palm. "Mamma—"

"Do not lie to me, Sylvester. I've had enough of your lies."

"Mamma, this is not the time for this conversation, nor am I in the place. Please allow me to come home first, then I will tell you everything. We will go to brunch."

"Fine. But you need to come home, Sly. It has been too long. There are people here who need you."

*I know Mamma, and I suspect my Vincenza is one of them.*

"Sì. Give me another week, possibly two. I will be home. I swear to you."

"Please rest, mio figiio. Te amo."

"Te amo, Mamma. It is good to hear your voice."

"Yours too. I cannot wait to hold my boy in my arms again."

I disconnect the call, and my fingers dance over the touch screen, dialing the next phone number.

A single ring resonates through the speaker before it's answered. "This is Sullivan."

"Have I been away so long that you now answer the phone as though you are a CEO, mio amico?"

"Sly?" Sully questions in disbelief. "You take my jet to California, then step into the fog and disappear, never to be seen or heard from for months, and the first thing you do when you *do* call is mock me? Hi! So great to hear from you, pal."

"Ciao, Sullivan. I hope you are well," I snark, fighting against the smile creeping onto my lips.

Sully scoffs, and I sense he is genuinely upset. "You've got some nerve, Sly. Do you have any idea what your family's gone through? What I've gone through?"

"I was shot," I say simply, as though my recent injury could excuse me from all my other transgressions.

"I know."

"You weren't worried?"

"OF COURSE I WAS WORRIED," Sully booms through the phone. I hear rustling, then the sound of him expelling a breath. "Look, Sly. You left, and things got really hard. Your parents were devastated, and Enzo was left to pick up the pieces. He's pissed at you—more than I am. I was just his wingman to try and cheer your mom up. You broke her heart, man, and honestly, you broke mine, too. Thought we were better friends, but you up and cut me off."

"There are things you don't know—"

"No, Sly. There are things *you* don't know." His words freeze me in my spot.

"What things?"

An annoyed laugh resounds through the speaker. "Is this your number now? Or is this a burner phone you're going to chuck after we hang up?"

I scrub my hand down my face. Neither of these conversations are going how I expected them to. "This is my number now."

"Good. I'll call you when I'm ready to talk to you."

"Sully, I've called to apologize."

"Well, I'm not ready to hear it, man. I'm glad you're not dead, but for the last however many months, you might as well have been. I've got a lot going on at work right now, I have to go."

He ends the call, and I'm left sitting on my bed in confusion. Years of friendship, yet I hadn't expected this reaction from him. Sully is happy-go-lucky. Everything rolls off his back. He's funny and light-hearted.

I truly hurt him by leaving.

When Vinnie hadn't shown up at our meeting spot, the only thing I could think about was my broken heart and the feeling of betrayal. I never stopped to consider how my loved ones would feel about my leaving.

I ran away without further consideration of those around me. The errors of my ways flash through my mind like a neon sign and I realize how selfish my behavior was.

Returning to New York is no longer a question in my mind. I must go. Ridgewood has been my salvation, but it's time for me to leave, as difficult as it may be. I just need to fulfill my promise to Nixon and help him plan his cousin's funeral first.

Then I need to figure out how to say goodbye to the friends who have become my family.

# Chapter 8

## *Vinnie*

My stomach rumbles as I look at the grab-and-go options at the upscale market, Fraîche. Practically drooling over every choice, I find it difficult to make a decision on what to eat, even though I'm starving. I left my office early today; my afternoon meeting was canceled, so I decided to take the rest of the afternoon off.

I wanted to go home—to *my* home—and have a few hours of peace before I ended up back at August's penthouse. But first, I stopped for something to eat. It didn't feel right to go home and eat all the food Cecilia had stocked up on for herself, so here I am, perusing the options and struggling to make a decision.

It's been a week since I returned from Ridgewood. A week since August took his anger out on me for leaving. Internally, my ribs are still bruised. Every motion I make sends a zing of pain through my body and causes me to grit my teeth. Walking hurts. Sleeping hurts. And forget about laughing.

But it's not like I've been doing too much of that lately.

Externally, a large yellow bruise spans my left side. The physical evidence of where August kicked me, hidden from sight. But the memory still haunts me.

Slowly, I make my way to the salad bar and am impressed with how it looks, so I decide to make one. Picking up a box to build it in, a few fall after being stuck together. I groan, already feeling the pain that's about to shoot through me.

My jaw clenches as I bend, reaching for the boxes on the floor. I suck in a sharp breath between my teeth as my body screams in protest.

"Here, let me help," a smooth, strong voice says behind me. From where I'm bent, I look over and see the face of a man I haven't seen in months, and surprise runs through me.

"Sullivan?"

He gives me a lopsided grin as he bends to reach for the box I haven't picked up yet.

"Hey, Paladino." As he straightens, his eyes dart to where I can feel my blouse has ridden up slightly, and I quickly pull it back in place, praying the bruise didn't peek through. "Please, call me Sully."

"What are you doing here?" I ask, suddenly feeling frantic and full of nerves.

Sullivan Rochester is Sly's best friend. Or at least, he was. I'm not sure if he's been in touch with Sly since he left. Other than at the occasional charity gala, our paths never cross. Seeing Sully like this so soon after going to Ridgewood, my mind immediately questions whether Sly sent him or if this is truly a coincidence.

Sully shrugs, holding up a box of organic cereal in his hand, and giving it a shake. "Same thing as you are, I suppose?"

A nervous laugh bubbles past my lips. "Oh. Yeah. Yes, of course."

Lifting my hand, I play with my locket—something I've found myself doing more and more of lately. It's becoming a nervous habit.

Sully tracks my movement, and for the briefest of moments, I see his eyes narrow before they bounce back to mine, and he grins again. "How are you doing?"

His question freezes me in place. The context of it could span so many facets, and my brain goes blank, unable to conjure a simple answer.

How am I doing…mentally?

Physically?

Emotionally?

Since Sly's been gone?

At this specific moment?

My face must reflect something conducive to my thoughts because he laughs. "You look like I just asked you to multiply seven-hundred and fifty-two by three-hundred and sixty-nine."

Reaching out, he touches the top of my shoulder, and I can't help but flinch at the contact.

Confusion contorts his face. "Vinnie, are you ok—"

"I've got to go," I say immediately, snapping out of my stupor and cutting off his question before he can finish asking it. "It was good to see you, Sulliv—Sully. Take care."

Abandoning my empty salad box, I rush from the store and out onto the busy Manhattan sidewalk. I don't stop once I'm outside, though. Instead, I cross the street, walking until I see a small alcove to step into. It takes a minute for me to catch my breath, my chest heaving with anxiety as the air cycles through my lungs hard and fast. My vision swims for a moment, and I tip my head back, taking a deep breath through my nose.

My reaction was irrational—I know that. But seeing Sully made me think of Sly, and thinking of Sly…

I have to stop. I need to put my emotions aside and continue forward with my plan of marrying August, even if it kills me.

The wedding is a week away. My final dress fitting is *tomorrow*.

Everything is in motion.

*Sly is safe.*

And I'll do everything to keep it that way.

When I walk into the bridal boutique, I'm immediately handed a glass of champagne by a smiling woman. There's a light scent of rose permeating through the air and soft music playing on the sound system.

My mother's voice carries over the music in a squeal

of delight as I thank the woman and move toward the bridesmaid dresses she's browsing through while waiting for me.

She's still upset I went with light pink and gray as my wedding colors—she was pushing for lavender.

"Oh, honey! You look gorgeous," my mother gushes, pulling me in for a hug. I'm careful not to spill my champagne on her as she does.

Before the dress fitting, a hairstylist and makeup artist came to the apartment to go over wedding looks and did a sample makeover. My hair is curled to perfection, left loose down my back, while my makeup is pristine. Dramatic, but also timeless.

When I saw myself in the mirror for the first time once they had finished working their magic, my eyes became misty. I looked every bit of the bride I'd always imagined I would be—I just wasn't marrying the right man.

Now, as I make my way across the store for my final gown fitting, I feel overwhelmingly nauseous. My dress is on a hanger beside the three mirrors surrounding a single, circular pedestal for brides to stand on and admire the gowns they're trying on.

And I will admire my gown. It deserves it—my dress is stunning. Everything I always dreamed of.

Flowing tulle with floral lace detailing, cut in an A-line that features a gorgeous, full train. The long, gauzy sleeves cuff at my wrists, giving it a fairy-like feel as it sits off my shoulders. Paired with a diamond tiara fit for a princess, I'm able to forgo a veil, although my mother is still trying to fight me on the issue, begging me to wear a traditional cathedral veil.

Sighing deeply, I run my fingertips against the exquisite fabric.

For a moment, I let myself envision my wedding day. A wedding day where Sly is the one standing in front of the altar wearing a black tuxedo, his hands clasped behind his back as he watches me walk down the aisle to him. My heart aches at the vision, and I bite my lip to keep myself from crying.

"Your dress is magnificent, sweetheart. It's perfect for you," my mother's voice breaks through my thoughts.

I plaster on a smile and turn toward her. "It's what I've always imagined."

Bringing the champagne flute to my lips, I tip it back and drink down the bubbles, emptying it in one go.

"Good afternoon, Ms. Paladino! Mrs. Paladino! Will anyone else be joining us today?" the saleswoman, Veronica, greets, stopping in front of us. She's enthusiastic, practically beaming as she looks from me to my gown.

"Just us," I confirm.

"Excellent, let's get started then!"

Metal scrapes metal as she pulls the hanger from the rack and sweeps her arm beneath the gown to carry it into the fitting room. I follow her in as my mother takes a seat on the plush, button-tufted white couch. Once I step into the spacious changing area, Veronica pulls the curtain behind me.

"Your hair and makeup look stunning. Was today your test run of them?"

"Yes," I say as I unzip my summer dress and slip the sleeves down my shoulders. My tone is clipped, and while I feel slightly guilty—it's not this woman's fault I'm filled with dread—I still can't find it in me to pretend to ooze happiness like I know is expected of me. Holding the dress against my breasts, I give her a weak smile. "May I have some privacy? I can get into the gown myself and will shout if I need help."

The woman's face falls, but she nods. "Of course, Ms. Paladino. I'll be right outside if you need me."

"Thank you," I say as she slips past the curtain.

As I pull my wedding dress from the hanger, I hear her making conversation with my mother, asking her if she's excited about my 'big day'.

Holding open the dress, I step into the sea of tulle and pull it up to my waist, twisting it slightly to get a good grasp on the zipper. I zip it as much as I can before twisting it back and stuffing my arms into the sleeves.

Once the gown is on, I reach my arm behind my back, gritting my teeth as I push past the discomfort and pull the zipper up the rest of the way.

Then I take a moment to look at myself in the mirror.

My reflection shows me a picture-perfect depiction of

a bride, ready in every way for her wedding day. She's lovely, the woman in the mirror. Her gown fits perfectly, her hair and makeup complementing the aura of the dress.

But on the inside, the woman in the mirror is dying. Her death is slow, but little by little, she's fading away. Not only is she mourning the loss of a relationship she barely got to nurture, but she's saying goodbye to the vibrant, happy woman she once was.

The Vincenza Paladino I grew to become is slipping through my fingers faster than I can comprehend. I miss the woman I once was. The woman I was before August forced me to become his bride, threatening to destroy the man I love if I were to resist.

What should be the happiest day of my life—the happiest time of my life—is a death sentence to my soul.

Swallowing thickly, I turn away from the mirror and pull the curtain open. My mother immediately begins to tear up, something that she's done every time she's seen me in the dress.

"I'm sorry!" she exclaims, dabbing the corner of her eyes with a crumpled-up tissue. "You're just so stunning, sweetheart. I can't wait for your father to see his little girl."

The corners of my mouth turn upward, but I know my smile doesn't meet my eyes. Stepping onto the pedestal, I fluff the skirt of the gown and run my hands down the front.

"How does everything feel?" Veronica asks, cocking

her head to the side as she inspects the dress from behind me.

"Great. The last round of alterations was perfect."

"Wonderful!" She claps her hands together. "Do you have the headpiece you planned on wearing to try on today?"

"I left it at home," my mother supplies. "I completely forgot about Vinnie's hair and makeup appointment prior. That was my mistake."

"It's fine, Mother, don't worry."

"Not a problem! I'll leave you two to admire the gown for a moment while I have my colleague settle the remaining paperwork. I'll just be a few minutes."

"Take your time," my mother says through a smile. She stands and comes over to me, brushing the hair away from my shoulder. "Are you okay, Vinnie darling? You seem off. Sad, almost."

Knots twist in my stomach. Concern shines through my mother's dove-colored eyes, and it kills me that she's picking up on the emotions I'm obviously failing to conceal.

"I'm fine," I lie. "Just tired. I actually feel like I'm coming down with something."

She gasps. "Oh, no! Let's get you out of this dress and home so you can relax. You can't get sick—we have such a busy week ahead with the rehearsal and then, of course, the wedding. This would be the worst time for you to catch something."

She shoos me off the pedestal, pressing her hand

against my lower back to turn me in the direction of the fitting room.

My dress drags elegantly behind me as I walk, the fabric making a soft swishing sound.

Following me into the room, she starts to unzip the back of my gown.

"No!" I shout as I turn quickly to pull away from her. I don't think—I just react, which startles us both.

Her eyes widen, her soft features scrunching in confusion, but she takes a step away from me. "I'm sorry, I—"

"No, I'm sorry. I don't know why I reacted like that. I'm just not feeling like myself."

"Oh, honey," she sighs. "I'll call Ross and have him bring the car around for you."

"Thank you."

"Of course, sweetheart," she says as she slips past the curtain, leaving me alone.

A single tear slips out, and I wipe it away before more can fall. Pressing my palms together, I bring them to my face and steeple my nose, taking a few deep breaths.

The nausea is back, rolling through my stomach aggressively.

Reaching behind, I unzip the gown and step out of it, breathing deeply as I do to try to keep the nausea at bay. The bile creeps up my throat as I hang the dress, and the moment the hanger is situated on the hook, I can't hold back.

Spinning, I spot a small wastebasket on the floor in

the corner of the dressing room and rush to it, dropping to my knees and leaning over at the same moment my stomach retches its contents.

My ribs burn as I dry heave, my stomach completely empty. Tears prick my eyes. I'm on my hands and knees, holding my hair back in one hand as I pray my stomach stops roiling.

The curtain flies open and soft footsteps rush in. A hand takes my hair from mine, and another rubs my back in gentle, circular motions.

"Oh, sweetheart, you weren't kidding," my mother coos. "It's okay, let it all out."

A small gasp sounds from behind us, and I assume it's the saleswoman, though I don't care enough to check.

"I'm sorry," I croak, leaning back on my heels, and wipe my mouth with the back of my hand in a very unladylike manner.

"It's okay," my mother consoles, but her hand falls away from my body, and she stills.

Turning my head to look at her, I see her staring wide-eyed at my side, and I realize I'm wearing only my bra and panties—my bruises on full display.

Her eyes sweep over the rest of me and finally meet my own, and I see her face morph into sadness. A thousand silent questions are asked, but not uttered aloud.

"Vinnie—" she starts, but I shake my head, my eyes cast to the floor, no longer wanting to see the look she's giving me.

Standing, I turn away from her and pick up my

sundress from where it sits folded on a chair. "You wouldn't believe what happened," I say dismissively, pretending like the lie I'm constructing is no big deal. "I came home last week, and the housekeeper had left a puddle on the floor from when she mopped. I slipped and launched myself into the credenza. Can you believe that?"

*God, I hope she does.*

She adds her own fake laughter alongside mine as I pull the dress overhead and settle it on my body. Without asking, she comes over and zips the dress. Once it's in place, I face her and smile.

I can see she's skeptical, unsure if she should believe me. Her expression hardens for the briefest of moments before she smiles. "You really must be more careful, darling."

My heart sinks with her response. There's a large part of me who hoped she'd wrap her arms around me and tell me not to marry August, because I don't deserve a man who is abusive, right? The little girl in me is desperate for her mother to get her out of this situation.

I really shouldn't be surprised that she's choosing to ignore the signs, though it does break my heart. She's always been concerned with appearances, and to her, there's no better match for her daughter than the most prestigious former bachelor in Manhattan.

Or maybe she truly is naïve and is taking my story at face value. My mother is sheltered, and as much as I adore her, she often doesn't use her head.

Fighting back more tears, I give her a tight smile and straighten myself. "I will, don't worry."

The saleswoman clears her throat awkwardly, garnering our attention again. I'd forgotten she was lingering at the edge of the fitting room. My cheeks heat, hating that she just witnessed that exchange with my mother. "Everything is ready to be settled up at the front, ladies. Whenever you're ready, I'll meet you there."

I nod, and my mother smiles at the woman. "Thank you, Veronica. You've been a gem through this whole process."

Squeezing my shoulder, my mother turns her attention back to me. "I'll have the bridal boutique sign an NDA, sweetheart," she whispers. "Don't you worry."

I stand there, dumbfounded, as my mother follows the saleswoman out, her words ricocheting through my mind.

Maybe my mother isn't as naïve as she portrays. I'm left wondering if she really is more concerned with appearances than she is with her own daughter.

# Chapter 9

## *Sly*

Saying goodbye to Ridgewood is bittersweet.

In every way, this city became my home. The people in it became my family.

Yesterday, we laid one of our brothers to rest. Every member of the Sinners Warlord and their families showed Preston respect by attending his funeral. Among the attendees were officers from the Ridgewood Police Department, and all the staff members from Andromeda, the bar the Sinners live above.

The service was short, but I have no doubt it was everything Preston would have hoped it'd be. Myself, as well as five other Sinners—Preston's cousin Nixon included—were pallbearers.

Burying Preston felt like a door closing on my time in Ridgewood. I'd had the week after being discharged from the hospital to spend time with my closest friends here, and now it is time for me to leave.

As I stare out at the tarmac in front of me, my

phone vibrates in my pocket. Reaching down, I see Sully's name flash across the screen as it rumbles in my hand.

I debate not answering, already feeling irritable from the day. My mood is somber, bordering on anger from the circumstances surrounding Preston's death that I cannot bring myself to let go of. The phone continues to vibrate in my hold, and though my gut tells me to send it to voicemail, I answer, unable to ignore my best friend.

"Sully," I greet, cupping my free hand over my other ear to barricade some of the noise from the plane's engine. "This isn't a great time. I'm on the tarmac."

"You're coming back?"

"Sì. I land early tomorrow."

"Good. That's good, man."

His voice sounds off—strained. Like there is something he needs to say, but is avoiding it.

Movement catches my eye, and I look up to see a flight attendant standing in the open doorway of the plane. She gives me a small wave, beaming at me from the top of the stairs that lead up to the small private jet I booked, signaling it's time to leave.

"They're waiting for me to board. Say what is on your mind, amico."

From the other end of the call, I can hear the rustling of paperwork. He must be at the office late.

Sully lets out a short groan. "I ran into Vinnie a couple days ago."

"And?" I begin climbing the stairs toward the grinning stewardess. I'm not surprised he ran into Vinnie—Manhattan is huge, but also incredibly small.

"She—uh, she was acting strange. When I said hi, she was really dodgy. Almost like she was hiding something."

"Okay?" I'm not sure where he's going with this. There are many reasons why she could have acted awkwardly. It may have been as simple as she was having an off day.

Regardless, my time to speak to Sully is running out. He needs to tell me the point of his phone call, and quickly.

"I don't know, Sly. She kept playing with her necklace. Touching it absentmindedly as she looked around the market, avoiding eye contact with me. She seemed nervous and jumpy."

The mention of a necklace garners my attention as I sit in one of the plush seats on the aircraft. As I lean back against the cushions, the stewardess steps up into my line of sight and mouths, *"Would you like anything to drink?"*

I shake my head, giving her a quick smile to be friendly, then turn my attention back to the conversation, my heart rate accelerating as my mind races and gravitates to the worst of thoughts.

"Did she seem like she was in danger?"

"No. Maybe? I don't think so—it was just almost like she was afraid someone would see us together, but there was a moment where I tried to touch her shoulder and she flinched…she also bent to pick something up and… Can we actually talk in person when you get back? Maybe I'm overexaggerating things."

My brows furrow, the entire conversation confusing me more with every word that flows from his mouth. I cannot think of a reason as to why she would be afraid to be seen with Sully. Aside from August, Sullivan Rochester is considered one of the most eligible bachelors in Manhattan and comes from a very powerful family. If anyone saw them together, they probably wouldn't give it a second thought considering who *she* is too. But her behavior just seems not like her, and I can't help but think the worst.

"Maybe it was just because of who I am? She knows we're friends," he offers.

My mind considers it, though deep in my center there is a nagging pit that grows. "Perhaps. You did not notice anyone else in the store with her?"

"No. She was alone, from what I could see."

"Hmm," I rumble, mulling over the thought. My mind drifts back to the necklace.

"And the necklace?" I ask him, wondering if it's the same she wore in the hospital room back when I first noticed the locket around her neck—a piece of jewelry I can't recall from our time together. It piques my curiosity now, in the same way it did then.

"Yeah, like one of those heart necklaces that open up."

"A locket."

"Yeah, a locket. She kept playing with it, which, as I

say it out loud, doesn't seem weird. But it was just a combination of everything. I know I don't really know her. It just seemed like odd behavior for anyone. Thought you should know."

Something about Sully's encounter doesn't sit right, but I cannot place what about it bothers me the most. I know I will have plenty of time to consider my thoughts when I am forty-thousand feet in the air.

"Thank you for telling me, mio amico," I tell him, knowing I need to end the call.

"Yeah, of course. It's been a while since we've seen each other, but I know how much she meant to you, and knowing you, I'm sure she's still important. I wouldn't feel right sitting on this information."

"I appreciate it. It is odd, and I'm not sure what to make of it, honestly. But I will find out."

"I know you will. If you need me in any way, you know where to find me."

"Thank you, Sully. Truly."

"Travel safe," he says, and then he disconnects us, leaving me to reflect on his encounter with Vinnie. Her behavior seems odd, but what I can't stop thinking about is her playing with her necklace.

I flip the phone over in my hand a few times as my mind wanders. What bothers me the most is the *type* of necklace it is.

Perhaps I am reading too far into things.

As I flip the phone upright in my hand, my fingers brush across the screen until I've reached Vincenza's contact, and I push the button to connect us.

The click of the phone sounds against my ear, and it goes straight to her generic voicemail, robbing me of the opportunity to even hear her voice.

Before I can continue to think about things further, the pilot comes over the intercom to greet me and warn that we are five minutes from takeoff. As he speaks, I put my seatbelt on and switch my phone into airplane mode.

Leaning my head against the headrest, I turn to my right and look out the window, relaxing into my seat as the plane begins to taxi the runway.

It gains speed, and before long, we ascend, pushing forward into the California sunset. Ridgewood's airport is small, and it only takes moments before the plane is leveling above the city.

The buildings sparkle against the hues of purples and blues as a thin coverage of clouds comes in over the tops of them. I can't help but smile at the beauty of the small city I called home for these last few months, but as I stare down at the skyline, I feel a small twinge of excitement to see the extravagant skyscrapers of Manhattan.

Exhaling a deep breath, I let my eyes close as I settle in for the next six or so hours of my flight.

*Goodbye, Ridgewood.*

Anticipation bubbles in my chest as I walk up the steps and into my parents' home. The first thing to assault me is not the scent of the meal that is being prepared, or even the comforting smell that *is* their house. It's my mother.

Quite literally.

The palm of her hand meets the back of my head as I walk through the door before she pulls me into a tight hug. Tears stream down her face as she pushes up on her tiptoes to squeeze around my neck.

"I cannot believe you put me through that, Sylvester Lucchetti! You are lucky you did not cause me a heart attack."

Kissing her on both cheeks, I gently run my hands up and down her arms as though I am warming her. "Please forgive me, Mamma."

"I already have," she says, pulling me back into another hug. I inhale the scent of her—the perfume she wears mixing with the scent of garlic from whatever she's been cooking. She smells of my childhood—of *home*.

In the arms of my mother, I let go of some of the pent-up stress I've been holding onto and allow my eyes to shut for a moment.

When I open them once more, I see Papà and Guilio emerge from Papà's office from over her shoulder.

My eyes meet my middle brother's across the room.

"Look what the cat dragged in," Guilio muses as he walks over. "I'd ask if you were healed enough to hug, but I can see Mamma doesn't care if she re-injures you, so I won't either."

She lets me go so Guilio can pull me into a hug. As he does, he claps my shoulder affectionately. My brother's welcome is warm, but from behind him, Papà scowls.

Guilio releases me, and I step toward Papà with my hand extended, nervous for my reunion with my father, as though I'm a small child again.

His eyes drift down at my outstretched hand, and he shakes his head. "You take off without a word, cut contact with your entire family, get yourself *shot*, tell us not to come while you're in the hospital for more than a week, and *then* you have the audacity to extend your hand to me?"

My head drops with the shame of his words. I'm embarrassed by my actions, though I've had a reason for each one. I'm about to apologize—what else can I do—when he takes my hand and uses it to pull me toward him into a hug.

Papà is a little shorter than I am, about four inches. He rests his chin on my shoulder. "Don't ever do that to your Mamma and me again. Do you understand me?" He exhales a shaky breath, and I can feel the stress in his shoulders through his hug.

"I won't, Papà. I am here to stay."

"Good," he says, squeezing tightly again. Then he releases his grasp, stepping backward to look me in the eye. "Your injuries?"

"Healing. I feel much better. Not perfect, but getting there."

"Excellent. I'll take a look at them later."

"Thank you." I tip my head in a nod. "Where is Federico?"

"Out," Mamma supplies. "He has a girlfriend now. They're inseparable."

"And Lorenzo?"

Guilio's eyebrows shoot up when I use our cousin's full name.

"Right here, *Sylvester*."

Whipping around, I see him standing in the doorway—he must have just arrived. His arms are crossed over his chest, which is accentuated by the white button-down shirt he wears. Clearly, my cousin has increased his gym routine since I've been gone, and I can't help but wonder if it has something to do with the Paladinos.

When I left, he was in the thick of the feud, trying to gather information to take them down. He'd been jumped by a few of their men when he was caught snooping.

Seeing Enzo stirs anger within me that's been lying dormant. He was the last person I saw before I left Manhattan—he'd sought me out to interrogate me about my relationship with Vinnie, and ultimately helped force my hand in leaving.

He was partially responsible for my abrupt departure—a piece of information I know he's kept to himself. "Ciao, cugino. I was wondering if you'd be a part of my welcome committee when I returned home."

"I'm surprised you have returned home, *cousin*." His

voice drips with sarcasm, thickening the tension in the air between us.

From my peripheral, I can see the change in the posture of the family who surround us. Curious eyes are watching, and Enzo knows it too if his smirk is any indication.

I hold my tongue, biting back the words I want to say to him. There will be another time and place.

Storing the anger away, I smile at him. "Sì, it was time. Although Ridgewood was humbling. You should visit there sometime."

Sensing the disdain, Mamma steps forward and places her hand on my shoulder. "Son, are you hungry? The kitchen is a mess from dinner preparations, but if you are hungry now, I can create a lovely brunch. How does that sound?"

"It sounds great, Mamma, grazie." I toss another look at my cousin, my eyes narrowing as I follow Mamma's lead.

Enzo's annoyed scoff echoes through my parents' foyer.

As I walk, my phone vibrates and I slide it from my pocket, seeing Sully's name and message.

SULLY

**Can we meet later and talk?**

I will have to message him back later—right now, I must speak with mia madre.

The closer we get to the kitchen, the more the scents

of her cooking intensify, bringing my mind to a place of nostalgia.

She pins me with a stare the moment we're alone, and immediately begins to move effortlessly around her kitchen, gathering things to make brunch. Mamma has always had a talent for not taking her eyes off you when she's upset—something she continues to prove to me as an adult.

Taking a seat on a barstool, I rest my elbows on the countertop. "It is good to see you and be back home. Whatever you're preparing smells delicious."

"Don't try to sweet talk me, figlio," she scolds, waving a wooden spoon in my direction. "This is not a matter I will let you off the hook easily for. Now, tell me why you left your home."

Her words cause me to wince—a reaction I cannot stop in time.

Her eyes soften slightly with my reaction. "Mio dolce ragazzo, per favore confida con tua madre. Cosa ti stà succedendo?" *My sweet boy, please confide in your mother. What is going on with you?*

Shaking my head, I switch to Italian as well. "Questo non è né il momento né il luogo, Mamma." *This is not the time nor the place, Mamma.*

My eyes bounce to the open walkway, then back to her.

"Per favore. Parliamone più tardi." *Please. Let us discuss this later.*

"Va bene, ma è meglio che tu vada a parlare con il tuo papà. Non sono così sicuro che sarà così indulgente." *Fine, but you better go speak with your Papà. I'm not so sure he'll be as forgiving.*

Setting the wooden spoon on the counter, she begins measuring out ingredients into her large mixing bowl. I watch as she mixes together avocado oil, milk, eggs, and sugar. Once she has a handle on what she's doing, she looks up at me again.

"Andare." *Go,* Mamma pushes in the voice she only uses when she leaves no room for argument.

Relenting, I stand from the stool and round the corner, pressing a soft kiss to the side of my mamma's hair as my hand comes to hold the other side of her head.

She sighs softly, and I can tell how frustrated she is with me.

"Ti amo, Mamma," I say before releasing her.

As I walk from the room to go search for Papà, I hear her tell me she loves me too, and I know that while she means it wholeheartedly, I still have a lot of missed time to make up for.

I just hope the other people in my life aren't as upset with me as she is.

# Chapter 10

## *Sly*

"We need to talk," Enzo tells me as he rounds the leather couch in my family's study, swirling a lowball of whiskey as he walks.

Already seated, my legs are spread wide in front of me as I perch my elbow on the armrest, my own whiskey in hand. I've been waiting for him, knowing this moment was coming.

We'd made it through a lovely day spent with my family, catching up. They listened to stories of the Sinners and filled me in on everything that's been happening here in New York.

Dinner was delicious. Mamma made my favorite dish—spaghetti and meatballs with her homemade sauce. But as she and Federico cleaned the kitchen, and Guilio and my father retreated to his office to discuss my brother's newest hedge fund, I made my way to the study, knowing it was only a matter of time before Enzo followed.

"I'm surprised you waited this long to seek me out."

"Because we've had so much time to speak alone? You're lucky I stayed."

"And you're lucky I am sitting here, willing to hear what you have to say after you all but drove me out of town," I hiss.

Looking at the empty fireplace, I force myself to take a sip of my whiskey, letting the alcohol sit on my tongue while I bite back the rest of the words I want to say to him.

He's silent for several minutes, taking a seat next to me on the couch, but he doesn't sit back. Instead, he props his elbows on his knees and stares straight ahead like I am.

"You fell in love with the enemy," he says simply, his voice devoid of emotion.

"She is not the enemy," I growl. "She is not responsible for her father's actions."

We turn to face each other at the same time, both of us on edge.

"She shares the last name and the DNA of the man who killed my dad. That makes *her* the enemy, just as much as he is."

"If you truly believe that, then your ignorance runs deep. She is the kindest, most amazing person I have ever had the pleasure of knowing, let alone loving."

He scoffs, shaking his head in disbelief. "Then why did you leave? Why is she marrying another man?"

My jaw tics as I grit my teeth. Looking down at my glass, I curb my anger and swallow my pride. "I don't know. There is something off with the entire scenario that I cannot figure out."

I can feel my eyes well with tears again and I tilt my head toward the ceiling, shaking it slightly. I have never been this emotional of a man, but when it comes to Vincenza, it's like my soul is torn in half, and the piece I still possess is battered and bloodied, laid out in front of me.

When I look back at my cousin, his expression has softened as he watches me.

Lorenzo has been my best friend since I was a child. We grew up together. Became brothers after his father passed. This wedge between us cuts almost as deeply as the one between me and Vinnie.

"She came to visit me in Ridgewood after I was shot," I continue. "I could feel the love between us was just as powerful as the day I left. The way she spoke— the way in which she let me hold her and touch her. Yet, she still insisted she was marrying him. Something is not right, Enzo. I just can't put my finger on what it is."

The words flow from my lips as though there is no animosity between us. He is simply my cousin again, and I am no longer angry. There are still many things we need to speak about to repair what has been broken, but at this moment, I just need my cousin.

"August is a piece of shit," he says after a minute of thinking. "While I've been researching Joseph, I've been looking into August, too. They're both terrible excuses for humans."

"Why are you researching them?"

Enzo's eyes darken, narrowing slightly as a smirk graces his features. "To destroy them."

I sigh and pinch the bridge of my nose. "Enzo—"

"The Paladino family has gotten away with far too much, Sly. I won't let this go. Not until I feel the weight of what they've done lift from my shoulders. It's been a heavy load to bear since I was a child. The Paladinos are not a good family, despite how much you say you love Vinnie. You *know* this."

"Sì, I do. Her brother—*August*. They're not good men."

"Neither is their old man."

I nod, agreeing with my cousin but silencing my words. I expect the conversation to be finished, but what he says next surprises me.

"Does she really mean that much to you?"

Swallowing the lump in my throat, I nod. "The world. Trust me, cugino, I never thought I would fall for a Paladino. I fought against it for a long time, but ours is a love that could not be stopped no matter how much I tried."

There is a turmoil in his eyes, but after a moment, his head bounces with a few soft nods. "I'm not sure I can ever accept her, given who she is. But if she makes you as happy as you say she does, I won't stand in your way."

My chest inflates with relief. It's not acceptance, but it's a start, and I feel the anger between us dissipating.

"Grazie. Having to choose between la mia famiglia or amore mio is not something I want to do. I am confident you will grow to love her. She has that effect on people."

"We'll see," he says skeptically. "So what are you going to do about the wedding, now that you're back?"

"What is there to do about it?" I ask. "She says she is set in her decision. There seems to be some hold over her, making her committed to seeing this through."

"And that's enough to keep you dormant? That doesn't seem like the Sly I know."

"Sully told me something that's been bothering me. He ran into her at the market, and she was acting strange. She was jumpy and wouldn't make eye contact with him."

"Well, that's not surprising, since Sully is a giant child. Maybe she just doesn't like him?"

A small chuckle leaves me, but it doesn't feel sincere. "I don't think that is it. He said she was playing with her necklace a lot, almost in a way that was subconscious."

"Not exactly a red flag, but I'll take your word for it as being odd. So what do you think is going on?"

"I'm not sure," I tell him honestly. Exasperation fills my chest—a sense of helplessness.

"Isn't the wedding soon? Next weekend, right?"

"This weekend." I swallow thickly. "The wedding is this weekend."

Silence fills the study again, and moments later footsteps approach before Mamma pops her head around the door. "Would you boys like some gelato?"

Enzo laughs, standing with his glass in his hand. He tosses back the remaining sip of his whiskey and walks toward Mamma.

"Zia, do men eat gelato?" he teases.

She pushes the door open further and pulls the dish towel from her shoulder, swatting it at his chest lightly. "Yes, Lorenzo, they do. Antonio, Federico, *and* Guilio are already enjoying their bowls. You're never too old for gelato."

Mamma meets my gaze from across the room and offers me a smile.

"You're right, Mamma," I agree. "You go on, Enzo. I have a quick phone call to make, then I will join you both in the kitchen."

Unspoken words pass between us as he looks over his shoulder at me.

*Yes, I am going to call her.*

He nods, then gently pushes his palm against Mamma's back to guide her out of the room. When the door's soft *click* sounds behind them, I remove my phone from my pocket.

As I unlock it, I see Sullivan's text message from earlier. I forgot about it and never responded, so I call him first.

The phone rings twice before he sends me to voice-mail, and a banner message illuminates across my screen.

SULLY

**Can't talk right now!**

Shaking my head, I find Vinnie's contact instead.

The phone rings and rings, but when I'm certain it's about to turn over to voicemail, her soft words float through the speaker.

"Hello?" Her voice is quiet, but I can hear her smile.

"Hello, piccola ladra," I say as I stand, unable to resist smiling myself.

"Sly," she breathes, and my name on her tongue is like music to my ears.

"How are you, Vincenza?"

"I'm good. Busy. Are you out of the hospital? How are you feeling?" Her questions rapidly fire, and I imagine the look of concern on her face.

"I am healing nicely. The pain is minimal, and sì, I've been discharged from the hospital. I'm home now."

"Oh," she says softly. "I bet your friends are incredibly relieved to have you back." There is a fake layer to her tone, and my brow furrows at the way her voice grows higher as she says the words I can tell she doesn't mean.

"I'm in Manhattan."

She gasps.

"Meet up with me, piccola ladra. Let me see you again."

"Sly… We've said our goodbyes…"

"I am not ready for goodbye. I love you too much to say goodbye to you. Meet up with me."

"I *can't* meet you, Sly."

"Vinnie…"

"I can't. If I see you again…" Her voice cracks, and the splintering radiates through my heart.

I can sense where this conversation is heading, and even though I'm putting her on the spot by asking her to meet, she can't possibly be blindsided by it. She knows where my heart lies.

Annoyance blooms with me with the realization that I am physically so close to this woman, yet mentally we're so far apart. She has no reason to marry August—no reason in which she will tell me—but it's the unknown that plagues my mind and causes me to wonder.

"You'll what, Vincenza?" I bite, hating my tone, but unable to hide the emotion that flows through me. "You'll allow yourself to *feel* the truth? What happened between us while I was in the hospital…what I felt… what I *feel*. I know you felt it too."

There's a silence on the other end of the phone, and I almost think she's hung up. But her soft breaths indicate that she hasn't, and seconds later I hear her inhale a sharp, shuddering breath.

"I won't be able to stay away," she whispers, and even though I cannot see it, I hear the quiver in her voice.

It breaks me.

Sitting back down on the soft leather couch, I run my hand through my hair. "You don't need to stay away, piccola ladra. I'm back, and if you want to be with me—if you break off your engagement with August—there will be no questions asked. I will not let the past haunt us, Vincenza. I will spend our future protecting you. Cherishing you. I love you. I haven't stopped loving you."

"I *can't*." Her voice is pleading, filled with turmoil and strife.

My hand balls into a fist as I bring it to rest on my thigh, slamming it down in frustration. "Vinnie—"

"Just…*please*, Sly," she cuts me off. "I can't do this. My wedding is the day after tomorrow. I'm marrying August."

"Tell me why you were acting strangely when you ran into Sully at the market."

"He told you he saw me?" she asks, surprised.

"Sì, of course he did."

Leaning back against the sofa, I settle in, forcing myself to regain my composure as I cross my ankle over my knee. The only thing I want to do is race out of this house and go find her, but I know in my heart that will not solve anything in this moment. I need to *hear* her.

A soft crackling rustles against the phone speaker as though she's adjusting it.

"I wasn't feeling well when I saw him," she says matter-of-factly.

My jaw clenches at her casual response.

She's not telling me something. I can hear it in her voice that she's avoiding the truth, and I can't ignore the nagging feeling deep in my stomach—something Sully mentioned repeats itself continuously through my mind. There are two things, actually, but only one I will address at this moment, *needing* to know if my instincts are correct.

"Vincenza," I begin, hoping my voice comes across calmer than I feel inside. "How long have you worn a locket?"

Through the speaker, I hear a small gasp. "I—what does my necklace have to do with this conversation?"

"It has everything to do with this conversation if your necklace means what I think it does," I growl, unable to conceal the exasperation in my voice.

Pushing to my feet again, I begin to pace in front of the unlit fireplace. "How long have you worn a locket, Vinnie?"

It's silent on the other end of the line, but I know she's still there. Squeezing my eyes shut, I beg her to tell me without saying the words aloud.

"I purchased it after you left," she tells me so quietly, it's barely a whisper.

My heart falls to my stomach, crashing past the other organs as it sinks deeper and deeper, her words one step closer to confirming my fears.

As calmly as I possibly can, I ask the question I'm terrified to know the answer to. "Is he hurting you, Vincenza?"

We both go quiet once the words leave my lips—the only sounds coming through the phone are those of our soft breaths.

She doesn't answer the question.

"Are you using your safe word, piccola ladra?"

*Locket.*

Her safe word.

The word she'd selected as her safe word when she first learned of my preferences in the bedroom. The word selected for if things became too much for her.

As a pleasure dominant, I have no intention of ever hurting her, but the line between pleasure and pain is thin, and everyone has a limit, so I made her choose something that would indicate she felt uncomfortable, in pain, or just simply wanted things to end. All she needed to do was say the word and I would stop what I was doing immediately, no questions asked.

Perhaps this is her way of telling me without words that, whatever was happening, she wants it to stop.

It's entirely possible that I am reaching with my assumption, but when Sully told me she mindlessly toyed with her necklace—her *locket*—during his entire encounter with her, it brought back memories to her in my hospital room. She played with the locket then, too, when she was lost in her mind or trying to avoid the heaviness of some of our conversation.

A door slams in the background, and Vinnie sighs. "I'm getting married in two days, Sly. I can't do this. I have to go."

"Answer the question, Vincenza."

I hear her walking, and another door shuts lightly. Then, water begins to run in the background.

"I know you don't agree with my choice, but it's time for you to listen to me," she says, her voice low. The water sounds close to her, and it makes me think

she's turned it on for a reason. A deep feeling of protectiveness rushes through me, but then she continues on,
cutting through my thoughts. "I don't love him, Sly. But
I *am* marrying him on Saturday. My mind is set in this
decision. I'm sorry."

A smile upturns my lips despite what she's just said,
and hope blossoms in my chest.

*Hope.* I haven't felt that in many months.

*She doesn't love him.*

She's already told me as much, but to hear her reit-
erate it resonates differently this time.

"Do you love me, piccola ladra?" I ask, praying
she'll tell me the truth. The only thing I want to hear is
that she still loves me, too. Everything else we can
handle together.

I stop pacing and hold my breath until she answers.

"Sly…"

"Do you love me, Vincenza? Because love is not a
strong enough word for what I feel for you. My entire
existence was created simply for you. My heart calls to
you. It sings your name, and beats solely for you. I
would move Heaven and earth if—"

"Of *course* I love you, Sly. God, I love you so much
it's killing me. Every day, you're all I can think of.
You're the only reason I get up in the morning and lay
my head on the pillow at night."

"Then *why?*"

"I have to go. Please, feel some semblance of peace
knowing my heart is yours. It will *always* be yours, but

there are things I can't explain to you. *Please*, just let me go."

"Is he hurting you?" I ask again, the unanswered question pushing its way to the forefront of my mind again.

"I have to go."

The line goes dead, and immediately a roar bellows from my chest as I throw my phone. It lands with a thud against the couch and I see a new shade of red.

My rage is a deep shade of burgundy, so dark it's nearing black.

She never answered the question.

She was jumpy and nervous when Sully saw her.

She flinched when he reached for her.

Her silence speaks volumes, and with sudden clarity I realize the answer has been in front of me this entire time.

I feel my monster clawing his way out, and this time I have no intention of pushing him away.

August is hurting the love of my life. Physically, and likely threatening her in some way. Vincenza is a strong woman. She wouldn't agree to marry him—especially if he's putting his hands on her—unless there is something monumental being held against her.

I can *feel* it. Hear it in the words she doesn't speak aloud.

But I have no proof. Not yet, anyway.

As the monster within me claws closer to the surface, I know what must be done. A plan begins to form in my mind and I know exactly how I can guarantee Vinnie's safety for the rest of our lives.

Leaving was the worst thing I could have done for us, and it's time to start making up for lost time.

The first thing I need to do is get her far, far away from August.

Then I'll ensure he never sees the light of day again.

# Chapter 11

## *Vinnie*

"You seem off, sister," Luciano tells me as we take a corner table at the small cafe down the street from my office. It's rare our lunch breaks align, but I moved an appointment to take Luce up on his invitation.

I busy myself by placing a napkin in my lap. When I look back up at my brother, he's watching me closely.

Shrugging, I say, "Pre-wedding jitters."

He smirks and shakes his head. "Why don't you stop lying through your teeth and tell me what's going on with you? Your wedding is tomorrow. You look like one of my clients, not a woman who's getting married in less than twenty-four hours."

Luciano is one of the most prominent divorce attorneys in Manhattan and recently gave all the wives on the Upper East and West Side something to talk about when he decided to do the exact opposite of his partner, Simon Gamble, and align himself with only female clients whose husbands were ready to run them through the financial wringer.

My brother has a knack for sniffing out lies like a bloodhound.

"Do you want the truth?" I ask, then bite my tongue as the waitress comes over with our quiche and cappuccinos on a tray. I smile at her as she sets them down. "Thank you."

"Of course. Enjoy," she tells us both with minimal eye contact before she walks away.

"Obviously," my brother quips in a bored tone. He still hasn't stopped scrutinizing me and I shift uncomfortably under his gaze.

"The wedding is a farce," I tell him, tilting my chin upward to push my strength forward. All I want to do is cry. "I'm not marrying August because I love him. I don't even like the man. Hate him, in fact. I'm marrying August because I have to."

Luciano rolls his eyes and shakes his head again. "Baby sister, do you think I'm dense? Anyone with eyes can see that you despise August. The question is, *why* are you marrying him? What does he have on you?"

Anger suddenly overtakes me, my temper rising so quickly I have to force myself to keep my voice low. "Why do you think he has something on me?"

"Surely you aren't agreeing to this just to make Mother and Father happy."

"I—" My stomach roils, and I look down at my hands situated in my lap. How do I tell him that the life of the man I love is on the line? "It's not as cut and dry as you're making it out to be."

"Everything can be simplified, Vinnie. So I'm going to ask you again. Why are you marrying a man you have no feelings for?"

Sly's face flashes through my mind as I decide how much I want to tell my brother. He's never been one to conform to the feud between our two families—he's always been more of the black sheep—but he grew up in the same toxicity I did and with that, the seed was planted from a young age.

Still, I long to confide in someone other than Cecilia, and my brother has always been there for me. Growing up, he was my protector, and though we've drifted apart over the years, I feel like confiding in him may just bridge the gap between us.

Picking up my cappuccino, I take a sip and gather my thoughts.

"Last fall I fell in love," I start, taking a deep, shuddering breath as I look up at my brother. "We were together in secret until August's proposal shifted us off our axis. He asked me to run away with him, or to come clean about our relationship, and the afternoon I was supposed to meet him with my decision, August showed up at my apartment with a file of photographs. He'd been having us tailed for weeks."

I purposely omit that August had slapped me and knocked me unconscious. That's a detail I plan on keeping to myself.

"By the time he left, I was too late. Sl—the man I

love thought I didn't want to be with him, that I was choosing August. And he left town."

My brother narrows his eyes and takes a slow bite of his quiche, listening to my every word. I can see the wheels in his head turning. "Yet there's a reason why you haven't tracked him down to tell him otherwise. What hold does August have over you, V?"

Tears line my eyes, and I grow so exasperated it all begins to bubble to the surface. I am *not* this woman. August shouldn't have this power over me, but fear for Sly's life holds me so tightly, I can't break free. Logically, I know in my heart if I told Sly, this could all be over, yet there's that small part—the two percent of me— that screams, '*but what if August kills him first?*'

And that's the part that keeps me rooted in my decision.

Telling my brother won't change anything, still I hear myself whisper, "August is threatening to kill him if I don't comply with his demand to marry him."

I hear my brother chuckle and I glare at him from beneath my lashes. "Oh, sweet, naïve sister. You're a *Paladino*. Do you truly think that the St. Jeans hold more weight than the Paladinos in this city? Your little lover boy's life isn't truly at risk, August has just manipulated you into believing it is. Who is he, anyway?"

"You don't know August like I unfortunately have come to, Luciano. Trust me on this one. I wouldn't be putting myself through hell if I wasn't one-hundred percent positive his life would be in danger if I were to back out."

"What reason would August have to threaten this man's life? You still haven't told me who he is."

"And I won't," I tell him, shaking my head. "It's not important anymore. What is important is that his life is safe—protected—because tomorrow as of five p.m., August will get what he wants."

My brother's lips purse and he leans back in his chair, relaxing into it as he looks at me skeptically.

Wanting a distraction from the conversation, I let my eyes wander out the window, and I watch the cars as they pass by. The air constricts in my lungs when I see an all black Ducati amongst them. I stare at the driver, scrutinizing his build, his posture, his everything, wondering if it's Sly.

I only breathe again once he passes.

"Tell me, Vinnie. I can help you if you tell me who he is." My brother breaks through the fog in my mind. Slowly, I turn back to look at him.

"I *can't*," my voice cracks. *I won't.*

Luciano doesn't press me further, and slowly our conversation drifts into mundane chit-chat. We don't speak of tonight's rehearsal dinner, or the pre-wedding Paladino brunch, but I can tell there's more he'd like to say.

By the time we stand to part ways, my heart feels heavy, and I dread going back to the office for two more hours.

I'm looking down at my phone as I breeze through the lobby of my office building, when I hear a voice call to me, the melodic echo bouncing through the space. "Miss Paladino!"

Stopping, I turn toward the reception desk and smile at the woman standing behind it, her arm in midair. She's new, and I can't recall her name, but her smile is vibrant as she tucks a lock of her platinum blonde hair behind her ear.

"Sorry to interrupt you!" she says as I walk toward her. "You had a gentleman stop by while you were gone. I told him you had left for the day. I apologize—I hadn't realized you'd be back."

My heart plummets into my stomach, my entire body freezing in place. Salvia lodges in my throat as I try to swallow through the clash of panic and excitement that runs through me, my thoughts immediately jolting back to Sly.

"That's okay. Did he leave his name?"

She doesn't need to say it. Not really. My instinct is already screaming his name, wondering if he's still around, or went elsewhere to find me.

"I'm sorry, he didn't. Once I said you'd left, he didn't stick around. For what it's worth, he was strikingly handsome. Looked familiar, but I couldn't quite place where I'd seen him before. Well-groomed beard. Accent."

*Probably the newspapers. His face has been plastered across since news broke of his injuries.*

*Headlines reading, "Son of Renowned Manhattan Surgeon shot in California Drive-by."*

I can feel my body begin to tremble. "How long ago was that?"

"About thirty minutes or so, maybe forty." My head bobs as she speaks.

"Thank you so much," I reply with shaky breath, and before she can answer, I'm walking away. My heels click against the tile flooring as I rush toward the revolving door, desperate for fresh air.

I should have known he would show up here—that he'd try to see me—but my delusional self had hoped he'd simply give up.

As soon as I'm back outside, the warmth of the summer day envelops me, and in conjunction with my heart rate, a thin layer of sweat immediately prickles at my hairline.

Cars speed past where I stand on the sidewalk, my arm outstretched in the air to hail a cab. The sound of zipping tires against asphalt and motors revving does nothing to calm the pulsation of nerves zooming through my bloodstream. After a moment, a yellow taxi pulls alongside the curb and I waste no time pulling open the door and climbing inside. Grabbing my phone from my clutch in lieu of buckling my seatbelt, I dial Cecilia's number as I tell the driver, "Greenwich and Vestry."

Loyal to a fault, she answers on the second ring. "Hey."

"Hey. Are you home?"

"Yeah," she says through a yawn. "I just woke up from a catnap."

"Lia, I think he's on his way to the apartment right now."

There's a rustling against the speaker, and I picture her sitting up on the couch. "He, who?"

"Sly," I tell her, then gasp when the cab driver slams on the brakes and lays on the horn.

"Watch it, ya idiot!"

My fingertips curl along the edge of the cracked leather seat.

"Where are you?" Cecilia questions.

Pinching the bridge of my nose, I close my eyes. "I hopped in a cab. Listen, if he shows up…"

"I'm not even home," she singsongs into the phone, and I sigh with relief.

"Thank you," I breathe.

"Look…I understand why you're going through with this, and why you're avoiding him, Vins, I really do. But don't you think there could be some other solution? Maybe if you just talk to him, you guys could figure out a plan."

"Trust me, I've been over every possible option in my mind. I don't trust August as far as I can throw him, and I just can't take that risk. *Especially* now. Sly almost died, and it had nothing to do with August."

"Exactly. Repeat that sentence again, Vinnie. Sly almost *died*, and it had *nothing* to do with August. It's like he's been given a second chance. Don't you think you should take advantage of that?"

I'm quiet, and she lets the silence stretch, not pressuring me to answer. For several minutes, neither of us speak and it's like her presence is with me in the car instead of just on the other end of the line. It's calming, and I appreciate that she's just being in the moment with me as I think about her words and the feeling in my chest.

All too soon, the driver pulls in front of August's building—a historical site that's been transformed into luxury condominiums at which he owns the almost nine-thousand square foot penthouse.

Reaching into my clutch, I grab my wallet, fish out a few bills, and hand them to the driver.

"Thank you," I tell him as I climb out.

"Does August know he's back?" she asks at the same time as the doorman greets me, "Ms. Paladino."

I smile and dip my head in a nod as I pass through the door that's held open for me.

"I can only assume." I address Cecilia's question. "I suspect if he does know, I'm about to find out."

The elevator pings and I step inside, holding my electronic keycard against the card reader for the penthouse floor. The doors are painfully slow as they close.

"Do you want me to meet you there before the rehearsal? Ride with you guys and act like a buffer? I could ask Ross to bring me."

"No, it's okay." I watch the numbers ascend above the elevator doors.

"I wish you'd let me help you..." her voice trails off, the sadness behind her words like a shot in the heart.

"I know," I tell her, smiling sadly to myself. "I have to go, I'm almost there. I'll see you tonight though, okay?"

"*Please* be safe," she stresses.

"Always."

*As safe as I can be around a grenade that's liable to explode at any moment.*

Hanging up, I slip my phone into my clutch right before the elevator doors open up. When they do, a nauseating symphony of erotic sounds echo from all around. Skin slapping against skin, obnoxious, high-pitched moans. Guttural groans.

Stepping into the foyer, I'm immediately greeted with August's bare ass, and the sight of him pounding into a woman bent over the arm of the couch, whose face I can't see.

"Welcome home, wife," he groans as he readjusts his hand so he's pushing the woman down further into the cushions.

"I'm not your wife yet," I practically growl. "New friend?" I drop my purse onto the table and kick out of my shoes, haphazardly leaving them right in the middle of the floor.

The second I step foot into this gilded cage, I shake myself free of everything I've been taught through my upbringing. Manners, filter, and kindness be damned. August is insistent about this union and shackling himself, so I will be pulling against the chains and making life as difficult as possible for him.

His thrusts increase and I roll my eyes. It's nothing I

haven't seen before. He's done this practically weekly since forcing me to move in here.

"You know I like my women willing, Vinnie. Are you ready to take her place yet?"

"Not a chance in hell," I spit, giving him my back as I walk to the guest bedroom—my bedroom.

"Then I'll keep fucking whomever I please!" he shouts, and I hear the woman cry out from what sounds like pain, not pleasure.

"You do that," I call over my shoulder as I round the corner.

I barely make it into the room I refer to as my own when I hear him over the moans of the woman—she's coming, or she's a fabulous actress. "Be ready to leave in two hours, *wife*."

I cut off the rest of his sentence and use my bare foot to slam the door closed, twisting the lock for good merit.

One-hundred and twenty minutes until I have to become an actress myself.

# Chapter 12

## *Sly*

Stalking had never been a part of my plan, yet I find myself speeding down Columbus Avenue in the direction of Vincenza's Central Park Tower apartment.

The summer sun beats down against my black leather riding jacket and gloves as sweat drips from my forehead beneath my helmet. Weaving through the cars, I pay close attention to the road, forcing Vinnie out of my mind as I focus on making it to her building safely, but as quickly as possible.

She wasn't at work. The woman at the reception desk was less than informative when I asked questions, attempting to gauge Vinnie's whereabouts.

The clock is ticking—in just over twenty-four hours she'll be walking down the aisle toward a man who doesn't deserve her. Toward a man I heavily suspect mistreats her.

The light ahead turns red, and I look left and right

as I approach, not bothering to slow my speed as I run the light. Horns honk at me but I pay them no mind and continue onward.

Finding a place to park my motorcycle, I rip the helmet from my head and deposit it onto the seat before I trudge toward the massive building. The doorman gives me a sideways glance, yet opens the door for me, regardless.

The ride in the elevator takes an eternity as I work to steady my breathing, my heart hammering behind my rib cage with every escalating floor. When the elevator dings and I step into the small foyer that allows me to knock on Vincenza's door, I hesitate.

My mind spirals in the many ways this could go. But I raise my fist and knock before I let my thoughts get too carried away.

Though the apartment seems quiet and empty, I suddenly hear a small bump of furniture.

"I know you're in there," I say, trying to keep my voice steady. "I just want to speak to you for a moment, piccola ladra. *Please.*"

Moments pass before soft footsteps draw closer. My heart feels as though it may explode at any moment from how quickly it beats. Biting my tongue, I wait with bated breath for her to open the door.

From inside, the locks begin to disengage. When the doorknob twists and finally opens, I am surprised to see Cecilia standing in front of me. Her hair and makeup are done, but she's wearing a plush bathrobe, which she pulls tighter around her.

"Hi," she says, crossing her arms in front of her chest.

"Hi, Cecilia. I apologize for disturbing you. I am here to see Vincenza, is she in?"

Sadly, she shakes her head. "She's not. She's getting ready at August's."

"Getting ready?"

"For the rehearsal."

"Oh." How could I have not realized there would be a rehearsal tonight?

A sinking feeling begins in my sternum and quickly falls to my stomach. This is truly happening.

Tomorrow is the wedding.

For some reason, knowing there is a rehearsal makes it much more real.

Looking down at the floor, I consider asking Cecilia for August's address, or the location of the church. What good would it do, though? If I have any hope of swaying Vincenza before it's too late, I must do it when she's not overwhelmed with tonight's event.

"Thank you for your time," I tell Cecilia, with the most pathetic excuse for a smile I can muster.

Turning back toward the elevator, I press the call button.

"Sly," she says, and I look back at her over my shoulder. "She loves you. You have no idea the lengths she's going to because of her love for you. Maybe you can still sway her at The Manhattan Grand."

My brows furrow in confusion, and she shakes her head like she wants to say more, but doesn't.

Instead, she closes the door, putting a very clear barrier between her and my impending questions.

The brief conversation has done nothing to ease the concern that builds within me. *The lengths she's going to because of her love for me?* What does she mean by that? Her mention of The Manhattan Grand is also oddly worded, and leaves me wondering if Cecilia has just given me Vincenza's location.

Seeking clarification, I stalk back toward the door, raising my fist to knock again, but instead stay frozen in my stance, trying to piece the puzzle together.

Everything I've been told in the last few days swirls through my mind, but the only clear sentiment—the one flashing through my mind like a neon sign—is screaming, *'you have to stop this wedding'*.

Dropping my fist, I turn and head back to the elevator and push the call button again. The doors open immediately and I step inside. As they begin to close, I reach into my pocket and pull out my phone to make a call to the one person I know will be able to help me by whatever means necessary.

It rings continuously, and just as I think it will turn to voicemail, a gruff, slightly muffled voice greets me. "Miss me already, pookie?"

"Perhaps. Do you have anything keeping you in Ridgewood, amico? I know we spoke about you coming to visit, but I would appreciate the trip happening sooner than later."

"How soon?" His voice is clearer now. He must have taken his helmet off.

"How quickly can you get on a flight?"

The elevator doors open and I walk out, nodding at the doorman as I pass by. New York's background noise envelopes me as I walk to my Ducati.

"You footing the bill, Lucchetti?" Gravel crunching floats up to intermix with the sound of his laughter.

"Yes, Nixon, I am footing the bill."

If there is one man I know can help cause a distraction and assist me with stopping the wedding, it's Nixon.

"Fantastic. I can be on a flight out tonight—give me two hours to pack my shit and get to the airport. Make the flight out of SFO."

Nixon was the man who "found" me when I first arrived in Ridgewood. He recognized something in me and knew I would find a home within the motorcycle club he was involved in. Though skeptical, I accompanied him to meet the president and was welcomed in.

Well, perhaps not *welcomed*, but the club's president, Cain, didn't turn me away.

I owe a lot to Nixon. His friendship is not something I take for granted.

"Grazie, amico mio."

Nixon grunts. "See you soon, asshole."

I arrive at my motorcycle right as we end the call and pick up my helmet that rests on the seat where I left it. Before I slip it on, I toggle to the group message with Sully and Enzo, sending them a message.

My apartment. 30 minutes.

Their responses come in immediately, so I read them before putting my helmet on.

SULLY

Someone's demanding today.

ENZO

It's three p.m. on a Friday. Some of us
have jobs, cousin.

Shaking my head, I type out, 'It's important' as I kick my leg over my bike and straddle the seat. The engine roars to life, vibration igniting through the entire motorcycle.

ENZO

It better be life or death by the way
you're summoning us.

Can you guys meet me or not?

SULLY

I still can't believe you kept paying for
your apartment even though you were
gone for almost a year. Should have
known you'd always come back.

ENZO

Because that's what's important
right now.

SULLY

Oh, c'mon, Zo. Don't act like you didn't
sneak in there and cry yourself to sleep
on his couch a time or two.

ENZO

How many times do I have to tell you?
Don't call me Zo.

SULLY

Alright, Zo-Zo.

# Chapter 13

## *Vinnie*

Crystals shimmer from the low lighting of The Cordelia, a posh restaurant the St. Jeans rented out for the rehearsal dinner. Soft music plays over their speaker system as dishes clank from the fifty guests in attendance for this meal. This *celebration*. Both sets of families, close friends, and the wedding party.

Despite not wanting bridesmaids and groomsmen, August relented when my mother fought him tooth and nail on it, insisting that one's wedding day is nothing without being surrounded by the people who love you.

We settled on two each. Raina and Cecilia as my bridesmaids. Joseph and August's younger brother, Orlando, for his groomsmen.

The restaurant sparkles with radiance as everyone enjoys their food, starving after leaving the church. The sea of people around the table are the picture of perfection in their expensive tuxedos and beautiful dresses. I am wearing a mid-length white dress that accentuates my curves and suffocates me both in the literal and mental sense.

I wanted to wear black out of sheer principle, but I knew Mother would have a coronary.

With Raina sitting on my left, holding my hand beneath the table, I'm able to attempt to enjoy myself as I nibble on the filet mignon on my plate, zoning out while the people around me talk amongst themselves.

"You okay?" she leans in and asks under her breath. I nod subtly and place my fork down in order to grab my chardonnay.

I take two large gulps as she squeezes my hand. On my right, I feel the heat of August's gaze on me before he leans closer.

"Shall I get you another, darling? Maybe if you drink enough, I'll get to test drive the car before I buy it tomorrow."

"You're disgusting," I tell him through my teeth as I smile widely. My mother is watching from across the table, her eyes glittering in the light.

It makes me sick, the way she pretends like nothing is wrong. She saw my bruises, yet she hasn't said another word about them.

"You know," Raina whispers. "I can have you out of here in ten seconds flat. Say the word, I'll create a diversion and we'll be gone."

"Tempting," I whisper back, taking another sip of my wine.

"You really don't have to go through with this, sis."

"Oh, but I do."

She doesn't know everything—not even close. If she did, I know she'd go absolutely feral on August. That's just how she is. My reverse Sour Patch Kid friend. First she's sweet as candy, everyone's golden girl. But piss her off and her personality can flip. The childless version of a Mama Bear.

All Raina knows is that I'm head over heels in love with Sylvester Lucchetti and I'm refusing to be with him because August has threatened his life. That's the main purpose—the entire plotline of this marriage.

The only saving grace is that I've had time to snoop around to try and arm myself with as much knowledge as possible since being under the same roof as August. When he's not around, I cherry pick everything I can, trying to figure out *why* he's going to such lengths for this.

Although I don't have all the details, what it comes down to is the Paladino legacy. Paperwork has been drawn up, presumably for us to sign, indicating that once August and I are legally married, he will become the heir in line to my father's underground drug trade— not me—if I am to inherit it. Whether August plans to sign everything over to Joseph is a piece of the puzzle I have yet to find, but having August in charge certainly is a leg up for my brother.

The best part of all of this is if Joseph would simply have a conversation with me and believe it, he'd know I don't want anything to do with Father's empire.

He can have it.

And it *will* go to him, without all of this—the

marriage, the threats—even happening. Luciano won't want it, not with a flourishing practice of his own, and logistically, Joseph is next in line.

Apparently, my brother doesn't understand how lineage works.

When I attempted to have a normal adult conversation with August about it, he turned violent, grabbing a fistful of the underpart of my hair and tugging me so roughly down the hallway, it nearly ripped from my scalp. When he released me, he shoved me into my bedroom, knocking me to the floor, and spit on the carpet beside me.

I haven't tried to bring it up again.

Further down the table, a glass clinks, and I see my uncle Marcel stand. "A toast to the happy couple! Please help me by raising your glasses. It has been a few years since I have seen my favorite niece, but on behalf of my family, I'd like to thank the Paladinos and the St. Jeans for including us in the festivities. Vinnie, you have grown into a stunning woman, and I am so happy for you. Cheers!"

A round of cheers erupts through the table, and to make a point, August presses a firm kiss against my cheek.

My stomach roils thinking about having to actually kiss him tomorrow to seal our vows. Turning my head to pull away, I lock eyes with Cecilia. She's been acting strange all evening, but we haven't had a chance to talk. My eyes flit toward where I know the restroom is, and she reads between the lines, pushing her chair backward as she stands and politely excuses herself.

Squeezing Raina's hand, she follows suit as she releases me, and I slip into my mask before turning back to August, purposely raising my voice more than necessary and touching his shoulder as I stand. "I'm going to use the ladies' room. I'll be back."

Once the three of us are inside, Raina flips the lock behind me as I rush to the sink and place my elbows onto it, holding my head in my hands.

"I hate this."

"Then let's get the hell out of here!" Raina basically shouts. "I don't care if I have to pull a Janet and have a nip slip to distract everyone so you can sneak out the back. Just tell me what you need me to do, and it's done."

Shaking my head, I look at Cecilia through the mirror. "What's going on with you tonight?"

She bites her lip, then sighs. "Sly came to the apartment."

I groan through the way my heart pangs. "Of course he did."

"What did he say?" Raina asks, placing her hands on her hips.

"Not much, he was just looking for you, Vins." She hesitates. "But it wasn't so much as what he said as what *I* said."

Spinning toward her, I pin her in a stare. Raina does the same, and I watch as Cecilia's cheeks stain pink under our scrutiny.

"I told him you loved him, and that you're going to great lengths for that love… It just slipped out. I'm sorry, Vinnie, but also I'm not. I want him to fight for you. You deserve to be in a marriage with someone you love—who loves and adores you, and worships the ground you walk on. That's Sly, not August."

"I'm under no illusion that it would be August," I snap, the tears pricking my eyes. "This marriage isn't about love. Hell, it isn't even about *me*. But I'm committed, and you both know that, so I'd appreciate it if you stopped trying to talk me out of it and just supported me through it."

"Oh, Vins, we *do* support you," Raina tells me softly. "Which is why we're trying to get you to see this entire thing from a different perspective. An outside perspective. You have so many options, marrying August should be the very last one."

"I don't understand why it's so hard for everyone to understand," I growl, so incredibly tired and frustrated of having to explain myself over and over. I get it. They love me and are worried, but they also know that the threat against Sly's life is very *real*. "August is a terrible person. Beneath his *'charming former bachelor persona'* is the devil personified. He has people behind him, hidden in the shadows, doing his dirty work. There's no doubt in my mind that if I don't comply with what he's demanding of me, he'll go after Sly. He's proven it with his PI following Sly all the way to California. And that's not a risk I'm willing to take. I will gladly chain my life to August's if it means Sly isn't pulled into the bullshit August *and Joseph* have entangled me in."

By the time I finish speaking, there's a half-moon indentation from my nail in my palm bleeding because of how deeply I've curled my fists.

Cecilia and Raina are both silent, looking at me with a mix of remorse, and dare I say, pity.

Their expressions enrage me. I love them so much, but right now I don't want to be around them.

"I need some air," I say and immediately leave the restroom, letting the door swing shut behind me.

Fury grips me tightly when I only make it two steps before a hand curls around my bicep, squeezing it tightly beneath the lace sleeve of my dress. I look down at the hand before I look up at the face it belongs to.

"You're right, *wife*. I do have people in the shadows working for me, and I'm so glad you recognize that. My threats aren't idle, Vinnie. I will happily kill your little boyfriend to keep you in your place," August's slimy voice penetrates through the air next to my ear.

Lifting my chin, I hold his gaze. We both grit our teeth, feeling the tangible tension between us in this power struggle.

His grip on me tightens further.

"What's going on here?" my father's voice sounds out. Both of us snap our heads in the direction of his voice, and from the corner of my eye I can see August slip his smile into place.

"Ah, Maurizio. Headed to the gentlemen's room?"

August tries to deflect. Loosening his grip on my bicep, he slides his hand down my arm and reaches for my hand.

No longer caring about appearances, I move my hand away from him.

My father's eyes bounce from me to August with a crease in his brow. When his eyes connect with mine again, I can see them searching for answers.

So badly, I want to crumble at my father's feet and tell him *everything*. I've silenced myself for so long—not talking to him about the deeper parts of my life in fear of his opinion, rejection, or wrath. But for the first time in years, I want to tell him.

Still, I continue to silence myself and bite my tongue, giving him a weak smile.

August shifts next to me, clearly unsettled by the silence. Taking a few steps to close the distance to my father, he claps his hand against his shoulder and turns his body. "Come, I'll accompany you. I was on the way to the men's room myself before your radiant daughter distracted me."

As they begin to walk away, I lean against the wall behind me, mentally exhausted.

*If my father turns around to look at me again, I'll tell him everything. I'll run after him and confess how August has been treating me, my love for Sly, and that this entire wedding is a sham.*

*If he looks at me, it'll prove that he has an inkling of suspicion that something isn't right.*

But my father never turns around. He just continues down the hallway with August's arm around his shoulder, completely entranced by the man who is fooling everyone.

# Chapter 14

## *Vinnie*

"Miss Paladino! Are you excited for your big day?" Marcia, the head housekeeper at my parents' house, asks as she fluffs the couch pillows beside me, doting on me as I relax into the sofa with a fresh latte in hand.

I smile politely over the rim of the mug. "Of course," I drawl before taking a sip of the hot liquid.

"You'll be the most exquisite bride, Miss. I can't wait to see the photos," she continues to gush as she moves on to fluffing the cushions on the loveseat across from where I sit.

It's eleven-thirty a.m. and we just finished our intimate family brunch. Mother thought it'd be nice to have one last meal as just our family, and August opted to do the same with his. Sitting around the dining table, just me, my parents, and my three brothers, made it easy to pretend like everything was normal.

For a moment, I was able to retreat to the memory

of when family brunch was exactly that—a simple meal between the six of us.

Even Joseph seemed to be in good spirits today, which put me on edge slightly. It feels like he has the upper hand in some capacity, and that makes me uneasy.

After brunch, Mother sent me to relax for a while and asked one of the kitchen attendants to make a latte for me while the housekeepers set up our spa treatments.

My mother hired a manicurist and massage therapist to treat me and her before I leave to go get ready with Raina and Cecilia in a few hours. I want to get ready at my apartment, but my mother insisted on booking a suite at The Manhattan Grand hotel, just down the road from the church.

Next to me on the plush, velvet couch lies a full itinerary of the day on embossed paper. I can't take my eyes off the words *wedding ceremony*.

This is actually happening.

The day is here.

Excitement buzzes throughout the Paladino residence. Staff members are extra cheerful as they go through their daily tasks, watching my mother dance around with a smile on her face.

Looking at her these days breaks my heart—shatters it, really.

*How can she not see the pain on my face and the hurt in my eyes?*

She's been so hyper focused on this wedding, engrossed in every detail.

I love my mother, but I pray if I have children one day that the gravity of her mistakes will be so ingrained into me there won't be a shadow of a doubt that I would miss something so blatantly outlined on my child's face.

Although I can't fully blame her. I am fully aware I have the power to speak up—to protect myself better and to put an end to this—and I'm choosing not to.

Still, it doesn't dull the ache of knowing my mother either doesn't see it, or is purposely ignoring it.

"Out," Joseph's voice commands suddenly, and I whip my head in his direction just in time to see Marcia straighten herself and scurry from the room.

Joseph closes the French doors behind him and strides over to the fireplace, picking up a photo of the two of us when we were children. He scoffs at it before setting it back down and pinning me in his stare. "Ready to become Mrs. St. Jean?"

He doesn't try to hide the smirk on his lips.

"No need to hide your glee, Joey. I'm sure you're getting something out of this union, I just haven't figured out what."

He sits on the loveseat across from me. Leaning forward on his thighs, he steeples his fingers over his mouth. "I'm getting a lot out of it, actually."

"Care to elaborate?"

Sitting back, he drapes his arm over the cushion behind him. "Well, for starters, it eliminates the cross-contamination. Did you honestly think you could fuck a Lucchetti and keep it a secret?"

My heart falls to the bottom of my stomach, along with my expression. I suspected August told him, but he has yet to bring it up until now. Hearing him confirm he knew about my relationship makes me ill.

Schooling my features, I tighten my lips into a line and watch him closely, waiting to hear what he has to say next.

"You're not as *sly* as you think you are, baby sister. Pun intended. At least you didn't pick that pathetic excuse for a man, Lorenzo." His features twist up at the mention of Sly's cousin. "Still though, not like the other one is any better. Way to be a loyal member of this family."

"You don't know him at all," I seethe. Pushing to my feet, I stand, my shins hitting the coffee table as I take a step toward him. My finger raises, pointing at him. "What about our family loyalty, Joseph? You *hate* me and you don't even have the human decency to tell me *why*."

Not wanting me to have the upper hand, he stands too, taking a step forward. Although my brother is a full head taller than me, I find myself not cowering.

It feels good to grasp a little of my power back.

Joseph's voice drops to a low growl as he stares down at me, shooting daggers through his eyes. "You *should* know why."

"Well, I don't."

"BECAUSE HE LOVES YOU MORE," Joseph explodes.

His mouth snaps closed, and the room becomes so quiet you could hear a pin drop. My heart splinters, tears immediately springing to my eyes as I continue to look up at my brother. For the first time in what feels like years, I feel like I see bits of the brother I used to know reflecting through his navy irises.

"It didn't matter the grades I held or the achievements I accomplished," he continues. "The awards, the hard work—they were all overshadowed by *you*." His voice is like venom, thick and icy, seeping into my veins. "All you had to do was exist, and you became Father's favorite."

"I never asked for that, Joseph! I never even accepted that role—never wanted to be the favorite! I'm not even sure that's true. He loves us *all*."

His eyes are dark and cruel as he stares down at me, hardly two inches from my face. He's so close I can feel his spittle as he speaks. "It doesn't matter. It's still a fact. He puts you before any of his sons."

I shock myself by not stepping away to put distance between us. As intimidated as I am, I refuse to cower. I want answers. I'm *owed* them.

"So, what is your endgame? Obviously you and August have a plan. I'm not obtuse, Joseph. I know you've been planning and calculating for months. So tell me. What are you after?"

A sinister laugh floats from his lips and I'm surprised when it's he who steps back. Joseph begins to pace with short steps in front of the coffee table that separates us.

"Well, I suppose it won't hurt to tell you now, since the wedding is tonight, anyway." He stops and watches me for a moment, then sits back on the couch, resuming his relaxed position from earlier.

"When our father inevitably hands the business over to you, it will be August who takes over on your behalf. There's a bit of paperwork you'll have to sign this evening as soon as your marriage license is signed." A smile pulls across his face. "Of course, making sure you don't end up with a Lucchetti is another perk."

"When has Father even said he's going to give it to me, Joseph? *You're* the one involved in it. It makes no sense as to why you think he'd skip over you and hand it to me."

"All my life, I've been in the shadow of my baby sister. You get everything I want. You take *everything* from me!" Joseph snarls, his teeth clenched. A vein bulges on his forehead. "It wouldn't shock me one bit for Father to hand everything I've worked for over to you."

"So all this so August can take over the business—a business that I have absolutely no interest in—on my behalf? How does that benefit you?" I ignore the comment about Sly.

"It's a partnership, baby sister, and your document won't be the only one signed tonight. The details are none of your concern."

"I beg to differ."

Suddenly, Joseph stops and steps into my space

again, the coffee table a welcomed barrier as he leans toward me.

"All you need to know, Vinnie, is everything I've ever wanted will be *mine*, and *you'll* no longer be a Paladino," he snarls.

His words catch me off guard and completely obliterate any sense of confidence I've been holding on to. An overwhelming sense of fear washes through my body as his words sink in, and I realize just how unpredictable he is.

He sidesteps around the coffee table and toward me until we're toe to toe. "Make no mistake, Vinnie. This is *my* time. And I will stop at nothing to make sure my plans are carried out successfully. Your new place is by August's side—silent, and with a goddamn smile on your face."

The next several seconds are tense as we stare at each other. My heart beats frantically, my chest rising and falling in rapid succession. Words swirl through my mind but I can't get a sentence to form, too speechless from the clear malice my brother harbors for me.

"Vinnie! Darling," my mother's voice singsongs from outside of the doors. As she pulls them open, Joseph grabs ahold of my hand and stretches it to the side as his other hand comes to rest in the middle of my back so it looks like we were getting ready to dance.

"Oh! There you are, Joseph. Your father is looking for you, sweetheart."

Dropping his hands, he takes a step back and smiles wildly at her. "Thank you, Mother. Vinnie and I were just practicing our brother-sister dance for tonight. You know I have two left feet."

A laugh of disbelief bubbles up and I shake my head, frustration radiating off me in waves.

"That's so sweet," my mother exclaims, beaming at my lying, manipulative brother. "I hate to break up the bonding time, but Vinnie, our massage therapists are ready for us!"

Joseph leans forward and gives our mother a peck on the cheek. "I'll leave you two to it."

Pushing his hands into the pockets of his slacks, Joseph strides from the room, and I watch him go, shaken to my core at the altercation we just had.

Paying my mood no mind, my mother loops her arm through mine and pulls me out of the den. "I'm so excited for our girl time, Vinnie! We're going to get all pampered before it's time to get ready for your wedding. I can't believe today is the day, can you? Aren't you just so excited?"

Sighing deeply, I let a single tear fall and look to the side so she doesn't see it. Reaching up, I swipe it away before it can fully slide down my cheek, then I look straight ahead with a smile that feels like plastic.

"Absolutely elated, Mother."

"This is the start of your forever."

*Or the end of it.*

# Chapter 15

## *Sly*



I pace around my kitchen, anxiously awaiting Enzo and Sully to arrive. Nixon is on his way from the airport now, having arrived an hour ago after a long overnight layover.

It feels as though my worlds will soon collide. I'm not sure I'm prepared for my friends in Manhattan to meet my friend from Ridgewood, as I am uncertain how they will get along. I don't doubt that Nixon and Sully will hit it off, but Enzo is the wildcard.

SULLY



ENZO

Crossing the living room, I unlock the door and open it. Immediately, Sully rounds the corner, his smile wide.

"Enzo is not right behind me, for the record," he quips as he saunters into my apartment. I leave the door open and follow him to where he's dropped down onto my couch. He props cognac-colored oxfords onto my coffee table. "What was so important you needed us here again? Didn't get enough bro time with us last night?"

Unamused, I cross my arms over my chest. "I have someone I want you to meet."

"Who?"

"I assume the tattooed buffoon who followed me up here is the person we're meeting," Enzo's gruff voice comes from behind me.

Turning, I see him walk through the doorway just as Nixon comes into view behind him, holding a duffel bag in each hand. His charcoal gray t-shirt shows off the new ink on his forearm, and his jeans look dirty, but his hair has been freshly faded on the sides and haphazardly styled on top.

"Says the man in the overpriced mafia get-up." He looks tired, evidence of his all-night travels.

"Overpriced? This is only a six-thousand dollar suit. That's nothing."

"My point exactly." Nixon follows Enzo inside, looking around at my apartment. Letting out a low whistle, he drops both bags where he's standing. "Dang, pookie. These are some fancy digs you have here."

"Nixon," I say with a smile, walking over to him. We clap our hands together and pull in for a hug, patting each other in friendly greeting. "How was your flight, amico?"

"Nothing special."

"You flew first class."

He shrugs, his smile widening. "So this is the other side of Sly Lucchetti, then? Marble flooring, fancy decorations, and…two dudes who obviously hate me for no reason?"

"Hey now," Sully scoffs, jutting his thumb in Enzo's direction. "Don't lump me in with the Italian dreamboat over here."

"I don't hate you, I just find it unsettling that you followed me all the way up to my cousin's apartment and when I asked who you were, you ignored me," Enzo replies dryly.

"It's a need to know basis." Nixon shrugs.

Enzo shakes his head and crosses his arms over his chest before looking at me and jerking his chin in Nixon's direction. "Where'd you find this guy? On the side of the road?"

"Actually, he found me at a tattoo parlor, but that is beside the point. I need your help. All of you."

"Just say the word," Nixon remarks.

But it isn't Nix or Sully who I fear won't help. My gaze connects with Enzo's, and I would be lying if I said my stomach didn't somersault at the thought of him walking out of my apartment when I ask the question.

"Vincenza's wedding is tonight," I say, never looking away from Enzo. "I need help to stop it."

His eyes narrow slightly, but his expression doesn't give anything away. From my peripheral, I see Sully and Nixon gesture their agreement to help.

My heart gallops in my rib cage with every moment that passes without Enzo's response until suddenly Sully erupts.

"Jesus, Enzo, give up the 'I hate that family' bullshit. Your cousin and best friend just asked you for help, and you're standing here making him wait for a response. Get over yourself, man, and let's help him get Vinnie back. *Especially* since August might be hurting her."

"What do you mean?" Enzo asks immediately, his gaze shifting to Sully. He may not like the idea of me being with Vincenza because she's a Paladino, but he would never sit back and allow a man to bring harm to a woman—no matter who her family is.

"You haven't told him?" Sully asks, shaking his head at me before turning back to Enzo. "I ran into her and she was acting really suspect. It made my spidey senses tingle. Something's not quite right."

It's with Sully's words that I insert myself once more. "Aside from loving her beyond measure, I could never let her marry someone who is hurting her. Even if she does not want to be with me, I will not let this wedding happen—but I need help. Are you in, or are you out, Lorenzo?"

Another long pause settles in the air before he

answers. My heart starts beating again once he says, "I'm in."

"Eccellente."

"So what's the plan?" Nixon asks, looking at me for direction.

A smile crawls across my face as the gears in my mind start warming up, a plan forming right behind my eyes. "Come, let me tell you what ideas I have so far."

Moving into my dining room, we all take a seat around the mahogany table, and I take a moment before addressing them. Staring down at my fingers, I pick a small piece of skin at the edge of my nail and think about how I want this to happen.

I start by telling them the one thing I know for certain. "By my hand, August will die today."

Sully's eyes widen, and he pales. He's never known the monster inside me—only Enzo has truly seen me in my darkest. Nixon seems unsurprised, but as members of The Sinners, there have been times where we have done things we are not entirely proud of, both together and individually.

"Vincenza has given me a few signs that he is hurting her, but rather than acting in haste, I have been planning a strategy that will not only end the abuse the love of my life has been facing, but also show the Paladinos—primarily Joseph—that the Lucchettis fight for and protect the people we love. Enzo, this will be a clear message that we have not forgotten Gabriele's death."

Enzo nods in agreement, and I continue. "The

wedding is at five o'clock at Saint Sebastian's church, but I need to see her first. If there is a chance I can put a stop to the wedding without resorting to violence, I will take it. But I am not above ending August to make sure the vows are unsaid, and frankly, I know with every fiber of my being that is how it will end. Vinnie will not agree to end the wedding—she has told me as much and I can tell there is something he has against her—but I will at least attempt before I take full action."

The men around me are quiet, waiting to see if I have more to say. When it is clear I do not, Nixon speaks first. "So, what are you thinking?"

"I have reason to believe prior to the ceremony she will be at The Manhattan Grand hotel. I wish to go there and speak to her. We will call that plan A. If I am unsuccessful, we will move to plan B."

"Which is?" Sully interjects.

"I suppose then I can be considered a wedding crasher."

"Tell me more," Enzo comments. "How will you know where to find her at the hotel?"

"Well, this is where I need help. Nixon, perhaps you will be best for this portion. Someone will need to visit the front desk and pose as a relative—perhaps one who has just come into town. Nixon will be best suited for this because no one will recognize him."

I run my hand along my trimmed beard, thinking about how to utilize Sully and his charms. "Sullivan, it would be great if you were a distraction. If Vinnie's mother, or someone else, tries to go up to the room, perhaps you can use your magnetism to distract them."

"And me?" Enzo contemplates. "I can't be held liable for what might happen if I cross paths with a Paladino."

"Your job will be done from afar, cugino. I need you to work on plan B. If I cannot sway Vinnie, I need to figure out how to get into that church undetected. Surely, the Paladinos will have top security working, and I need to know how to get past them. Is that something you can do?"

"It is."

"Anything else I should consider?" I ask, wondering if I've missed anything.

Enzo and Sully shake their heads, but Nixon is tapping his pointer finger against his lips—something he does when he's deep in thought.

"What is it?"

His eyes snap to mine. "It all seems too easy."

I am about to respond when Sully's laughter overtakes the room. "Just wait until you see this family. Their events are more secure than the presidential motorcade."

*Yet, not secure enough for me to sneak in undetected. I've done it once, and I'll do it again.*

Like the little thief she is, Vincenza stole my heart. Now, I'm prepared to do *anything* to steal her back.

# Chapter 16

## *Vinnie*

The moment my makeup artist spritzed my face with setting spray, the process of my hair began. The remanence of brunch sits in my esophagus like burning acid as the hairstylist curls and pins my hair into the wedding look of my dreams.

"Oh, sweetheart, you look stunning!" my mother coos as she watches through the mirror from the plush tufted couch behind me. She glances at the diamond studded Rolex on her wrist. "I'm so sorry I won't get to stay longer and see you right before the wedding. Your father insists that I ride in the limo with him."

A weak smile tugs at my lips. "That's okay, Mother. Go get ready."

"I have about five more minutes. Oh, Cecilia, don't you look picture perfect?"

Cecilia emerges from the en suite where her hair and makeup was being done as well. She's barefoot, wearing a light pink silk robe, and smiles warmly at my mother. "Thank you, Mrs. Paladino."

Raina passes her a flute filled to the brim with bubbly champagne as she passes by. She's wearing a matching silk robe, and is on her way to the en suite to trade places with Cecilia. From the small smirk on Lia's lips, I have a feeling Raina rolled her eyes at my mother's comment.

We're all a bit on edge with her presence. My two best friends know how much I've been dreading this day, and they're as frustrated as I am by my mother's ignorance about the emotions of her own daughter.

Time drags on as those five minutes tick by, but finally, my mother stands to gather her purse and air kisses me goodbye. "I'll see you when you walk down the aisle."

She turns again to give me one last look of adoration before the hotel door closes softly behind her.

"Thank fuck," Raina says from the en suite. Cecilia bursts into laughter, as do I, but the hairstylist doing my hair looks unamused. "Now we can get this party started."

Immediately, music blares from the bathroom she's in—a top 40 something I recognize but don't know the name of.

"Champagne?" Cecilia asks, lifting a fresh flute in offering.

"Sure."

"How are you holding up?" she asks as she passes it to me.

Bringing the glass to my lips, I drink a gulp while the stylist releases one of my curls from the styling wand. "Mmm hmm," I hum as cheerfully as possible. "T-minus one hour."

"Just say the word," Raina yells from the other room. How she even heard me is baffling.

"I'll go check on her," Cecilia muses, walking into the bathroom and leaving me to my thoughts.

Behind me, my hairstylist grabs an aerosol bottle, and a plume of chemicals clouds around my head as she sprays my hair. "Final touches, Miss Paladino."

I say nothing, but take another large gulp of my champagne.

Moments later, she tells me she's finished and encourages me to look in the mirror.

My hair and makeup are as beautiful as they were on the day of my final dress fitting. Absolute perfection and fit for a bride who is head over heels in love with her fiancé—not a woman who would rather be anywhere else, in anyone else's shoes.

"It's stunning," I tell her truthfully.

For a moment, I watch her clean up her belongings until Raina comes out of the bathroom. Her hair is a simple half up, half down style of soft waves that cascade down her back, with two small pieces framing her face. "You look amazing."

"So do you, babe."

"Are you ready to get in your gown?" Lia asks softly, approaching my dress. Her hand shakes slightly as she brushes it against the fabric.

Blowing out a breath, she finally reaches for my dress, pulling it from the hook and cradling it in her arms.

Shrugging my white silk robe from my shoulders, I stand in my undergarments as Lia brings the wedding gown to me.

The closer she gets, the heavier the pit in my stomach feels.

The three of us say nothing as they help me into the gown, delicately holding the sleeves so I can slip my arms through them. The moment feels so wrong. We should be smiling and laughing, feeling giddy for this once in a lifetime moment we're sharing.

But the room feels completely devoid of happiness.

Cecilia situates the tulle off my shoulders while Raina zips up the back. When they step back so we can all look at my reflection in the mirror, I notice tears lining Lia's eyes.

"For what it's worth," Raina says as she blows out a shaky breath to hide the quiver in her voice. "You look absolutely divine."

"Like a queen," Lia's voice is melancholy.

"Like a Paladino princess." I can't push away the sadness in my voice, and a single tear rolls down Cecilia's cheek.

The sound of the hotel room phone ringing cuts the somber moment short, and Cecilia hurries across the room to answer it. Raina and I glance at each other, and I wonder who would be calling.

"Hello?"

The hairstylists whisper their goodbyes and well-wishes to me before they quietly leave the room, and I return my attention back to Lia.

Her brows crumple together as she listens to whoever is on the other end. "I don't recognize that name. Hang on."

Covering the speaker of the phone, she looks at me. "The front desk says your cousin Tate is here to see you?"

Immediately, my heart rate picks up. "I don't have a cousin named Tate."

Removing her hand from the speaker, Cecilia tells the front desk she'll be right down and hangs up.

"I'll go see who it is," she says as she pulls on a pair of leggings under her robe, before untying the bow in the front and shrugging it off. Quickly, she throws on a chambray button down.

Within seconds, she's out the door, not bothering to close it softly as she makes her exit.

"Why would someone pretend to be your cous—" A knock on the door slices through her sentence.

We both turn to look at it.

My eyes narrow as I shrug at Raina, assuming Lia left her keycard. Crossing the room, I answer it, expecting her to be there.

All at once, the air leaves my lungs with a harsh *whoosh* as Sly comes into view on the other side of the doorway, staring at me with a fire in his eyes I haven't seen in months. He's wearing his signature all black look, this time with jeans and his leather motorcycle jacket over a t-shirt—looking like sex and sin, and making the butterflies dance in my stomach like they do every time I set my gaze on him.

"Sly," I whisper, as he takes a step toward me and cups my cheek with his hand.

"Hello, piccola ladra." His eyes roam down my body, taking in my appearance in my wedding gown. "Wow. You look breathtaking, Vincenza."

He drinks me in, and as he does, a flood of emotion slams into me. I should be wearing this dress for *him*.

Walking down the aisle to *him*.

Reciting my wedding vows to *him*.

*But we've been robbed of what should be the happiest day of our lives.*

Lifting his gaze, he looks behind me at Raina.

"If I may speak with the bride for a moment... alone," he requests with such poise, it leaves no room for argument.

Raina lifts her arms before bringing them back down to pat the sides of her thighs. "Let me change really fast."

She winks at me as she goes back to the en suite and shuts the door behind her. It barely clicks into place before I'm spinning back toward Sly.

"What are you doing here?"

His eyes blaze with confidence as he leans forward and kisses me softly. As he pulls away, his thumb brushes my cheek. "Convincing you to marry me instead."

"I hope you can," Raina mumbles, emerging from the bathroom, and not slowing as she sees herself out.

Once alone, Sly's lips descend on mine again, not giving me a moment to respond. Not that it matters, because the moment his lips touch mine, I'm completely under his spell.

His kiss starts off slowly, but quickly ignites my blood. Warm tingles radiate over my body, desire instantly pooling between my thighs as he tangles his hand through the curls of my hair. Cupping the base of my skull, he presses his thumb against it to tilt my head back, deepening the kiss.

A groan vibrates through him, and I eagerly match it with my own.

I feel him *everywhere*, yet the only place he's touching is my head.

The magnitude of his presence shocks me to my core. I hadn't realized how badly I craved him until his skin touched mine. But I know this is fleeting. Only for a few moments.

Pulling away, I break the kiss and allow my forehead to rest against his. "You shouldn't be here."

"Yet, there's nowhere else I could imagine being."

"It's my wedding day," I argue, forcing myself to stay strong.

"Sì, and witnessing you in this gown is doing something to me, Vincenza. I have dreamed of this day a million times, and it is clear the fantasy did not do the reality justice."

A whimper catches in my throat and I close my eyes. With a strained voice, I admit, "I've dreamed of it, too."

"Piccola ladra, I understand that there are things you are not telling me, but I need you to understand something as well. I will do *everything* in my power to protect you. What do I have to do to get you to call the wedding off?"

"I *can't*, Sly."

I expect him to argue—to fight back like he has with every other conversation—but he doesn't this time. We've gone around in circles so much, and it makes me weaker, my resolve crumbling little by little with every heated conversation.

This time though, his eyes simply search mine, and I can see the moment something clicks into place for him. His demeanor changes—the light in his eyes dims.

It feels like a bullet to the heart.

"Very well," he says, nodding once. His tone is colder than it was before, a little more detached.

It breaks another piece of me.

Sliding his hand down my sleeve, he takes mine and gently tugs me over to the white tufted couch in the center of the room, guiding me to stand in front of it. Neither of us sits, but he drags his hungry eyes up and down my body again, and my stomach tumbles.

Sly's fingers graze across the intricate lace flowers near my breasts. He takes his time, moving around me to take in every last detail. Bracing his hands on my hips, he turns me so we're both facing away from the couch, my back to his front.

A chill runs through me as his lips ghost the side of my ear, his warm breath against the sensitive skin.

I'm hypersensitive to his every movement and touch, my body begging for more of it. The thin fabric of my panties rubs against me as I shift on my legs, the friction almost too much as my heart races and I wonder what he's going to do or say next.

"Sei assolutamente stupendo." Though I don't understand his native tongue, when he speaks, my knees weaken with his words, and I know I'm lost to him—a willing captive in the tortuous web he's weaving in an effort to get me to call off the wedding.

My heart feels like it might explode from how quickly it's beating, my breaths becoming more shallow.

Able to read my body perfectly, Sly drags his lips down the column of my neck, allowing the back of his fingers to follow.

Gently, he bites the curve of my neck to my shoulder and causes my heart to stop when he whispers, "Lift your wedding gown, piccola ladra."

# Chapter 17

## *Sly*

Vincenza's eyes meet mine in the mirror, her cheeks flushing.

Dragging my hands down her body, I crumple the fabric of her gown in my palm and start bunching it higher. Her hands meet mine and she continues to pull up more of the dress, exposing her legs inch by tortuous inch.

Slowly, I kneel behind her. "You are absolutely exquisite, piccola ladra. Every part of you was made for me." Leaning forward, I press a soft kiss against the back of her thigh. Her knees buckle slightly in response, and she lets out a soft moan.

"This isn't fair," she whines breathily. "I know what you're doing."

My teeth nip at the delicate skin of her inner thigh. "What is that, exactly?

"Swaying me with your touch." She gasps when my fingers brush against the lace of her panties.

"Mmm," I hum. "And is it working?"

Hooking my finger in the fabric, I pull it to the side, dragging my fingers through her wetness. She's soaked for me, and I can't wait to draw pleasure from her body as many times as I can before she leaves this hotel room.

"I'm set in my decision, Sly," she says, tipping her head back. Her eyes are closed, hips rocking slightly. Her body is begging for my touch, and as tempting as it is to continue taunting her, I am working on a timeframe.

Ignoring her answer, I pull her panties down and let them slide from her legs. She pushes up on her tiptoes as she steps out of them, kicking them aside.

Sidestepping on my knees, I grip her thighs and guide her to turn with me. "Bend over, piccola ladra."

Spreading her wide, I am gifted with the magnificent view of her most intimate places, and immediately I bring my mouth to her. Her arousal coats my tongue as I swipe it through her folds, savoring the taste.

"I have missed you, Vinnie. Every day that passes and you are not in my arms is like dying a thousand deaths."

"I've missed you too," she admits. "So much, but Sly, I can't…"

I cease her words when my thumb connects with her clit, swirling the nerve with the exact pressure I know makes her lose all sense of control. Her knees buckle again as my finger works in conjunction with my tongue while it slides inside of her.

"Oh my God," she moans, arching her back as she

presses further into me, leaning her forearms and elbows on the couch. In her hands, she continues to grasp as much fabric of her gown as she can hold.

"Piccola ladra, I have spoken to God about the pleasure I am about to give you and he has willingly turned an eye for this moment. Address me, not Him."

But I don't give her the chance to. Instead, I increase the rhythm of my tongue and finger, and bring her to orgasm quickly.

Crying out, she slams her open palm against the couch cushion. "*Sly*. Sly, Sly, Sly, Sly, Sly," she chants.

My cock strains against the fabric of my pants and I reach down, grasping it in hopes of waning some of the pressure.

"I do not wish to ruin your hair, Vincenza. So sit on the couch and spread your legs for me."

I'm nowhere near done with her yet.

She obeys and lowers herself onto the couch, pulling her gown up past her hips. The image of stroking my cock and coming all over her beautiful wedding gown flashes through my mind as she scoots herself to the very edge of the cushions.

Staying on my knees, I place my hands on her thighs and press her legs open as far as they'll go, not giving her any time to recover from her orgasm before I suction my lips around her clit and begin my ministrations yet again.

I'm hopeless when around her, wanting to succumb to her every want and need.

"Sly," she moans. "Please…I'm so sensitive. Let me take care of you."

"Absolutely not," I grumble, never removing my mouth from her. My tongue caresses her opening in long, languid strokes. Dragging my hands further up, I slide them beneath her, cupping her cheeks as I use my thumbs to spread her wider.

I eat her like a starving man devouring his first meal in days. Everything about her—from the noises she makes to the roll of her hips, and the sweet, delicious taste of her arousal—makes me painfully hard. Desperately, I want to sink inside of her, but even more, I want to bring her to orgasm so intensely her pussy will vibrate with aftershocks throughout the ceremony.

At least until I arrive to stop it.

Using the tip of my tongue, I massage her clit in precise circles, teasing it as I shift my hand and sink two fingers into her. With a soft bend of my fingers, I begin to massage her G-spot in the same tempo as I tongue her clit.

Moments later, the most beautiful sound erupts through the quiet room as she comes again on my tongue. I lap her up, holding her thighs firm as she tries to close them. Her hand fists my hair as she simultaneously pulls me closer and pushes me away.

When her body relents, melting against the couch, I sneak a quick glance at my watch.

Our time is running out.

Standing, I look down at her pussy as it glistens. It's beautiful, and as my eyes drag up her body, I take in her flushed appearance. She looks thoroughly satisfied, but so badly I wish to hear her come a few more times. "I desperately want to continue to pleasure your body, piccola ladra, but I'm afraid I must go in a moment. So, stand up."

Instead of listening, she slides from the couch and sinks to her knees, reaching for my belt. "Let me make you feel good, Sly. I want you in my mouth."

Taking a step back, I shake my head. "As much as I would love your lips around my cock, I would much prefer to feel your pussy as you come all over it."

Bringing my hand to my belt, I unhook it before working the rest of the fasteners. Pushing the denim down my legs, along with my boxer briefs, I sit on the couch. My pants shift down to my calves as I spread my legs, getting comfortable.

I watch as Vinnie's greedy eyes drag over the lower half of my body, licking her lips. Without further instruction, she climbs onto me, straddling my legs as she holds onto the back of the couch and lowers herself.

She takes me fully and we both groan in unison when I'm fully seated inside of her.

"Dammit, Sly," she moans, but she doesn't continue her thought.

She doesn't have to. I can feel the way her body speaks for her. *She's still mine.*

Holding onto the couch with one hand, she uses it as leverage to slide up and down while her other arm holds her dress. Every time she takes me, she clenches her walls, milking my cock harder with each roll of her hips. Yet, her movements are slow and deliberate. Drawing pleasure from both of us. Making this moment count.

*She thinks it will be our last.*

Using my hands to guide her hips, I close my eyes and whisper, "You were made for me, piccola ladra. A perfect fit in every capacity. Please, don't marry him."

"That's not fair," she argues.

And it truly is not fair of me to ask—I already know she will not be marrying August St. Jean today. Still, I wish she would be the one to call things off, though I know in her mind she has good reason not to.

I'm just not sure what her reasoning is.

"Ti amo," I tell her—reminding her she is the one for me.

"Sly," she moans again.

Reaching between us, I use my thumb to stroke her. My release is so close I fear I won't be able to hold it off much longer.

Since the day she left my hospital room, all I have thought about is her touch.

My body aches for her, always.

With my dominant hand, I guide her hips up and down my shaft faster, pushing us both to the brink of release. When her pussy tightens around me, I know she is close, and I rub her clit vigorously as I let myself go. My balls tighten, cock twitching inside her as ropes of hot cum line her walls. At the same moment, she cries out, her own orgasm ripping through her body even harder than the last.

Quiet panting fills the room, and it takes us both several minutes to come down from our exquisite releases, chests heaving as we catch our breath.

As Vinnie's breathing slows, she leans forward, capturing my lips in a kiss that screams everything her words will not. Her lips are soft against mine, and I reach up to tangle my hand in her hair, cupping the base of her head to deepen it. It is in this position that I love holding her most—where I feel like she is forever in my arms, as she is in my heart.

Kissing her back with unrelenting force, the love I have for her flows through me as though it's a tangible being, intense and powerful. The magnitude of said love knows no bounds, and somehow, even clearer than before, I know she will marry me today instead.

My silent proposal intertwines with her silent *yes*.

With a kiss, I allow myself to daydream of when I will finally get the opportunity to propose, and the look on her face when I do. A smile pulls at my lips at the mental image, and Vinnie pulls away, smiling at me as she traces her fingertips against my cheek.

Lifting on her knees, she slowly glides up my cock, releasing me from her warmth before she pushes backward to her feet and stands.

Leaning forward, I cup between her legs before she can step away further, dragging my fingers through my cum as it slides out of her. Smearing it against her inner thighs and all around her greedy pussy, I smile. "With every step closer to him, you'll feel the evidence of my release on your skin. You're *mine*, Vincenza, and no promise of matrimony will keep you from me."

Her cheeks redden slightly as she pushes back a smile of her own. "Your mouth is filthy, Sly Lucchetti."

I can hear it in her voice that she doesn't fully believe my words. Not yet. But within the hour she will.

"Only for you, piccola ladra. My mouth was made entirely for you and your pleasure."

She turns back toward the mirror and picks up her panties, stepping into them as best as she can with the large skirt of her dress. Our eyes connect through the mirror, and I watch the shudder of her chest as she expels a shaky breath.

Knowing it is my time to leave, I stand and redress myself before coming up behind her. My hands trace up the intricate detailing on her sleeves before I wisp her hair from her shoulder and press a kiss to the column of her neck.

*You're mine, Vincenza Paladino, and in less than one hour, we will show the world that our love is stronger than your fake engagement.*

# Chapter 18

## *Sly*

Every step I take away from Vincenza as I cross her hotel room feels like a searing hot knife cutting through each organ in my body, stopping at my heart. The tip of the knife pokes at the it, pricking it with pain each time my foot touches the ground.

Walking away from her is never easy, regardless if it's only for a while.

With the wedding ceremony beginning in just twenty minutes, I had to force myself to leave the room. There are still plans to make.

My hand hovers on the doorknob as I sneak one final glance at the bride.

*My* bride.

Vinnie looks breathtaking. Her cheeks are extra rosey, and she looks thoroughly pleased—because she is. Sitting on the couch, her eyes flare as she watches me go, and I can't help but wish I was inside of her mind, listening to her thoughts.

"Ti amo, piccola ladra," I say before pulling open the door and taking a step into the hall. As the door closes behind me, my heart surges as I sense a presence.

Turning quickly, my hand immediately reaches beneath the back of my jacket, clasping my pistol.

"Relax, Lucchetti. I'm here to talk to you about my sister, not further the war." The eldest Paladino is leaning against the wall next to the door, the sole of his shoe propped up against it as though he doesn't have a care in the world—or a wedding to attend.

"Luciano, is it?" Of course, I already know. I'm buying time, trying to analyze his body language to figure out why he is here.

He scoffs. "Don't act naïve, Lucchetti. We're past that, despite this being our first meeting. The noises I just heard come from that hotel room—which I intend to permanently burn from my mind later—confirm my suspicions."

My eyes narrow. "Which are?"

"My sister is truly head over heels in love with you. So what are you going to do about it?"

I don't ask him how he knows about us. Perhaps she told him, or perhaps he simply has worked through the pieces of the puzzle.

My attention returns to the closed door at my back as footsteps draw near. Luciano hears them as well and grabs me by the arm, steering me further down the hall and around a corner. As soon as we're out of sight, I shrug out of his hold.

I have no intention of clueing him into my intentions, but curiosity gets the better of me. "What exactly is there to do about it, stronzo?"

As Luciano shakes his head slowly, I see his jaw clench. "Stop it."

Surprise rattles me, and I am aware my expression is not hiding it. "You want me to stop the wedding?"

"I want my sister as far away from August St. Jean as humanly possible. Do I want her with a Lucchetti? Absolutely not. But I want her to be happy. Am I confident that you're the only person who can stop this wedding? There isn't a shroud of doubt in my mind."

"Why put so much confidence into a man you hate?"

"My father hated your uncle for a shady business deal that went down between them years ago. My life, my business, and my happiness have nothing to do with my father's businesses nor do they have anything to do with your family."

"Your sister said something similar to me once."

"She's a smart woman, which leads me to believe that you're not shady like your uncle was."

"My father wasn't shady," Enzo growls, coming around the corner. Sully and Nixon are on his heels.

Sully looks between me and Vinnie's brother, then at Enzo. I can practically see the wheels in his head spinning as he assesses the situation at hand.

Lifting his palms in front of him, he says, "Whoa, whoa, whoa. Gentlemen. I'm not sure what we just walked in on, but there's no reason to be uncivil. We were just on our way to grab Sly and we'll be heading out." To further his point, Sully tips his head in the direction they just came from.

"Relax, amico. It seems as though Luciano is interested in forming a partnership," I tell my friend.

From my peripheral, I see Nixon on high alert, looking Luciano up and down.

"We're not *partnering* with a *Paladino*," Enzo seethes through clenched teeth.

I walk over to him, placing my hand on his shoulder. "Calm down, cugino."

"Yes, calm down, Lorenzo," Luciano prods, his smirk widening. "I *want* Lucchetti to stop the wedding, and I will do whatever he needs help with. No part of me wants my sister to marry that asshole. The more I look into him, the more sick it makes me that she's even had to endure him for this long."

"I have tried many times to convince her to call it off…"

His eyes snap to mine. "Of course she's not going to call it off. *You're* the reason she's even so hell-bent on going through with it."

Immediately, I feel the blood drain from my face, my features drooping in combination of shock and horror. "What do you mean, *I'm* the reason?"

Sighing deeply as though he's bored, he crosses his arms over his chest. "I thought Lucchetti men were intelligent—surgeons run in your family."

Closing my eyes, I feel my hands ball into fists. My jaw pops with how hard I'm clenching my teeth. "What.

Do. You. Mean. I'm. The. Reason," I repeat, enunciating every word.

"August is blackmailing her into marrying him by threatening to kill you."

The group grows so quiet you could hear a pin drop. For several seconds, all I can do is study Luciano to determine if he is lying.

Finally, Sully laughs boisterously. "There's no way."

Luciano runs his hand over his freshly shaven face. "It's what my sister believes." He tips his chin in my direction. "When she told me about the situation, I tried to tell her there was no way August would be able to pull something like that off—the Paladinos have way more influence in this city—but she was so convinced he would, she refused to believe my words."

"Why did you not come to me immediately?" I ask, my stomach twisting from the weight of this revelation.

"She never told me who the man she fell in love with was, just that August had threatened to kill him. I didn't know it was *you* until you stepped out of her hotel room. I came to try and convince her again to call it off, but then I heard noises I hope to never hear from my sister again, and took a walk before coming back to see if I could speak to her. Your timing was impeccable when I made it back to her door."

"You told me you were here to talk to me."

"Indirectly. I was here to talk to her, but seeing you presented an entirely different opportunity. Now, we are on borrowed time as it is. Are we going to come up with a plan to stop this wedding or not?"

"We already have a plan," Sully states, and immediately Enzo barks, "Sully," in warning.

From behind me, Nixon finally speaks up. "I trust him."

Looking over my shoulder, his eyes connect with mine. Nixon has a knack for knowing when people are lying or using certain situations to their advantage. Him saying he trusts Luciano's word is not something to take lightly.

"You've been in the man's presence for five minutes," Enzo hisses. "He's a Paladino. I don't trust him as far as I can throw him."

"That's something you're going to have to put aside for the sake of Sly to help stop this wedding," Nixon replies, pushing off the wall he was leaning against to come join us in the middle of the hall. He glances at the tattered timepiece on his wrist. "The ceremony is starting in a few minutes. Put aside the bullshit and let's get Sly his woman back."

Enzo huffs in exasperation, but relents. "Fine. Let's do this."

"Were you able to figure out security?" I ask my cousin.

He shoots me a sharp look. "Yes, I figured out security."

"Just say the plan, Enzo. We're running out of time." Nixon's tone leaves little room for argument—I can see what little patience he has at this point.

Enzo's eyes bounce back in Luciano's direction, but he continues. "They already have men stationed at every entrance of the church, and in both corners of the balcony. Security is in all black tuxes, and they each have on a clear earpiece for communication. The best course of action is to simply infiltrate."

"Are they packing?" Sully asks.

"Of course they are," Luciano confirms.

"How do we know the second you burst in and make your objection, they won't shoot?" Sully continues. He's out of his depth with this mission—his family is not confrontational, or the type of family to get their hands dirty.

"Who's in charge of the security team?" Nixon asks no one in particular.

"Capaul," Luciano tells us. "The family butler. He's been on my father's staff longer than I've walked this earth. He heads the security team whenever needed."

Nixon rubs his chin. "What's his background in?"

"Retired secret service."

"Retired? How old is this guy?" Sully questions.

"Old," Luciano confirms. "But he knows what he's doing."

Glancing down at my wrist, I check the time. We need to expedite this conversation. Directing my question at Luciano, I ask, "So, how do we convince him to have his team stand down upon my arrival?"

"All depends on what you plan to do while you're in there. If you give them a reason to shoot, they will. If a member of the Paladino family is threatened, they'll eliminate the threat."

"And if the threat is directed only at August?"

A wide smile crawls across Luciano's face, and I can see the glimmer in his eye. Dare I say, there's a hint of approval in there?

"I suspect they'll hold their fire to wait to see what goes down. I have it on good authority that the security team isn't a huge fan of his, either."

"Not shocked," Sully blurts.

Nixon clears his throat. "I hate to be a cuckoo clock, but you need to get your ass changed and down to the church."

Luciano checks the time on his phone, sliding it from his pocket to peek at the illuminated screen. "He's right. Vinnie should be heading out any second. We need to move. Anything I can do to make this run smoother?"

"Sì," I tell him, pulling my phone from my pocket. Pulling up the new group message between myself, Sully, Enzo, and now Nixon, I click on the addition sign in the top corner to add a new contact to the chat. "What is your number?"

Enzo groans and begins walking down the hallway, away from us. Nixon tips his head and follows, while Sully waits with me. "We went from three to five awfully quick," he muses as Luciano recites his number and I punch it into my phone. "There's no way this wedding is happening."

Stretching out his hand, he offers it to Luciano, who takes it. The two men shake cordially, then Sully disappears down the hall in the direction Enzo and Nixon went.

"I'm going to put an end to this," I tell Luciano, once it's just the two of us again. "I love your sister more than life itself. I'll go to the ends of this earth for her. But make no mistake, Luciano. Your sister will become my wife. I will never walk away from her again, no matter the circumstances."

Slapping my shoulder, he grasps it tightly and looks me dead in the eyes. "Now's your chance to prove it, Lucchetti."

# Chapter 19

## *Vinnie*

What should have been a five-minute drive to St. Sebastian's takes us nearly twenty thanks to a fender bender blocking a lane, causing NYPD to have to direct traffic. It seems appropriate that I'd be late to my own wedding.

An omen, some would say.

As we pass the collision, the morbid thought of wishing it was me in the car that crashed passes through my mind.

The drive has been quiet as I stare straight ahead—other than to look at the accident—laser focused on the closed partition as Cecilia and Raina each hold one of my hands in their lap. The air is thick with the summer heat and unspoken words. Finally, I can't take it anymore.

"Look, I know I'm basically on my way to my own emotional funeral right now, but marrying August won't change *me*, you guys. We're going to go in there, grit our teeth through the ceremony, then enjoy the reception. It's an open bar, so we're going to utilize it."

Drinking away my sorrows doesn't seem like the best of choices considering where I'm expected to sleep tonight, but there's no way I'll make it through everything without a few drinks in my system—and I'm not a drinker.

Truly, a glass of wine, *maybe* two, is my limit. There's nothing I hate more than the feeling of being hungover.

Well, that's a lie.

I hate August more.

"It just feels a little hard to celebrate—" Cecilia begins, but Raina cuts her off.

"—but if getting wasted is what you want, getting wasted is what you'll get, babe."

"Thank you." I squeeze both of their hands at the same time and turn my head to each of them to give them a small smile. "Your support means the world to me."

"We'll *always* support you," Cecilia stresses. "Even if we don't agree with the decision, remember?"

"That being said," Raina interjects again. "There's still time to hijack this limo and make you a runaway bride."

My thoughts drift to Sly and the time we spent in my hotel room—moments that I'll always treasure. Though, I hope one day I'll forget the look in his eyes and the way the light extinguished when I told him again that I was still going through with the wedding. Seconds later, a startling visual of Sly in an open casket plagues my mind and I immediately start shaking my head.

"No. I have to do this."

When the driver pulls the limo alongside the curb in front of the church, I look out the window at the magnificent structure, sighing deeply. I've always admired St. Sebastian's. It's tall, pointed pinnacles, the stunning stained glass windows that decorate the front. Even the cross that rests on the highest point of the building sparkles against the summer sun.

Under any other circumstances, I'd feel a sense of peace knowing I was about to marry in the church I grew up in.

Our driver comes around to open the door, and Raina slides out first, accepting his hand for assistance. Cecilia leans forward and grabs the bouquets, handing them to me one at a time. I pass both mine and Raina's to her as she stands outside the car, then slides forward on the seat to follow her out.

Cecilia is out of the car faster than I can stand up straight, helping me smooth and fluff my gown on the dirty New York sidewalk. Taking my bouquet from Raina, I silently walk up the stairs that lead to the entrance.

Two men from my father's security team stand in front of the doors in tuxedos, their hands crossed in front of them. Clear, coiled earpieces sit in their ears and I can see one of them is speaking into the headset he wears, likely announcing my arrival.

When I stop in front of them, the one who was

talking tips his head in greeting, wordlessly opening the door.

The moment I'm over the threshold, I see my father waiting in the foyer. The heavy wooden doors leading into the church are closed, but even the dense oak that blocks us isn't thick enough to hide the chatter of excitement from the guests that are inside.

"Sunshine, you look stunning." He kisses the side of my temple. "Are you ready?"

"As I'll ever be," I answer honestly, but he misses the sarcasm in my voice. Looking over my shoulder, he gives a curt nod to someone, and within seconds I hear music from inside the church begin.

In my peripheral, I see a man push off the wall and approach my friends. "Miss Lancaster, Miss Burns— they're ready for you."

One at a time, they come to give me a hug.

"I love you," Cecilia reminds me as she squeezes me tight.

"I love you, too." The look on her face is solemn as she backs away and takes her spot in front of the doors.

Raina steps forward and grabs my face in her hands, not caring about my makeup. She holds my gaze as she keeps her voice low. "You will get past this. You are a strong, amazing, *selfless* woman, and your sacrifice will not go without praise. Keep your chin up, babe. I'll be right beside you—today, and *always*."

Unabashedly, she kisses me on the nose. I hear my father's deep chuckle beside us, and my heart races, though I know he couldn't have heard her. She walks away to go join Cecilia, standing behind her as they line up to enter.

My father steps toward me, arm extended with his elbow bent for me to take.

Like the dutiful daughter I am, I slip my hand into the crook of his elbow and we line up behind my bridesmaids.

Then the doors open.

Emotion clogs my throat when I see how full the church is. My vision blurs as I take it all in—not a pew is empty as a sea of faceless bodies fills every inch, with some people even standing in the back.

My stomach rolls.

A violinist begins to play the soft melody of Bach's "Arioso" as August's brother, Orlando, steps out from the right, offering Cecilia his arm. She takes it and they begin to walk down the aisle where I know August waits. I refuse to look that far, not wanting to see him until I absolutely have to.

What's the point? I have to look at him for the rest of my life.

When they reach the halfway point, Joseph steps out and offers Raina his arm. As she takes it, he looks over his shoulder at me, his expression giving nothing away. Our gaze meets, and his eyes harden. There's not an ounce of the boy I once knew left in him—my big brother, my best friend. In his place is a man I don't recognize, playing the part of my brother. The moment is fleeting before he turns back around and faces the church, and he and Raina begin to walk down the aisle.

My father and I step forward. All eyes turn to us as though I'm a magnet, and suddenly it feels like I can't breathe.

Standing there, with everyone looking at me, I mentally black out, slipping so deep into the recesses of my mind, I don't realize my father is squeezing my hand with his free one until I hear his voice cut through the silence my mind has created.

"Sunshine…Sunshine, it's our turn. This is it."

Whipping my head toward him, I search his face, looking—internally begging—for some indication that this is all just a bad dream. But as a bead of sweat drips from his forehead I know that it's not. The tuxedo he wears, the heavy gown I wear, the church full of people…this is real, and I'm very much about to metaphorically end my life for the man I love.

"Let's go," I say, and take the first step forward.

Before my heel even touches the ground, the gentle whoosh of bodies ripples through the air as every single person stands and turns toward us.

Beaming smiles and soft whispers line the rows as we pass by, every step numbing me more. I look around at the church I was raised in, taking in the sight of the evening sun dancing through the stained glass windows, the colors settling on the marble floor.

When I finally look up at August, I'm met with a smile that overtakes his face. A smile I would think was genuine, if it were on anyone other than him.

Stopping in front of him, he takes a single altar step down so he is level with us, standing before me and my father. They shake hands, and after, August clasps his in front of himself, waiting for his next cue.

My father and I bow in front of the altar before he reaches for August's hand and places mine in it.

Stepping forward, I cast a glance at Raina and give her my bouquet as I turn to stand beside August. She takes it and goes to sit with Cecilia and my family in the first pew. Across the aisle from them, the groomsmen—my brother Joseph included—sit with August's family.

As the music comes to a close and the chatter of the guests quiets, the Monsignor readies himself to speak.

Monsignor Jacoby, who has been the same man whom I have listened to every Sunday since I was old enough to sit through mass, wears a white vestment instead of his usual black with purple trim, and his circular bifocals rest on the bridge of his nose.

"We welcome everyone here today to share in the joy of the union and celebration of Vincenza Mae Paladino and August William St. Jean. We begin in the name of the Father, the Son, and the Holy Spirit. May the Lord be with you."

"And with your spirit," hundreds of voices repeat.

Recognizing our next cue, August and I turn toward each other and he takes the hand he isn't already holding so that he's clutching both. My palms begin to sweat under his gaze, but I refuse to give him any eye contact.

Instead, I stare at the knot of his tie and allow my mind to drift to Sly.

Sly and his striking hazel eyes. The soft smile he reserves just for me.

I think of his touch, and my body can't help but react with a shiver.

The telltale sign of tears prick the back of my eyes, and I bite down on the inside of my bottom lip to keep myself from outwardly reacting.

As the monsignor continues on through the beginning part of the ceremony, I keep my view cast downward, looking at my hands still clasped in August's. I hate it. The feel of his skin against mine. The knowledge of what's to come as soon as this ceremony is over.

Briefly, I think about how grateful I am that August's family is not Catholic and our families decided not to do a full traditional mass, or make us suffer through Pre-Cana.

I would have never made it through the two hours it would have taken from beginning to end of a full mass wedding, and there's no way I would have made it through six months of marriage classes through the church with August, pretending as though I'm actually invested in our *relationship*.

As it is, the words the monsignor is speaking don't register in my mind. Neither do the readings given by our loved ones, or the time that passes during the ceremony. It's like I'm having an out-of-body experience, and it isn't until August squeezes my hands to the point of pain to get my attention that I realize what is about to happen.

It's almost time to recite our vows of consent.

"Vincenza and August. Have you come here today, before God, your families, and each other, to enter into a marriage freely, wholeheartedly, and without coercion?" the monsignor asks.

We're meant to answer together, but as August recites, "I have," the words taste like bile on my tongue. I can't get them out—my voice is barely above a whisper as I attempt to say the same.

August squeezes my fingers again, and I clear my throat, willing my voice to stay strong. "I have."

The way my heart crumbles after I utter those two words is beyond explanation.

"Are you prepared to join in Holy Matrimony as you come together to follow the path of marriage, united as one, to love and to honor each other as long as you both shall live?"

"I am," August and I repeat in unison.

It feels as though he's physically ripped my chest open and is clutching my heart, squeezing it tighter and tighter with each declaration the monsignor speaks.

"Are you prepared to lovingly accept God's children and bring them up according to the love and law of Christ and his Church?"

"I am," we repeat, but mine comes out as a sob.

The thought of children with anyone other than Sly is the final nail in my metaphorical coffin. There's nothing left of me to break.

A vision of Sly and I walking hand in hand with a toddler by our side appears like a flash of lightning in front of my eyes before it quickly swirls away, as though it was never there.

Looking up at August, my eyes meet his, and reflected, I see everything I'm losing by standing before him.

Every piece of me screams inside—the strong woman I once was begging to be set free again, trying to claw her way out. I don't recognize myself, and as I glance down at the gorgeous white gown I'm wearing, every thought I've forced out of my mind over these last several months slams into me.

*You're a coward.*

*A fake.*

*Sly doesn't deserve a woman like you, but you deserve a man like August.*

*You're not the Vinnie Paladino you pretend to be.*

I don't realize a tear has fallen until August reaches up to brush it away, leaning into the role of the loving, doting groom he pretends to be.

"As it is your intention to enter into Holy Matrimony, it is time to declare your consent and commitment before God and His Church. August, recite your commitment."

August smiles widely. "With pleasure. I, August William St. Jean, take you, Vincenza Mae Paladino, to be my lawful wife. I promise to have and to hold you from this day forward, for better and worse, in sickness and in health. I will love and honor you through all the days of my life until death do us part."

Reaching up, he wipes at his eyes, putting on a good show.

Then he glances at the monsignor, and suddenly it's my turn. My heart pounds in my chest and my vision swims.

This is it. This is truly it.

"Amen," Monsignor Jacoby closes. "Vincenza, recite your commitment."

*I can't.*

My esophagus feels as though it's closing on its own, my chest rising and falling as I struggle to breathe.

"*Vinnie*," August growls through teeth gritted in a charming smile.

He's squeezing my hands so tightly, the tips of my fingers are as white as paper.

"I…" I begin, but the words I don't want to say die on my tongue.

A sudden *bang* erupts through the church as one of the doors slams against the wall. My head whips toward the sound, and the sight of the man at the other end of the aisle is enough to have me falling to my knees.

*What is he doing here?*

# Chapter 20

## *Sly*

Getting through the Paladino's security was more of a challenge than we thought, despite having the help of Luciano, and I'm nearly too late by the time I'm able to get inside of the church.

The only thing I can think of is getting to Vincenza before she speaks her commitment.

Pushing open the door as quickly as I can, it slams against the wall with force, causing every head in the room to turn in my direction.

It takes mere seconds for my eyes to collide with Vinnie's, and I see the moment her knees buckle. August holds one of her hands and reaches out to catch her with the other.

As he holds her steady, he looks up at me, and even from across the room, I can see his eyes darken. "Lucchetti."

In the same moment, Vincenza's father is out of his seat, bellowing my name. "*Lucchetti!*" The woman next to him—Vinnie's mother—grabs onto her husband's wrist and pulls him back down to the pew.

Releasing his hold on Vincenza, August takes a step away from her into my direction. Pulling my Glock from its holster beneath my jacket, I aim the barrel directly at him as I walk down the aisle toward them.

Nervous murmurs, small screams, and a few sobs sound throughout the crowd at the sight of my weapon. I pay them no mind—not even giving my attention to the Paladino family as I hold my gaze on August.

Adrenaline rushes through my bloodstream, my monster fully unleashed—prepared and excited. Not an ounce of remorse flits through me for what I'm about to do.

August looks ready to tear me limb from limb, and the only thing that flickers through my mind is him raising his hand to the love of my life.

He deserves to die.

Baring his teeth, August takes the altar step down. "If you think you can—"

*God, please forgive me.*

Squeezing the trigger, I fire my weapon.

Screams erupt throughout the church as the gunshot echoes through the grand vaulted ceilings, and August's lifeless body crumples to the floor. Vinnie's scream is prominent against the others, her hands covering her mouth as she looks at the corpse beside her in disbelief.

For the quickest moment, I lock eyes with Luciano, who gives me a quick nod as he sits next to his father, which I hope means he has reached the head of security and ordered them to stand down.

He must have, since I am still breathing.

When I make it to Vinnie, I see the red splatters of blood across her dress, her chest, and a little on her hands. Surprisingly, her face is spared of August's blood.

"Piccola ladra," I breathe as I take an altar step. "Are you alright?"

It's an idiotic question—there is a dead man laying on the floor in front of her—of course she's not alright.

Still, I do not trust her family, so as I see movement from my peripheral, I briefly look over at where they are and raise my Glock, pointing it at Joseph Paladino. "Don't you dare try anything, stronzo," I growl in his direction before sweeping the direction of the gun over to Vinnie's father.

"What are you doing here?" Vinnie asks, still in shock at my abrupt entrance.

From beside us, the priest—monsignor?—begins to whisper a prayer.

"I would never let you marry a man who harms you, Vincenza. As it is, the only man you should be marrying is *me*, and I hope you will."

Out of the corner of my eye, I see the man sitting next to Joseph begin to stand. "Sit down!" I snap, turning my gun to him.

Joseph mirrors the man as he pushes to his feet. "I'm going to ki—"

"Sit down, unless you're ready to join August in

death," I snarl, cocking the gun. The sound reverberates all around.

The man next to Joseph puts his hands in front of him, and they slowly sit back down. There's a wildness in Joseph's eyes as he stares at me—something dark and unrefined. I am mildly surprised when he lowers himself to the pew, yielding my threat.

Next to them both is a couple—perhaps August's parents. The man's face is beet-red, looking as though he's daydreaming about strangling me.

Narrowing my eyes, I send a clear, but silent, message.

*Don't even think about it.*

Next to him, the woman cries.

Slowly, when I am more certain Joseph isn't going to try anything, I reposition the barrel of my gun to face Vinnie's father, Maurizio, before turning my attention back to her.

Her eyes are glassy as she stares into mine. "You knew August was hurting me?"

"I figured it out, amore mio. You should have told me he was holding the threat of my life over your head. I would have protected you."

"I was protecting *you*," she whimpers, and I can see the truth in her eyes—and the fear. She believed August would have harmed me, all while it was her enduring the suffering.

Dropping my voice, I ask a question that's been plaguing me, one that I would shoot August's corpse again for, depending on her answer. "Piccola ladra, was he forcing himself on you? Did he hurt you in any other way?"

"No," Vinnie tells me, shaking her head. "He said he liked his women willing, and since I was not, he was waiting for our wedding night." A tremor runs through her body as she says the words, a clear look of disgust on her face.

Relief washes through me. "We have a lot to discuss, but I would like to save that for later. Right now, I would very much like to marry you."

Her eyes widen in surprise, and she glances at August's body as it cools at her feet. "*Now?*"

I can't help but to smile. She is beautiful, even when she is painted in red. "Sì, now. I can't wait another minute to make you my wife."

Still, my gun never wavers from being pointed at her father.

As though they can hear our conversation, Sully, Enzo, and Nixon appear from the side of the church and approach us.

A quiet layer of whispers settles among the guests as they watch my friend's approach—all wearing tuxedos, looking as though they're meant to be a part of the bridal party.

"And you all call me the dramatic one," Sully mumbles as he produces a black velvet box from inside his jacket pocket and hands it to me before sauntering over to where August's family sits, taking the seat next to the man who I presume is his father.

Without commentary, Nixon and Enzo pick up

August's body and carry him out of God's house. A trail of ruby-red blood drips across the white marble floor of the church, following behind them like an unwanted shadow.

I feel mildly guilty for the location of where I was forced to kill August, but I wouldn't hesitate to do it again.

I should have done it sooner.

Looking back at Vinnie, I lift her chin with my pointer finger. Her eyes—no longer full of tears—sparkle with a flicker of happiness that I haven't seen in months.

"Marry me," I repeat. "Be my wife. Make me the happiest man on this continent and the next. Let me love and cherish you as you deserve. Let me father your children and take care of the family we create together. Marry me and be my forever."

Without hesitation, Vinnie closes the distance between us and presses her lips to mine. "Yes," she breathes against my lips. "Yes. A thousand times, yes."

A collective gasp sounds, but I ignore the chatter and chaos as it emits around us. Instead, I take my time kissing my fiancée slowly and sweetly. "Ti amo, piccola ladra. Più di quanto le parole possano descrivere." *I love you, little thief. More than words can describe.*

Pulling herself from me, Vinnie smiles. "I love you."

Turning to the Father, I address him, though he looks terrified of my mere presence. I can't fault him for it—I can admit what I did in the church is horrific. "Father, please continue with the ceremony, but if you would, let us begin again from the statement of intention."

"Monsignor," Vincenza whispers, correcting me quietly. Placing her hand in my free hand, she gives it a gentle squeeze.

Shaking profusely, the monsignor turns his terror-stricken eyes to Vinnie. "Miss…Miss Paladino?"

Her smile widens, and she nods her head. "Please continue."

Her gaze follows the direction of my gun and she looks at her family for a moment. "Sly, please lower the gun. My father is unarmed."

"I don't trust him," I grit, staring at him as he stares at me.

"I understand," she tells me, her voice soft and sweet like smooth, golden honey. "But he isn't going to stop this. He would have already. *Please.*"

It takes me a moment before I am willing to tear my gaze from Maurizio and back to her. When I finally do, her gray-blue eyes shine brightly, and regardless of the tension I feel, a sense of contentment washes over me.

I flick my gaze to Joseph and take in his demeanor. He's seething—his hands in tight fists on top of his thighs—but he makes no move to stand, which surprises me, until my line of vision lands behind him.

Pressed against the base of his skull is the muzzle of a gun. The corner of Enzo's lips turn up in a sideways grin as he leans forward in the pew behind Joseph. Next to him, Nixon's arms are draped over the small space between the two other men, his own gun in his hand.

Satisfaction blooms in my chest, and I turn back to *my* bride, looking at her as I smile and say, "Please, Monsignor. You may continue."

With a shaky breath, he addresses me. "What is your name, young man?"

"Sylvester Lucchetti."

He nods and clears his throat. On his authority, the guests of the church quiet once again.

"Vincenza and Sylvester. Have you come here today, before God, your families, and each other, to enter into a marriage freely, wholeheartedly, and without coercion?" he asks, the tremble in his voice evident.

"I have," Vincenza and I repeat in unison. Releasing one of her hands, I brush my knuckles against the side of her cheek.

"Are you prepared to join in Holy Matrimony as you come together to follow the path of marriage, united as one, to love and to honor each other as long as you both shall live?"

"I am," we repeat, and I reach for her hand again, rubbing my thumb against the skin of her ring finger. Within moments, my ring will rest in that very spot.

"Are you prepared to lovingly accept God's children and bring them up according to the love and Law of Christ and his Church?"

It's all I've been dreaming of—life and a family with Vinnie.

There is no hesitation when I say, "I am." Her words collide with mine, and I cannot help but lean down to kiss her softly, knowing she's been picturing a future with me, too.

"As it is your intention to enter into Holy Matrimony, it is time to declare your consent and commitment before God and His Church. Due to the—er—circumstances, I will ask Vincenza to recite them first, so you have the opportunity to hear them, Sylvester."

"Grazie, Monsignor."

Vinnie beams at me, her gaze never straying from mine. "I, Vincenza Mae Paladino, take you, Sylvester Lucchetti, to be my lawful husband. I promise to have and to hold you from this day forward, for better and worse, in sickness and in health. I will love and honor you through all the days of my life until death do us part."

"Amen," the monsignor says curtly. "Sylvester, recite your commitment."

My heart gallops with excitement. I am about to make Vinnie my *wife* and show the world how much I love and adore this woman.

"I, Sylvester Lucchetti, take you, Vincenza Mae Paladino, to be my lawful wife. I swear to have and to hold you from this day forward, for better and worse, in sickness and in health. I will love, cherish, and honor you through all the days of my life until death do us part, and every moment in the afterlife."

"May the Lord, in all of his kindness, strengthen the consent you have declared before God and His church to bring fulfillment of his blessings to you." The monsignor clears his throat again, a line of sweat accumulating at his hairline. "What God has joined together, no one may asunder. Let us bless the Lord."

He raises his hands, signaling to the guests to repeat their part. Some do as a quiet ripple of "Thanks be to God," sounds throughout, but the voices are nowhere near strong or boisterous.

It doesn't seem to bother Vincenza, though, so I don't allow it to bother me.

"The rings," the monsignor says under his breath. Reaching into the pocket where I stowed the box Sully handed me, I turn it toward my wife so she may see her ring.

She gasps as the lid opens, revealing a four carat pear cut pink diamond set on a white gold band, with a halo of diamonds surrounding it. Behind it rests two white gold bands—a diamond band for her to wear when she prefers a simple ring, and a brushed band for myself.

Taking all three from the box, I hand them to the monsignor.

Resting them flat on his palm, he looks down at them. "Lord, bless these rings so that those who may wear them abide in peace and in your will, may remain faithful to one another, and may always live in mutual charity. Through Christ our Lord."

"Amen," echoes through the church as more guests join in for this blessing. I repeat them, and Vinnie follows as she grins, watching as the monsignor sprinkles our rings with holy water.

Handing me Vinnie's rings, he passes mine to her.

Positioning the band at the tip of my ring finger, she gazes lovingly into my eyes as she says, "Sylvester Lucchetti, receive this ring as a sign of my everlasting love and fidelity."

She pushes the ring up my finger until it reaches the base.

"Vincenza Mae Paladino," I begin, raising my voice slightly so all can hear as I align both rings to slide on her. "Receive these rings as a sign of my everlasting love and fidelity."

Making the sign of the cross, the monsignor closes. "In the name of the Father, the Son, and the Holy Spirit. Now, let us invoke God's blessing upon this bride and groom, and may favor with his help those on whom he has bestowed with the Sacrament of Matrimony. In the sight of God and these witnesses, I now pronounce you husband and wife. Sylvester, you may now kiss your bride!"

I don't wait another second before I close the distance between us and kiss my wife. Cupping the back of her head, I tilt her back, dipping her deeply as our mouths move together in perfect synchronicity. I want to ravish her, but our sins have already amassed in this blissful union, so I keep it as tame as I possibly can.

Too soon, I right her and break our kiss, but I never take my eyes off her. The monsignor then gives his final words to us and the attendees. "Go in peace to glorify the Lord with your life."

All around, guests resound, "Thanks be to God."

Leaning forward, I kiss her softly again before I

angle my body and scoop her into a bridal carry. She laughs as I start down the aisle, heading straight for the doors.

"We're supposed to walk down the aisle together as husband and wife," she scolds in a playful tone, wrapping her arms around my neck.

"I have waited far too long to have you in my arms again, Vincenza. This is me making up for lost time. You may never walk again, amore mio."

Nuzzling into me, she kisses the tender spot on my neck. "I love you, Sly Lucchetti."

"Ti amo, moglie mia."

*I love you, my wife.*

# Chapter 21

## *Vinnie*

"Vincenza! Vincenza, stop!" my father's voice echoes through the church as Sly carries me into the foyer. My stomach lurches hearing him call me *Vincenza* and not *Sunshine*, like he has since I was a child.

Over Sly's shoulder, I see a look I've never seen on my father's face before—one of disbelief, anger, and rage.

"It is your decision, piccola ladra," Sly tells me. His pace slows, but he continues walking toward the tall oak doors that lead outside.

I don't want to stop and face my father, but I know it's the right thing to do. I can't imagine what is going on in his head—there is so much he doesn't know, and considering all that transpired in the last thirty minutes, I know we need to talk. "We should talk to him."

"Of course." Sly sets me down carefully, allowing me to find my footing beneath the elaborate skirt of my gown. Reaching down, he laces his fingers in mine.

His touch is reassuring and whispers the unspoken promise of solidarity.

My father comes to an abrupt stop in front of us, his face red and angry as his eyes dart between me and Sly and down to our connected hands. A true moment of realization hits, carving along every feature of his face. I can't help but feel a wave of guilt slam into me, my heart sinking as the way he sees his daughter shifts before my very eyes.

"Vincenza?"

"Daddy, let me explain."

His brows furrow together at my use of a term of endearment he hasn't heard from me since I was a child, and he shakes his head. "Not here."

Footsteps of wedding guests draw closer, and he gestures toward a closed door off the foyer, opening it and disappearing inside. He doesn't check to see if we're behind him.

Tugging Sly by the hand, I follow my father.

As we enter the room, the lights are off, and the space is colder than the foyer. Ornate, antique mahogany furniture lines the office space, along with bookshelves, wingback leather chairs, and an unlit fireplace.

Behind me, the door clicks into place, and I glance over my shoulder to see Sly leaning against it, his eyes on my father.

Placing his palms on Monsignor Jacoby's desk, my father leans forward, his back grounded as his head hangs. He doesn't look at us—doesn't speak for several long, anxiety inducing seconds.

Taking a few steps backward, I lean against Sly. His hand encircles my waist, grounding me. "Daddy, I—"

"You married a Lucchetti," he finishes. The low, lethal tone of his voice causes my spine to stiffen. "You've embarrassed this family."

"I love him," I state, unwavering. Lacing my fingers through Sly's, I keep our hands intertwined at my stomach.

My father turns to face us. "You have no idea what you're saying, Vincenza. You have betrayed this family. Your entire life I have warned you against them. There's a reason we have been at war with them for decades—why the feud began in the first place. The Lucchettis are not a family to associate with, they're—"

"They're my family now, Father. *I'm* a Lucchetti now."

"I WILL NOT ALLOW IT," he bellows. "What he just did out there—"

"Was to protect the woman I love," Sly interjects, his voice calm as he addresses my father. Letting go of my hand, he sidesteps and puts himself between us. "You have no idea the things *my wife* has endured behind closed doors with that pathetic excuse for a man. The man *you* agreed to marry her off to."

My father's eyes meet mine, and I struggle for words, looking down and breaking our eye contact instead.

"You gave your blessing to force her into a marriage

with a man whom she not only despised, but who physically assaulted her. All because you trusted the word of your son, who is just as much of a monster as August was."

"You are a liar, just like your good-for-nothing uncle was," my father spits, and I can't believe the words as they fall from his mouth.

He doesn't *believe* him. Doesn't believe *us*. Or, he's choosing not to.

*He's ignoring what he saw during the rehearsal, just like I knew he would.*

Tears prick my eyes as I look at Sly, and he reaches up, lovingly rubbing my cheek with his thumb.

"Show him, piccola ladra," he says quietly, his eyes softening. "It's the only way he will *see*."

Forcing back a whimper, I nod and turn around so my back faces Sly. He understands my unspoken request and slowly lowers the zipper until it reaches just above the lace of my panties, keeping me covered as much as possible. Holding the gown to my chest, I lightly shake my arm as I pull it out of the sleeve, releasing the fabric so more of my skin shows.

As it floats from my arm, the fading bruises on my rib cage are exposed, and my father sucks in a harsh breath.

"He's been abusing your daughter, Maurizio. Right under your nose." There is no anger in Sly's voice as he delivers the harsh reality to my father, just sadness—in tune with the emotion plaguing me in this moment.

A pained look morphs my father's features as he

stares at my yellow and brown discolored skin. "I… Sunshine, why have you kept this from me?"

"What was I supposed to say?" Sadness and disbelief seep into my words. "You wouldn't have listened. You saw what you wanted to see, even when the warning signs were flashing before yours and Mother's eyes like a neon sign in a dive bar. Every time I wanted to confess, you sang August's praises and spoke of how much this wedding would be good for the family and for *business*."

"You should have spoken frankly about what was going on," he argues.

I scoff, pushing my arm back into my sleeve. "You would have ignored it, Father."

"And this?" He gestures between me and Sly, as Sly zips my gown again. "What is *this*?"

Before I can answer, Sly does. "I have loved your daughter since I was a boy, even if I was too young to recognize the signs until recent years. Our relationship should have never been kept a secret. The love I have for her is more powerful than words can fathom, Maurizio."

"Then where were *you* when this was happening to her? If you love her as much as you claim to, why didn't you intervene?" my father sneers, so angry, spittle flies from his mouth with every word he enunciates.

Remorse flickers across Sly's face, so I connect our hands again, giving him a soft squeeze. "Gone for foolish reasons. I believed she didn't want me, and truly loved him. It was only when she came to Ridgewood to find me, that I—"

"You went WHERE?" my father bellows again, his temper getting the best of him. It feels like he is honing in on the wrong details of the story as he tries to piece it together.

"Ridgewood, Father. California."

"It's where I have been these past few months," Sly adds.

"I took the first flight I could when I heard—"

The door to the monsignor's office flies open, practically falling off its hinges from the force of Joseph bursting into the room. It slams back into place behind him.

Pointing his finger toward Sly, he screams, "I'M GOING TO KILL YOU," as he stomps further into the room.

Instinctually, I position myself between Sly and my brother at the same time Luciano saunters into the room, his hands in his pockets as though this is just another Saturday evening.

"You will do no such thing," I challenge, mustering every ounce of strength I have to keep the quiver from my voice. "*You're* the reason this has happened."

"He couldn't if he tried, amore mio," Sly says under his breath as he presses a kiss to my temple.

"He *murdered* August, then *married* you. And you're casting the blame on me? My friend is dead."

"Your friend was a woman-beater," Luciano canters back with boredom.

"Stay the fuck out of this, Luciano," Joseph spits, then redirects his attention to Sly. "How dare you interrupt the wedding between my best friend and my sister, then have the audacity to *kill him*. You're dead, Lucchetti. I will bury you for this."

Spots of shades of red line my vision—bursts of scarlet, maroon, and ruby. My body begins to quake as I listen to every word my brother says, spewing his lies and accusations while my hearing sounds like I'm underwater.

"How did you bypass my security team, anyway?" I hear my father murmur, his brows furrowing in concern.

Luciano chuckles. "You're not the only Paladino man they're instructed to listen to, Father."

My father says something in response, but I can hardly hear the words. The feeling of the room caving in on me is heavy against my skin, and I feel myself losing control—not even Sly's touch keeping me firm on the ground. I've never felt this level of anger before, and it's on the precipice of erupting.

I try to keep it bottled, but as Sly rubs his hand rhythmically against the back of my neck, I can't contain it.

"YOU ARE THE PROBLEM, JOSEPH," I explode, turning toward my brother, pressing forward until we're inches apart. "YOU. Not me, not Sly. YOU. You, with your jealousy and your hatred toward me. You're completely and utterly blinded by the fact that you think Father will overlook you and hand his business to me. You purposely pushed this marriage into Father's lap, manipulating him into thinking the *union* would be beneficial, all so you could pair me with a man who would physically abuse me into submission. August is dead because of *you*."

My chest heaves with adrenaline, my breaths rigid and painful as I stare up into the darkened eyes of my brother. He looms over me, taking a step forward.

Before I register what is happening, he raises his hand, seconds from slapping me.

Preparing myself for the pain, I close my eyes and cower into myself.

But it never comes.

When I open my eyes, I'm surprised to see our father's—not Sly's—hand locked around Joseph's wrist, stopping him. "You have some nerve to raise your hand to your sister, Joseph. Get out of my sight. NOW."

Turning quickly, I plow into Sly's chest. One of his arms wraps around my body, while the other rests on the back of my head, holding me to him. "You're safe," he reassures.

A tear seeps from the corner of my eye, and Luciano meets my gaze from against Sly's chest.

"Get him out of here before I kill him myself," Sly warns, speaking to my eldest brother. Yet again, I'm surprised and confused.

*He just said that like they're friends.*

Luciano nods at Sly and moves in the direction of Joseph, grabbing our brother's bicep.

"Let's go," he says as I bury my face into Sly's chest

again, craving the closeness. Sly kisses the top of my head.

Moments later, I hear the door to the office close.

"Sunshine," my father begins, but Sly stops his words.

"I think this has been enough for one day, Maurizio. We're going to go."

My father takes a step toward Sly, crossing his arms over his chest. "I'd like to speak to my daughter. *Alone.*"

"My *wife* is exhausted, both mentally and physically, and I am taking her home. You may speak with her when we return from our honeymoon, Maurizio. I'd suggest you speak with your *son* first, and make damn sure he has no ill-intentions toward the woman we *both* love."

Sly's hand slides up my back and he drapes his arm over my shoulder as he ushers me from the room. I fight against the urge to look back at my father, and instead hold my breath, expecting him to say something as we walk through the door.

"Breathe, piccola ladra. Everything is alright." Sly rubs his hand against my shoulder and pulls the door open with his other, holding it so we can both go through together.

"The only thing that feels alright is that you're my husband. Everything else feels like a jumbled disaster."

A limo idles by the curb and when we approach, the back passenger door pops open. Sly lowers his hand to my back, urging me to climb in. He helps me lift my dress as I bend and slide onto the soft leather seat.

"Oh my gosh!" I exclaim when I see who's inside. "What are you guys doing here?"

"We overheard this one on the phone prepping his jet for you." Raina juts her thumb at Sully. "And there wasn't a single chance in hell I was going to let Romeo here whisk you off somewhere without saying goodbye."

Dropping to her knees, she walks on the floor of the limo over to me, tossing her arms around my neck. "I had a feeling he'd do something like that. You picked a good one," she whispers, masking it with a kiss to my cheek.

When she goes back to her seat, Cecilia crawls over to me next. Wordlessly, she holds me tight for several seconds. "That was terrifying and romantic, all at the same time. I'm so glad he put a stop to that sham of a wedding."

"Me too. And I'm so glad you're here."

"What a whirlwind few hours." She laughs her nervous laugh, and I know the chaos brewing through her mind. Cecilia is such a gentle soul—a laid-back woman who loves to be in the company of good friends, good books, and surrounded by her favorite comforts. Today was a lot for her.

It was a lot for all of us.

Still hugging her, I look over her shoulder and find Sully watching us closely. Giving him a weak smile, he returns it with a short nod.

"Where are Enzo and Nix?" Sly asks Sully, his hand

settled on my thigh. He hasn't stopped touching me, and I sincerely hope he never does.

"On clean up duty," Sully replies curtly, his eyes glued to Cecilia as she situates herself on the other side of me, causing me to press into Sly's side.

She's none the wiser, fixing her dress as she gets comfortable against the small leather bench seat that's meant for two.

"Where are we going?" I ask to no one in particular.

Sully scoffs, smirking as he runs a hand through his hair. My eyes catch on the light shining off the faceplate of his watch while he unbuttons the cuffs of his sleeves and rolls them up to his elbows. "The tarmac. Your plane leaves in thirty."

Shock courses through me as I turn to Sly.

A boyish grin pulls at his lips, and he pulls my hand into his. "We were just married, amore mio. We're off to our honeymoon."

I look at Raina, then Sully, and finally at Cecilia. All three of them smiling and nodding their heads.

My mind reels, still trying to catch up. "But I have nothing with me. My suitcase—"

"Will arrive shortly after you do. I'll make sure of it," Cecilia says matter-of-factly.

Pulling my hand to his mouth, Sly kisses my knuckles, brushing his soft lips against them before leaning over to whisper in my ear. His warm breath on my skin sends a shiver through me, and naturally I lean toward him.

Brushing the hair from my face, he skates his tongue along the velvety edge of my ear, his voice sending a current of arousal straight to my core. "Don't worry, piccola ladra. Where we're going, you won't need clothes."

# Chapter 22

## *Vinnie*

**M**y absolute favorite thing about the ten-hour flight to our honeymoon destination has been witnessing the joy that grows on Sly's face with every passing hour.

He refuses to tell me where we're going, but the constant stream of dark ocean below us clues me in to realizing it's some place European. Knowing my new husband, my instinct says Italy, but he refuses to confirm or deny.

Our honeymoon.

We're on our way to our *honeymoon*.

Giddiness filters through my system—soft tingles of excitement for the adventure that lies ahead.

"How long will we be gone?" I ask innocently, still hoping he'll reveal more about our trip. Sliding my hand over his thigh, I let my fingers travel dangerously close to his length as I lean over on the armrest of my seat. He catches my hand before it touches him, pulling my wrist to his lips, kissing the inside.

"Two weeks, amore mio. Unless you'd like to stay longer."

Two weeks is a long time to be away from my business, especially when I hadn't anticipated leaving. August and I hadn't planned a honeymoon—we were going to tell people we were going later in the year but then never plan it.

At least, I had no intention of ever planning anything. Why celebrate something that isn't worth celebrating?

Reaching over to the table next to me, I grab my purse and pull my phone out. The small white satin clutch glimmers in the light that shines directly on it. I'm grateful to Raina for bringing an outfit change with her in preparation of drinking and possibly dancing the night away. She shoved the Hermès overnight bag into my arms the moment the limo pulled up next to the plane.

I changed into her black midi dress once we boarded Sully's jet, and although I'm a little cold now, I'm grateful to no longer be wearing a bloodstained wedding gown.

Such bittersweet memories that dress will hold.

Bitter because I should have only ever put it on for Sly, never for August.

Sweet because, although it is bloodstained, I *did* end up marrying the love of my life in it.

I take a few moments to write a detailed email to my

assistant, letting her know she will need to take over for a while, and asking her to double check my calendar's accuracy. I don't go into detail about where we're going —not that I know yet—or why I'm suddenly leaving. I'm sure the news has already broken about the ceremony—she'll figure it out.

My heart stutters for a moment, thinking about the ceremony. The reality of what happened begins to set in, and a small wave of nerves hits me.

*Sly killed a man tonight.*

I look over at my husband, suddenly feeling sick to my stomach.

*Will he go to jail?*

His fingers dance across the screen of his phone, his brow furrowed as he clearly types a message to someone.

Looking back down at my own phone, I pull up the search engine and type in my name. Relief hits when the most recent article is from two days ago, highlighting my upcoming nuptials. I type in Sly's name, and thankfully, there is nothing new under his search, either.

"Mr. and Mrs. Lucchetti. We're about ten minutes from your destination," the stewardess with soft green eyes tells us as she passes by where we sit. She's been tidying up the cabin for the last thirty minutes, busying herself.

"Thank you," I say, offering a kind smile. Sly doesn't acknowledge her, too deep in thought. Gently, I touch his arm. "Is everything okay?"

Immediately, he turns his attention to me, his gaze softening. "Sì, piccola ladra." He expels a deep breath. "I was just speaking with your brother."

My jaw slackens as surprise overtakes me. "You have his number?"

"It's recent." He grins. "I had to bypass security somehow, amore mio. Luckily, your brother offered his alliance at the right time."

A smile upturns my lips—I owe my oldest brother a thank you. "What's he saying?"

"He and your father are working their connections with la polizia. When your father and brother spoke with us after our ceremony, my cousin Lorenzo, Sully, and my friend Nixon—you will meet him soon—they kept the guests seated. When your brother returned, the three of them let the guests leave one by one, but before they could, they needed to sign the NDA your brother gave them."

I can physically feel my eyes widen as my mind tries to absorb his words. "I have so many questions."

Sly chuckles. "Please, ask away."

Pressing my fingers against my temples, I rub them, trying to ease some of the building pressure. "First, how did Luciano even have copies of an NDA on hand?"

He reaches over and squeezes my knee. "As I said, amore mio. Your brother offered his alliance. When I left your hotel room, he confronted me, and we devised a plan. He had a short time to get the NDAs."

"But how did he even know you'd ne—" I question, but then I realize. "Oh."

"Sì. I had planned on ending August's life, Vincenza. Does that bother you?"

"No," I say without hesitation.

"It should. There is a darkness that lives within me. I didn't think twice before pulling that trigger."

"You had good reason."

"I did, and I will not hesitate to protect you by any means necessary if the situation were to arise again. Now, ask me your next question, piccola ladra."

"Why would Luciano have the guests sign NDAs when they are useless if a crime is committed?"

"Because, although the legality of the NDA would not hold up in a court of law, *fear* does. By obtaining a signed NDA from each guest, it sends a message—this day is not to be spoken about. The threat of the Paladinos alone is enough to keep quiet. Throw a Lucchetti in there…"

"Two." I smile. "I do believe I am the newest member of the Lucchetti family, am I not?" I take on a prim and proper fake English accent and bat my eyelashes.

Sly tosses his head back and laughs before he pulls me onto his lap. I do my best to adjust so that I'm comfortable as I wrap my arms around his neck and kiss him.

"Do you have any more questions, Vincenza?"

"None that can't wait," I say against his lips. He pulls back slightly to look at me, and I not-so-subtly grind my backside against his growing erection.

Groaning, his eyes flutter closed. "You drive me wild."

Moaning softly in response, I lean in and begin kissing up his neck slowly. Taking my time, I savor each graze of my lips against his skin.

"Miss?" Sly calls to the stewardess. He coughs as I nibble near his collarbone, unbuttoning the top button of his shirt. Seconds later, she peeks her head around the corner from where she's sitting in the jump seat.

"Yes, sir?"

Another button pops open and I slide my hand inside of his shirt, feeling his pecs as I glide my hand against his skin.

"Ask the captain to fly around for another twenty-minutes or so, and please allow us some privacy."

My fingers graze another button, popping it open before I move to the next, still sucking and nibbling at his neck.

"Certainly, sir," is the last thing I hear before Sly stands from his chair, deposits me into it, and spreads my legs wide.

Warmth heats my skin as the sun's rays peek through the transparent curtains in the bedroom, cascading across my back from where I lay on our bed.

When we touched down at Valerio Catullo Airport, I immediately knew where we were.

Sly brought me home.

The place where he feels safe and comfortable —content.

Verona.

Turning my head, I look over at him, still asleep on his back. His soft breaths expel gently from his lips with quiet snores, and I can't help but to reach out and touch him.

Dancing my fingers across the hard ridges of his chest, I trace every dip and groove of muscle, simply appreciating the man in front of me.

It feels surreal that less than twenty-four hours ago I was getting ready to marry a man I despised, only to protect the one laying beside me now.

The way I love Sly scares me. It terrifies me that it's all-consuming.

Undeniable.

*Unconditional.*

I thought this love only existed inside the pages of books, but to truly know it and feel it, is beyond any realm of reality.

I was willing to give up my life for him. I still am, but feeling his skin against mine reminds me that our lives are now joined.

He's my husband.

I'm his *wife*.

And no one can take that from us.

"Mmm, good morning, piccola ladra," Sly hums beside me, his voice thick with sleep. "Did you sleep well?"

Scooting closer, he lifts his arm so I can curl up as

close as possible.

"I slept like a baby."

"I am glad, amore mio."

"Whose house is this?" I ask, curious about the gorgeous villa we're staying at. When we arrived, Sly silently pulled out a key and let us in. I wanted to ask him when we came through the doors, but his lips were on mine before I could. Then he kept me thoroughly distracted the rest of the night.

A smile creeps across his face. Dipping down, he kisses my temple. "Ours."

"Ours?"

"Sì. I purchased this home during my time abroad. It's ours, now. What's yours is mine."

"Sly…"

"Shh," he breathes, and silences me with a kiss.

Parting my lips, he steals my breath as his tongue finds my mouth and we begin our familiar rhythm. It sends an instant wave of tingles through my body, igniting my desire.

Kneading my breast, Sly's hand engulfs it, flicking my nipple with his thumb.

"The things I want to do to you," he growls before kissing me deeper. Rolling on top of me, his length finds its place between my legs, already as hard as granite.

Sucking in a sharp breath, I lift my hips to meet where our bodies are trying to connect, spreading my legs to allow him entry. "Please," I shamelessly beg.

He groans, then begins lowering himself down my

body, but that's not what I want. Catching his arms, I shake my head. "No. I need you inside me. Now, Sly."

"Piccola ladra," he begins to argue, but my expression must be enough for him to easily relent.

His desire to give me the exact pleasure I seek is stronger than his instinct to give all the attention to only me.

Reaching between us, I wrap my hand around his shaft and begin to pump him from root to tip. His eyes darken as he looks down at me, propping himself on his forearms. "You may have the power to control me with a simple look, Vincenza, but make no mistake, I will not let you out of this bed until you are unable to walk from how shaky your legs are."

"All I want is you inside me, Sly. Filling me up. Marking me." My eyes roll to the back of my head as his fingers find my clit and expertly begin toying with it, alternating the pressures and ways he circles it. A long moan leaves my lips, and the rumble feels like it took some of my soul with it. "Oh my God."

Dipping two fingers into the wetness between my thighs, he uses it to smear around my entrance and clit before pushing them inside me. My hips lift and I suck in a harsh breath at the intrusion, but it's quickly welcomed and my legs fall open even further.

Still holding him, I align us and tilt my hips toward him. "Please," I ask again, and this time he obliges. Slipping through my folds, he pushes inside me until we're fully connected. Beneath my fingertips, I feel his shoulders flex.

Tilting my head, I meet his lips, kissing him with every emotion I possess as I take the reins and deepen it. His thrusts mirror each stroke of our tongues, letting me guide everything that's happening between us.

It feels as though time stands still. Like we're frozen in place together, secluded in our own bubble.

The most sinful bliss.

Flattening his palm against the bed, Sly pushes his other arm around my waist, and in one fluid movement, sits us upright so he rests against his heels and I'm on my knees.

With one hand tangling in my hair, Sly's other hand flattens against my lower back, holding me close as he kisses me and I begin to ride him. The position pushes him deeper inside me, and we groan in unison each time he bottoms out.

"Your body tells me you're close, piccola ladra. I can feel your walls clenching around me. Tell me, what do you need?"

But words fail me, the pleasure and overwhelming emotion of connecting with him so immeasurably stealing away any attempt at speaking.

Instead of pressing for an answer, Sly smiles sheepishly and reaches between us, playing with the sensitive bundle between my legs. Instantly, my body convulses, already so close.

Sparks ignite through me—the sweet sensation flicking down my spine and sending another rush of desire through my core.

"That's it, amore mio. Let go for me. Let me feel

your pleasure as it soaks my cock. Tell me what you need, Vinnie."

My hand wraps around the back of his neck as I use his body for leverage, sliding up and down him as quickly as my body will allow. "Fuck me harder," I breathe. "I want you…harder."

Shifting his hands to hold my hips, he begins guiding me as he pumps upward to meet me thrust for deliciously hard thrust, holding me in an angle where the root of him hits my clit with just the right amount of pleasure.

As he grunts with his own pleasure, I tangle our tongues, meeting him in a messy, teeth filled kiss. We're too lost in each other to care, the sounds of our skin slapping together and our pleasured sighs.

Within seconds, my orgasm slams into me and I toss my head back, breaking our kiss as I cry out with a strangled moan. Almost immediately, I feel Sly come, his cock twitching inside me.

Pressing our foreheads together, we both ride the wave, our chests heaving as we come down from it.

"Ti amo, piccola ladra," Sly breathes, his fingertips brushing against my back.

"I love you, too."

"But I am nowhere near done with you, either. Do you remember your safe word, Vincenza?"

He doesn't wait for me to answer before he's laying me on my back, pulling out of me. Positioning himself between my legs, he lays down on the bed and spreads my legs wide with a hand on each of my thighs. "Your safe word?" he asks again, looking up at me.

"You don't have—" I begin, but his stern look stops me from finishing my sentence. When my husband first told me he was a Pleasure Dom, having not been well versed on what it truly meant, I thought surely it wouldn't be an *every* time thing, but he's proven me wrong. He makes it his personal mission to ensure that I come at least twice, and that's only when we're in a less than ideal place.

I'm not complaining, but I sometimes feel guilty when he puts the sole focus on me.

Sighing, I relent. "Locket."

The left side of his mouth upturns in a smirk. "Eccellente," he says, lifting each of my legs to drape over his shoulders before sliding his tongue through my folds.

"Sly!" I squeal, acutely aware that his cum is dripping out of me. Bucking my hips, I try to pull away, but he only holds me firmer, lapping up both of our releases before suctioning his lips around my clit.

He shows no mercy as he pulsates the sensitive nerve and slips two fingers inside of me, drawing pleasure from my body purposely as he works me.

An endless slur of satisfaction elicits into the air, contrasting against the sound of his fingers pounding within me.

My toes curl in seconds and I cry out, louder than before, as an orgasm rips through me with the force of a tidal wave. Sensitivity overtakes me and I try to pull away, but Sly holds me in place, savagely lapping at my clit as he upturns his fingers to stroke my G-spot.

Black spots circle my vision, feral sonance flying from my mouth in incoherent nonsense as another orgasm slams into me again.

It feels as though my soul has left my body. Merciless spasms ricochet in my body as another orgasm cascades through me—something I didn't even know could happen.

The sensation is unlike anything I've felt before.

My limbs go limp as Sly dismantles my legs from his shoulders before he flips me like a rag doll, pulling my hips into the air. In one stroke, he's inside of me.

Leaning against my back, he pounds into me, sliding in and out with ease from how wet I am as I grip the pillow.

"Words cannot describe how amazing you feel, piccola ladra. So wet for me—gripping my cock like a vice. How many more orgasms can I pull from your body before we go explore my city, hmm, mia bellissima moglie?"

"I can't," I breathe.

"Oh, I guarantee you can, bella. Your body sings to me in a harmony only I can hear. Your pussy is weeping for me, drenching me in your desire. I know your body, Vincenza, and it tells me you can give me more." Snaking his hand around my waist, his fingers find my oversensitive clit and begin to rub it with slow, methodological touches. This time, it feels as though he's soothing my body after the intense pleasure he just extracted.

Melting against the pillow, I push my hips toward him, spurring his movements. He may know my body, but I know his too, and I can feel when he is holding back his own release.

With a rhythm of their own, my hips begin to sway as I grind against him. His sharp hiss gives me the confidence to continue, but it also encourages him. His fingers rub me faster, and my body betrays me with the familiar tingles that start to vibrate within me.

"I know what you're doing," I tell him with a shaky breath. Though it's extremely difficult, I maneuver my arm to reach beneath our bodies and cup his balls, massaging them gently as he slams into me.

A heady groan erupts through him, and he begins to slam into me faster.

The change in pace only increases the orgasm that threatens to detonate. "Faster," I beg, pushing my hips back with every thrust.

"Vinnie—" he groans, and I hear the hesitancy in his voice, but he doesn't stop.

"You won't hurt me. Fuck me faster," I beg again.

His hips increase their speed and I bite down on the pillow, loving the way his movements cause both pleasure with a mix of pain.

Needing more leverage, Sly moves his hands so both are gripping my waist as he pounds into me, harder than he ever has before. He's lost to the movement, his disjointed grunts filling our bedroom.

Knowing I'm close, I reach between my legs and rub myself, rolling my clit between my fingers before I start to circle it rapidly.

"Come, Vinnie. Play with yourself until your toes curl and you're screaming my name."

"You come," I argue. My eyes roll backward as he grips my backside, digging his nails into my flesh before he pulls back and smacks it with an open palm. It isn't hard—just enough to sting—but it sends a jolt through my core that immediately sends me soaring.

"Sly!" I scream into the pillow. At the same time, Sly groans a string of words in Italian that I don't understand. His cock twitches inside me, filling me up again as he comes.

Rather than let me go, his hands are all over me, touching every inch of skin as we catch our breath.

"Holy shit," I shudder, and he laughs.

"I love when you're authentically yourself, piccola ladra. You are bewitching when you are portraying the woman you were raised to be, but inherently sexy when you allow your true personality to shine."

Withdrawing from me, I hiss as the soreness immediately sets in. He scoots off the bed, then leans forward and kisses me as I sink into the soft mattress. "Stay here, my wife. I'll be right back."

I close my eyes as his footsteps draw further, then hear the sound of water filling the clawfoot tub in the adjoining bathroom at the same time as water flows from the sink. Moments later, the sink faucet turns off, and Sly's footsteps return. A hot compress is pressed between my legs as the weight of Sly's body sinks onto the mattress beside me.

"I am drawing you a bath, amore mio. Rose and eucalyptus bath oils have been added, as well as bath salts and bubbles. When you are relaxed, we will have breakfast, then explore Verona. How does that sound?"

"It sounds like I don't deserve you," I muse, turning my head to look at him. He's the image of perfection as he looks down at me, his dark hair astray with a few rogue strands flopping over his hazel eyes.

"Sì, you do, piccola ladra. You deserve every bit of happiness this world has to offer."

Emotion overtakes me—guilt filtering through my bloodstream like acid. We *need* to talk more about everything that's happened—I just can't bring myself to ruin the moment.

But Sly knows me better than I know myself. Reaching over, he wipes the tear with the pad of his thumb and bends down, kissing my temple. "We have our whole lives to discuss what happened, Vinnie. All that matters to me in this moment is that you are cared for and that you know how happy you make me. You made me the happiest man alive when you became my wife."

"I just want you to know how much I love you. How everything I did was because I thought I was protecting you. I see now what a mistake that was, and I'm so sorry, Sly. I'm so sorry."

"I don't want you to ever apologize for the decisions you made when you were trusting your own judgment. I trust your intuition, Vincenza. But from now forward, you need to trust mine. I will *always* protect, cherish, and love you."

"You mean everything to me," I whisper, the tears free flowing down my cheeks. "I love you so much."

"And I love you, piccola ladra. Now come," he says, wiping my tears again as he stands from the bed. Reaching down, he scoops me bridal style into his arms. "You have a bath to enjoy and I have breakfast to make."

Carrying me into the bathroom, he deposits me into the steaming bathtub where the delicious scents waft around me, and I relax into the hot water with ease, my entire body succumbing to the comfort as Sly kisses the top of my head and retreats to make us something to eat.

# Chapter 23

## *Sly*

Two weeks in the city I adore, with the woman I am irrevocably in love with, is not enough time. If I could convince her to stay here forever, I would.

Verona with Vinnie is a dream. We've laid under the heat of the sun, basking in each other's presence as we make love anywhere and everywhere we can.

We've acted as though we are tourists, sampling the cuisine and walking hand-in-hand through the popular destinations. Visiting Casa di Giulietta and seeing the architecture inspired by Shakespeare's Romeo and Juliet. Strolling leisurely over the Ponte Pietra, and sitting at the top of Castel San Pietro to enjoy the sunset as we overlook the city.

Tomorrow, we leave Verona and travel back to New York, but today… I've saved the best for last. Today I hope to watch Vinnie's eyes light up with wonder as I take her to the oldest library in the world, Biblioteca Capitolare. It has taken me nearly the full two weeks of our honeymoon to reserve the entire library to ourselves —something they were not inclined to allow at first.

Two hours is all we're granted, but it is better than nothing.

Knowing Vincenza's love for books, I could not allow her to leave my city without seeing its full history and beauty.

"Are you excited?" I ask, raising our connected hands to kiss hers. We have about five more minutes of walking before we arrive, and I can tell by the bounce in her step she's full of anticipation for her surprise.

"I don't see how you could have possibly saved the best for last, or so you say. Our honeymoon has been a dream, Sly. I couldn't have imagined it any more perfectly."

"Considering our wedding was not the way I would have planned it to be, the least I could do was give you a proper honeymoon, amore mio."

She shoots me a quick sideways glance. "It certainly wasn't what I dreamed of as a little girl but I've told you many times over the last couple of weeks—I wouldn't have it any other way. The wedding doesn't matter, it's the marriage that does. Marrying you is all I've wanted since we met."

"At age nine?" I quip, pressing my lips to her temple. Letting go of her hand, I wrap my arm around her shoulder and keep her close.

"Hmmm," she hums. "Maybe not at age nine. Definitely at age thirteen. Probably not at seventeen, though, but I did want to kiss you then."

Laughter erupts from my chest. "So many opportunities we had to betray our families. It is a wonder why we waited so long."

"Right person, wrong time." Vinnie shrugs, but a playful smile pulls at her lips.

We turn a corner, and Biblioteca Capitolare comes into view. Having seen it in person several times, I turn toward Vincenza to take in her expression, curious if any recognition will flash across her features. She scans her surroundings, but doesn't seem to realize where we are. As we come to a stop in front of magnificent architecture, she looks over at me, expectant and curious.

"I couldn't fathom the idea of bringing you to Verona knowing your love of literature, without bringing you to Biblioteca Capitolare. For the next two hours, the oldest library in the world lies at your fingertips, piccola ladra. To explore. To marvel in. Whatever you wish to do inside these walls will be granted."

Vinnie's eyes widen, and she pulls her gaze from me, looking up at the building. Her mouth opens and closes a couple of times before she looks at me with tears in her eyes. "Seriously?"

"Seriously," I repeat, grazing my thumb over her cheek.

She takes me by surprise when she squeals in delight, jumping into my chest and flinging her arms around my neck as she peppers my face with kisses. I barely have time to embrace her before she's grabbing me by the hand and pulling me into the building.

As we enter, immediately she sucks in a breath and

freezes in place, just as awestruck as I am by the sheer beauty in the entrance of the biblioteca. The scent of worn leather and old parchment fills the air, and two grand staircases encircle each side, with a small reception desk and museum cases on the lower level. A man wearing a light blue button-down shirt smiles and closes the book he's holding to greet us.

"Ciao. Benvenuti alla Biblioteca Capitolare. Siete i coniugi Lucchetti?" *Hello. Welcome to Biblioteca Capitolare. Are you Mr. and Mrs. Lucchetti?*

"Sì. Grazie per averci permesso di visitare la biblioteca in privato. Siamo in luna di miele e mia moglie lavora nell'editoria. Sono entusiasta di darle questa volta." *Yes. Thank you for allowing us to tour the library in private. We are on our honeymoon, and my wife works in publishing. I am thrilled to give her this time.*

"Grazie per la tua generosa donazione. Siamo lieti di avervi alla Biblioteca Capitolare. Se hai bisogno di qualcosa, non esitare a chiedere." *Thank you for your generous donation. We are happy to have you at Biblioteca Capitolare. If you need anything, please do not hesitate to ask.*

"Grazie," I tell the man, then turn back toward my wife. "Are you ready to explore, amore mio?"

"Yes!" she exclaims, and I laugh again, completely awestruck by the happiness radiating from her. Lacing our fingers together, she gently tugs me up the stairs and we spend the next hour exploring all that Biblioteca Capitolare has to offer.

From room to room I follow Vinnie, allowing her as much time as she wishes to take it all in, watching her fingers dust over the spines of the books as she admires the old literature. I'm enraptured by the way she never pulls her phone out to take photos, but instead stays present, enjoying each moment as it comes. What she does not realize is that I do capture the moments in photographs, and I intend to enlarge them and hang them in our home.

Stowing my phone as we enter the final room of the afternoon, I hear her soft gasp as we walk into the final grand library where leather bound books are kept in floor-to-ceiling mahogany bookcases. A gothic style chandelier hangs in the center of the room, with a few small wingback chairs beneath it. The lighting is low, and it takes a moment for my eyes to adjust and really focus.

The detailing in this room is marvelous. From the woodwork to the tiles, it radiates timeless elegance. There is even a ladder that rests along the bookshelves, and I notice it is on a track—something I have only seen in movies.

Vincenza spins in a circle to see it fully as she walks further in the space. "It's beautiful."

"As is the woman within its walls."

She looks over at me and smiles, wiggling her fingers so that her white gold, diamond wedding band sparkles in the low lighting. Her main band needs to be resized slightly, so she left it in the safe back at the villa, and I already miss seeing it on her finger. "You've already locked me down, you don't have to always be so charming."

"You think I'm charming you, *piccola ladra?*" Pushing my hands into the pockets of my slacks, I stalk toward her, pinning her in my stare. My cock hardens as I approach, her gaze lowering to where I know she can see its outline as it presses against the fabric.

"Yes," she breathes, as she takes a step backward. The way her breath hitches, I know she can read my thoughts.

I want her.

*Now.*

A smile pulls on her lips as she continues to retreat backward with every step I take until finally she's up against the works of literature. Pinning her with my hips, I reach above us and prop my wrist against the bookshelf, lowering my hips so I can grind my erection against her. "There is not a moment in time where I will stop charming you. You are my *wife.* You deserve every ounce of love, adoration, and respect that I have to give. I intend to cherish you, *amore mio.*"

Closing the gap between us, I kiss her deeply. She melts against my body, which only intensifies my need for her.

Our kiss turns frantic, her heart beating wildly against my chest as she reaches between us to palm my length with her hand. The friction feels like magic.

Reaching to her thighs, I hoist her into my arms and her legs wrap around my waist.

"We shouldn't do this here," she protests in the most unconvincing way.

Groaning in response, I take a few steps, leaning her

against the bookshelf's ladder, kneading her breast from the outside of her soft linen dress. But it's not enough. Pulling the fabric, I release it and lean forward, sucking her nipple into my mouth. My fingers grip her skin as I hold it tighter, pulling the taut bud into my mouth further.

A sharp hiss expels from between her lips, but I can already feel the roll of her hips as she seeks friction.

Releasing her breast, I help set her on her feet, but use my hand on her hip to keep her in place. "We are absolutely going to do this here, amore mio. There is nothing I want more than to hear your words of pleasure filter out into this room as I bring you to orgasm."

"Sly," she warns, but still I lower myself to my knees and pull up the hem of her dress. Gently, I press against her thighs so she settles against the rung of the ladder. "What if someone comes in? Our time here is almost up."

Positioning the dress around my shoulders, it tents me as I look up at her panty-covered pussy. A spot of arousal seeps through the white cotton, so I press into it with my thumb, rubbing her gently to start. "Let them. Heads will roll if they interrupt me before you come."

"But I—" she begins, but she loses her frame of mind the moment my tongue meets her center.

Through her underwear, I eat her as though its her bare skin, devouring her as I grasp the insides of her thighs.

"Sly," she moans, and I hear the soft clank of what I

can only assume is her ring against the wood as she holds on. "Keep going."

*I had no intention of stopping, piccola ladra.*

Tired of the barrier, I pull her underwear to the side, holding them as I continue. Her moans intensify with every lap of my tongue, and I savor the taste of her desire on my lips before I use the tip of my tongue to tease her clit, flicking the nerve.

Her hand flies to my head, and she fists the fabric of her dress, pulling my hair from beneath it, gripping tightly as she rolls her hips into my face. Without breaking my focus, I push on her calf, nudging her to drape it over my shoulder. In this position, she sinks lower on the ladder and takes more of a seated position on my face.

I love it. With my neck tilted back, I ravish her, my tongue pulling through her slick folds to her clit, swirling it as she cries out, no longer fearful of being walked in on, as her echoes of pleasure bounce against the books.

"Yes, yes, yes," she chants. "I'm so close, Sly. Right. There."

Her hips increase their rhythm as I work her with my tongue until she's to the point of collapsing, hanging by a thread on the edge where she teeters, her body so wound up I can feel the pressure building by the way she tenses her muscles.

"Oh my God," she cries again, and as I prod my tongue into her entrance and reach the pad of my thumb to her clitoris, she explodes around me. The beautiful melody of her pleasure-filled cries fill the room at the same moment I hear the sound of the large wooden door opening.

"Dio mio!" a man's voice shouts, and in the next moment, the door closes with a deep slam behind him.

Despite our intrusion, I don't stop my ministrations, determined to give Vinnie another orgasm as she rides out the last. It is my favorite thing to do—to see how quickly I can administer back-to-back climaxes.

Her knee presses against the side of my head as I push two fingers into her as deep as they'll go from the angle I'm in, and I work them rapidly with the succession I know turns her body into putty.

"Sly…please," she pants, her hands still fisting my hair. "We have to go."

"Not before you come on my fingers," I growl against her, refusing to remove my tongue from her skin. She tastes too sweet—I can't get enough.

"*Please*," Vinnie begs, this time pulling my hair roughly through her dress until I'm forced to bend my neck backward. Her dress slides down my face and my gorgeous wife comes into view looking flushed and driven to the point of madness.

I'm displeased to notice that she's fixed the top of her dress, yet simultaneously relieved that the man who just walked in on us didn't see my wife's bare skin.

"Vincenza—" I warn, swirling my thumb around her clit. "One more."

"I don't want to come on your fingers. I want your cock." Pushing from the library's ladder, she lowers herself, forcing me to remove my fingers from her, and reaches for my belt. Frantically, she unbuckles me, using one hand to unbutton my pants as her other hand pushes past the resistance of the band and wraps around my cock.

Groaning, my eyes shutter closed and my head tips back, overwhelmed by the feeling of her skin against mine. I'm impossibly hard in her hand, and can't resist the way my hips tilt into her grasp, chasing more of her touch. When the searing warmth of her lips wrap around my shaft, I nearly lose it.

Through hooded eyes, I watch as she takes me as deep into her throat as she can, working the base of me as she slides her mouth back and forth on my cock. Fisting her hair, I guide her a few more moments before pulling from her mouth. A string of saliva hangs from her lips to my cock as she looks up at me with wild eyes, and it makes me want to slam into her again and fill her throat.

But my wife has requested my cock, and I am here to do whatever it is she asks of me.

Together we stand, and immediately our mouths fuse together in a deep, wild kiss. She moans, sending vibrations into my own as I match it with a groan of equal fervor. As my tongue slides into her mouth, my fingertips grip the back of her thighs and lift her into my arms as I take the necessary steps back to flatten her against the bookshelf.

Trusting me to keep her steady, Vinnie reaches between us and pulls her underwear aside with one hand and with the other, she aligns my cock with her pussy. I don't waste another second before pushing into her.

"Hang on, amore mio," I command, and her arms instantly wind around my neck. Her legs tighten ever so slightly around my waist.

As her walls clench around my cock, I grab onto the shelves on either side of her head with both hands and begin pressing up into her, my speed gaining with every thrust.

I won't be able to push my release off for long with the way her pussy is milking my cock so perfectly, tightening around it each time I push deeper. Her body is wound tightly, too. I can hear it in the way she moans, feel it in the way her nails bite into the back of my neck.

"I can't fight it much longer, piccola ladra. You are too much of a temptation today, and as much as I'd like to take my time and make love to you amongst the classics, I won't last."

"Come with me, Sly. Together. Come with me." Her eyes are closed as she captures my lips and kisses me relentlessly. It temporarily stuns me until she begins mewling against my mouth and I feel her body climaxing.

Fucking my wife deeply, I white-knuckle the shelves I am holding and crash into my own climax. It hits me powerfully and I see stars as I grunt through the release I know is painting the walls of her pussy.

I only allow a moment for my body to reach completion before all too quickly I'm pulling out of her, tucking myself into my pants so I can help her fix her underwear and dress.

Once my bride is presentable, I press a chaste kiss to her lips. "Come—we are past due with our time. Let's go home before we get escorted off the premises."

Vinnie's eyes widen as I hold her hand, leading her to the door. "You don't think—"

"No, amore mio. I don't. But let's not risk it." From over my shoulder, I wink at her and pull open the thick wooden door.

The hall is empty as we make our way to the front of the Biblioteca Capitolare, and we are almost to the exit when I hear a voice from behind me. "Mi scusi, signor e signorina Lucchetti. Se potessi, per favore—" *Excuse me, Mr. and Mrs. Lucchetti. If you could please—*

"Quickly," I tell Vinnie as I push open the door and we run out, laughing like we're teenagers who were just caught in the janitor's closet. In a sense we are, just aged up and in a much more prestigious environment.

The door gives a shrill slam behind us as we jog down the three steps of the building and through the parking area. There's a side street we turn down and continue to jog for a few more moments before stopping to catch our breath. It's only then that we realize we've also been caught in a summer storm, which is perfectly reminiscent of our first true date.

Looking down at myself, my dark charcoal button-down is sticking to me like a second skin, my slacks equally as wet. I shake my head, laughing as beads of water go flying. When I look up at Vinnie, my breath hitches as I take in the state of her rain-soaked body.

Her sundress clings to her in ways I can only hope my body will later. Beads of water roll down into the valley of her breasts as her chest rises and falls. The tendrils of hair that frame her face stick to her, and her blue eyes blaze with unspoken need.

Wordlessly, we both connect like magnets and kiss like we need each other to breathe, not caring—in fact, *loving*—that the rain pours down upon us.

It is no secret that I find myself to be a romantic, but there could truly be no better way to end a beautiful afternoon getting lost in the books, than with a rain-soaked kiss on a quiet street in Italy.

But there is only so much romance a man can take. A heat ignites through my body, fueled by a desperation to claim and possess my wife so intensely and wholly, that it nearly knocks me over.

Our time in public is finished, and I'm ready to get her home.

And there is no doubt in my mind that she feels the same. Unabashedly, she rubs my cock from outside my pants and works her fingers to squeeze at the tip before sliding her hand down to where she can reach the outline of my balls. The simple touch makes my knees weak and my mind frenzied.

Scooping her into my arms, I opt to carry her the rest of the way, desperate to be inside of her again. "Come, amore mio. I need to get you home and out of these clothes."

The walk home is hurried as I carry my wife and try not to throw aside every moral I have and press her against a building in the middle of a busy area and fuck her senseless. The way she nibbles at my neck and whispers to me about how she can't wait for me to lick her pussy again is enough to drive me clinically insane.

I won't even attempt to be dignified and deny that as soon as I see the motorcycle I rented for our trip come into view in the piazza, I *run*.

# Chapter 24

## *Sly*

SULLY

Are you back on US soil yet?

ENZO

He's been back for the last week, you twit.

Yes, I told you the date I was coming back, Sullivan. I've been back for a week, as Enzo says.

SULLY

News to me. Why didn't you call? Or text?

Must I alert you of my presence at all times?

SULLY

Is that a legit question?

NIXON

He's been too busy fucking his new wife
into oblivion, Sully. Give the man a
break.

ENZO

Makes sense as to why you have yet to
visit your mother. I've had to hear about
her frustrations toward you all week.
She's pissed, you know.

LUCIANO

Could we not talk about who Sly has
been fucking, please? In case you
forgot, he married my sister. Why am I
getting these messages, anyway?

SULLY

I put you in the chat weeks ago, bud.
Welcome to the gang.

ENZO

Do not refer to us as a gang. Remove
the Paladino.

LUCIANO

Does my presence in your chat
bother you?

ENZO

Your existence bothers me.

LUCIANO

I'd love for you to say that to my face,
Lucchetti.

SULLY

I see the nuptials did nothing to ease
the disdain.

NIXON

Wow, big words, Sully.

Nixon, did you already head back to California?

SULLY

HAS HE NOT TOLD YOU THE NEWS?

SULLY

Also are we just ignoring the fact that Luce and Zo are trying to kill each other via text message?

Are either of them consenting to those nicknames?

NIXON

I've decided to stick around in New York a while. I'm at the airport now about to catch a flight home, but only to send some of my shit out here. Is it cool if I use your address, Lucchetti?

ENZO

No.

Of course, amico.

Do you have a place to stay when you return?

SULLY

No need to be so salty, Zo.

NIXON

I'll figure it out.

ENZO

Don't. Call. Me. Zo.

LUCIANO

While I'm stuck in this hellhole of a group chat, I might as well update you on the St. Jean situation, Sly. Would you prefer I call?

No, tell us all.

SULLY

Don't shut us out, new best friend.

NIXON

Do you have a serious bone in your body, Rochester?

SULLY

Not a one.

LUCIANO

The St. Jeans are pushing to press charges against you, Sly. They want you behind bars for killing their piece of shit son. As of now, the police are shuffling paperwork around, buying time. But the St. Jean's want to hang you out to dry with a premeditated murder charge.

ENZO

Not gonna happen.

How do you foresee me getting out of this?

LUCIANO

My father and I are working on it. Don't worry about it for now.

SULLY

See, the Paladinos are putting the feud aside. Lookin' at you, Zo-Zo.

NIXON

You really do love to poke the bear, don't you?

SULLY

I don't know about bears, but I love poking women…with my dick. Does that count?

ENZO

This is why no one takes you seriously.

Luciano, is it time for me to get representation?

LUCIANO

Are there handcuffs around your wrists?

No.

LUCIANO

Then no. Live life as usual. Take care of my sister. See you at family brunch, brother-in-law.

# Chapter 25

## *Vinnie*

"She's going to hate me, isn't she?" I ask Sly as we get ready to leave for his parents' house. I've been nervous all day, regretting our invitation to dinner when we should have made it lunch. Waiting all day to meet Sly's parents has been a slow torture.

Now, we're standing in the en suite of his apartment —*our* apartment—getting ready.

We're still deciding whether to call his place home or mine.

He looks at me through the mirror as he shaves beneath his jawline, creating crisp lines at the edge of his trimmed, short beard. "Why would you think that? She's going to love you."

"If I had a son, and a woman I'd never met, who my family had a less than desirable past with, just up and *married* him, I'd probably hate her. At least a little."

"My mother doesn't have a hostile bone in her body. She's going to adore you, piccola ladra. She always wanted a daughter. Plus, she's met you, remember? You were just a child."

"And what a lasting impression my family made with *that* introduction." My tone is sarcastic, and a little irritated, if I'm being honest.

The unease I'm feeling is tangible and lodged in my throat. I try to swallow it down, but the lump won't budge. Dropping my gaze, I rustle through my makeup case and pull out my blush.

"Vinnie."

Next, I search for my stippling brush, and push back the emotion that's overtaking my body. I shouldn't be so nervous, but I know the respect Sly has for his mother, and the last thing I can stomach is the idea that I will be a disappointment to her. Or worse, someone *she* doesn't respect.

Although, I'm not sure if I deserve the respect of the woman who made my husband.

"Vincenza," Sly's voice cuts through my brain fog, stern and rough. Looking into the mirror, his features are hard and serious. "Get out of your head."

Easier said than done as my thoughts spiral into self-deprecation.

Again, I drop my gaze, but this time I don't even pretend to search in my makeup bag. I simply press my palms onto the counter and let my head hang.

Seconds later, Sly's warm hands run up my arms and over my shoulders as he presses his palm against my collarbone and pulls me into his chest. "What is going on with you, amore mio? You've seemed off since we returned home."

"I don't know," I sigh, leaning my head back against him. "I've felt extra emotional this week. Maybe my period is coming early? Or maybe it's just the looming anxiety of the official family introductions this weekend. I'm really stressed about family brunch on Sunday. What if Joseph is there?"

"I hope he is. Your brother and I need to have a conversation."

"Which is exactly what I'm afraid of."

"And exactly why we're meeting my family first, Vincenza. They're going to love you, and you'll see how easy it is to set aside the animosity and blend our families."

"How can you be so sure? My father——"

"Will accept me as his son-in-law, or he will face the consequences. You told me on our honeymoon that you and I are family now. I would never ask you to choose between your father and myself, but as your husband, I can't help but hope I would be the man you choose to stand by when push comes to shove. Someday, when we have a family…"

"There's no question in my mind, Sly. You're my choice, forever and always. And yes, if my father doesn't accept you into his family, then we won't accept him into *ours*."

"Te amo, piccola ladra." He presses a kiss to my temple—something he does regularly and has no idea of the effects it has on my body. Instantly, I feel calmer, loved, and cherished by him. The simple, sweet act speaks volumes about how he feels about me, and the comfort it brings is unlike any other. "I can't wait for you to meet Mamma e Papà."

Sighing, I tilt my head, and he captures my lips gently, kissing me softly before releasing me to finish getting ready.

"Will you be ready in ten, amore mio?"

"I can be," I say with a smile as I reach for my hairbrush.

*As ready as I'll ever be, I suppose.*

When I envisioned meeting the Lucchetti family, the first thing I pictured was Sly and I standing outside of their home after ringing the doorbell, sharing a moment where he rubbed my back in comfort as I tried to keep the nerves at bay, and when the door finally opened, his mother would greet us and there would be a tense, silent trepidation in the air that would be difficult for us all to move past.

In reality, as we walk up the steps to Sly's family's brownstone, the image I conjured in my mind evaporates. Instead of knocking, Sly twists the doorknob and enters the home, tugging me along behind him by the loose grip he has on my hand.

"Mamma!" he calls as the door shuts behind us.

The Lucchetti home is warm in both color palette and temperature, with vibrant paint on the walls and colorful, plush accent rugs placed perfectly throughout.

As I look around, I hear Sly's quiet grunt of satisfaction behind me, and turn to see what inspired it. "What?"

He's slipping his shoes from his feet and sliding into a pair of slippers by the door with a wide smile on his face. "These pantofoles are new, amore mio. And pink. Mamma bought them for you."

Looking down at the light pink wool slippers, I notice the tag still attached to them. Picking them up, I examine them. They're my size. "She did?"

"Sì, of course I did. You are my daughter-in-law. The least I can do is buy you a proper pair of pantofoles for when you visit."

My breath catches at the sound of Sly's mother's voice, and I close my eyes, surprised and relieved at the lack of anger I hear in it. Sly squeezes my hand before turning to his mom. Opening my eyes, I turn toward her with a smile on my face.

"That was a sweet gesture, Mamma. Thank you. Let me introduce you to Vinnie—my wife."

Sly's mom is a striking woman, with gorgeous olive skin and vibrant hazel eyes, almost identical to her sons. Her dark hair is peppered with gray strands and she's wearing it in a twist. On her feet are a pair of slippers—*pantofoles*—-in a light shade of purple that matches the t-shirt style summer dress she's wearing.

Just looking at her makes me want to wrap my arms around her for an honest-to-God, genuine mom hug.

"You act as though I've never met her, Sylvester," she scolds, smacking his bicep with the back of her hand. Turning to me, she steps forward, her arms outstretched. "Ciao, dolce figlia. It is nice to see you again—we met when you were just a young girl. My name is Valentina, but feel free to call me Val." She reaches up and squeezes my cheek between her finger and thumb. "You have grown into a stunning woman. I can see why my son fell so hard for you."

"Thank you," I tell her as she pulls me into a hug. Her words twist in my heart, catching me off guard. "Thank you for having me tonight."

"The pleasure is ours," she coos. "Come. Are you thirsty? Hungry? I hope you have brought your appetite. Dinner will be ready shortly."

"Thank you. I'm famished."

"Eccelente."

"Is this her?" a deep male baritone asks from down the hall. Turning toward the voice, I see a man, whom I can tell is Sly's father, emerge from a room. Two other men follow him. One I recognize as Sly's cousin, Enzo, and the other looks like a younger version of Sly.

"Sì, Papà. Vinnie, my father, Antonio. Behind him is my cousin Lorenzo, and my brother Guilio." Tipping his chin at them, Sly asks, "Where is Federico?"

"He should be here any moment," Antonio tells us. Closing the distance, he reaches for my hand and pulls it to his lips, kissing the back. "It is nice to meet you, Vinnie." Clasping his other hand on top of mine, he gives it a soft squeeze before excusing himself and walking into what I assume is the kitchen.

Sly's brother steps forward next, taking me by surprise as he pulls me in for a bear hug. "Hey, kid," he greets. "Nice to meet ya."

"Guilio," his mother scolds, swatting at him. "Give the woman some breathing room."

Laughing, he lets me go and tosses a wink in my direction.

"Guilio," Sly warns, his voice stern, yet I can still hear the playfulness in it.

The interaction so far eases my nerves, and I withdraw a deep sigh, smiling at Sly. Draping his arm around my shoulders, he pulls me to him and kisses my hair.

After a moment of enjoying my husband's attention, I peek over at the man who hasn't said a word. He's watching us with scrutiny behind his dark brown eyes, his expression otherwise unreadable. Clearing my throat awkwardly, my anxiety makes me feel like I need to step away from my husband, but when I try, he holds me firmer.

"Lorenzo." He glowers, but his name is all he says.

"You may love her, cousin, but she's still a Paladino, and I don't have to agree with it."

His words send my heart plummeting to the pit of my stomach.

He starts to walk away, but Sly quickly steps forward, grabbing onto his arm to stop him.

"You may not like where she came from, but she is a Lucchetti now," he growls, his eyes narrowing into slits as he speaks to his cousin in a deadly tone. "You will respect my wife. If you do not, there will be more problems between us than the ones we choose to pretend do not exist. Have I made myself clear, *cugino*?"

Shrugging from Sly's hold, Enzo shakes his head, tossing a glare in my direction first. "Don't forget the blood that runs in her veins is the very same blood that *murdered* your uncle. She may be your wife, but she'll always be his daughter."

Stalking off down the hallway, a door slams seconds later, causing me to jump slightly. Instantly, Sly's warm arms are wrapping around my body again.

"I'm sorry," he whispers with his lips against my head.

"It's not your fault."

Guiding me into the kitchen, we rejoin the rest of his family—sans Enzo—and gather around the kitchen island while Val finishes cooking. The aroma is mouthwatering. Garlic and onion mixed with a fragrant sauce. The scent of freshly baked bread. A beautiful salad sits in the middle of the island, topped with an array of vibrant vegetables, and three bottles of homemade dressings sit beside it.

"Do you enjoy cooking, Mrs. Lucchetti?" I ask, unable to ignore my curiosity. I had always wished my mother cooked a meal of her own from time to time, but we always had a full kitchen staff. To this day, I have no idea whether my mother knows how to do anything in the kitchen outside of pouring herself a glass of wine.

"Oh, sì, my dear. Cooking is incredibly relaxing for me. Nothing makes me happier than knowing my boys are happy and fed."

"Have you always cooked for them?"

Her features scrunch slightly at my question, but then she must recognize the deeper meaning behind it. "I have. Cleaning is a task I cannot stand, so we have always employed a housekeeper, but never a chef. Mia madre had me in the kitchen with her the moment I could toddle." She laughs, smiling to herself at the memory. "I did the same with my boys, but it seems none of them have the cooking gene."

"I resent that, Mamma. I can hold my own in the kitchen," Sly chastises playfully.

"Well, I sure as hell can't," Guilio chimes in, making us all laugh.

"Give me another few minutes and dinner will be served," Val singsongs.

"Grazie, Mamma," Sly tells her, then turns to me. "Can I get you something to drink, amore mio?"

"Water would be great, thank you."

Sly steps away to grab me a glass, and I watch him navigate his parents' kitchen naturally, affectionately squeezing his mom's shoulder as he passes by her. A smile forms on my lips as I watch the interaction.

"Vinnie?" a deep rumble says hesitantly behind me.

Turning, I come face to face with Antonio. I had been too drawn into watching Sly and his mom, I hadn't heard him approach. "May I have a word with you?"

"Of course." My upbringing has me painting a smile on my face, even though I'm suddenly terrified.

Not of Sly's father, but more of what he might want to speak to me about.

"Let's have a talk in the study." His hand ghosts the middle of my back as he ushers me through another door off the kitchen and into a lovely room with rich leather seating and an exposed brick fireplace.

We both take a seat in adjacent chairs, and I sit up straight, crossing my feet and tucking my legs to the side with bent knees as I place my hands in my lap. My posture feels rigid—too proper—but I can't relax. Worry plagues me as I wait for what Antonio might say, my brain conjuring the worst-case scenario of how this talk might go.

*You're not fit for this family.*

*My son deserves better than you.*

*Your father murdered my brother, you're nothing to me.*

*You and my son need to get an annulment immediately.*

"You can relax, Vinnie. I didn't ask you to speak with me for the reasons you are probably thinking. Unlike my nephew, and until recently, my son, I learned to let go of my anger and resentment toward your family years ago."

Stunned, the only thing I can manage to say is, "Oh?"

"Life is too short. Being a surgeon, I have spent my entire adult years watching how a person's life can change faster than the blink of an eye—or from the bullet of a firearm."

I flinch, and Antonio leans over and pats the top of my knee in a fatherly way. "I don't blame you, Vinnie. I never have. You being with my son may have come as a surprise, but not an unwelcome one. I would never place blame on a child, regardless of what her last name is. Or *was*."

"You're not upset with me?" My voice is small, like a teenager being scolded after being caught sneaking back in at five a.m. The last five minutes spent with Antonio are like resurfacing years of fatherly conversations that should have happened with my own father but never did.

Strangely, it feels comforting.

Hearing that he doesn't resent me unleashes some of the anxiety built up in my chest.

"Of course not. I just have one question, and I wanted to ask it in private, without distractions, so I can look into your eyes and see the truth reflected. I am a very good judge of character, and an even better human lie detector. Answer truthfully, and I'll welcome you into this family with open arms. But if your answer is a lie, or I suspect you have ulterior motives, make no mistake, there will be another conversation happening after this one, but with my son. I do not mean that as a threat, I just want you to know that there is nothing more important to me than family, and if you intend to be in it, there will be no lies between us."

Shifting in my chair, I nod. "Ask me anything."

My heart rate accelerates, nerves surfacing as I anticipate what his question may be.

It doesn't matter that I'd never lie about the answer. Makes no difference that I intend to lay all my cards on the table when it comes to the Lucchettis, so they feel comfortable and confident in their son's marriage. I'm still utterly terrified that I'll somehow word vomit myself into a lie.

All I want is for the Lucchettis to see me as the woman their son loves, and not reduce me to a product of my last name.

I love my family, but I see the errors of their ways, and it's not how I want to live my life.

Scooting forward, he picks my hand up and wraps it between both of his, patting it as he looks me straight in the eyes and asks, "Do you truly love my son, Vinnie?"

Blowing out the breath held in my lungs, I answer him without hesitation and can feel tears welling up as emotion overtakes my body. "More than the moon loves the sun as he chases her through the days. I have *never* loved anyone the way I love your son, Mr. Lucchetti."

His eyes search mine for several seconds, and I hold my head firm, never breaking our gaze. For a moment, I wonder if he doesn't believe me, and I start to feel a wave of petrified nausea tumble in my stomach.

Suddenly, he stands, pulling me to my feet as well from the grasp he still has on my hand. Before I realize what's happening, he pulls me into his arms in a tight hug, and I instantly relax, trying not to be obvious when I take another deep breath to steady myself. But it's no use, because instant tears start to flow the moment his next words pierce through my soul.

"Please, Vinnie. You're family now. Feel free to call me Papà."

# Chapter 26

## *Sly*

**M**y fingertips trail up and down the smooth skin of Vincenza's arm as we lay in bed after a night of lovemaking.

Leaving my family's home left us both excited and appreciative of our future together. Dinner with them couldn't have gone better if I planned it.

The way my family welcomed Vincenza warmed my heart and provided further confirmation, and validation that I've made the right decisions in not only my life, but with the path I've chosen, and the amazing woman to spend my forever with.

Still, unease has settled deep in my bones and will not leave. Tomorrow looms over us like a thundercloud, and I know the concern I feel, my wife feels tenfold.

"Tomorrow won't go as well as tonight did," I warn her, although I know my words aren't needed.

She knows. With every fiber of her being, she knows.

Vinnie sighs, curling into my body further. Her leg is draped over mine, and the small curvature of her body conforms so perfectly against me, only reminding me further how well we fit.

"I'm not afraid anymore."

"Perhaps your father is ready to put the past behind him, as mine has. Luciano did say he is working with the polizia to keep the St. Jeans from pressing charges against me."

"Joseph is still a loose cannon, though. Now, more than ever. You killed his best friend."

"I killed the man who was physically abusing the love of my life. I would do it again, to anyone who dares think they can even look at you wrong. I should have stopped him sooner."

"Don't do that. I purposely kept you in the dark. I believed *he* would kill *you*. He was having you followed and leaving me photos like breadcrumbs."

"It seems as though we've both made mistakes and underestimated each other, amore mio. Never again. We are a team, and there will be no secrets between us."

Shivering, she inches closer, even though there is no space between us. "I'm worried Joseph will try to retaliate. August had been his friend for years, and now his plans of taking over our father's businesses are exposed. Father is furious."

"I will keep you safe, Vincenza. You have nothing to stress about."

"It's not me I can't stop fretting over."

Tightening my hold on her, I kiss the tip of her nose. "You worry about me too much."

"It's my job now."

"Mmm," I hum, nuzzling my nose against her cheek. "I can think of another job position I'd prefer for you, but it's not actually a job. Just a position."

Rolling her on top of me, my cock presses against her core as it juts from between her legs. She begins to rock against me, her pussy already wet, creating a layer of lubricant between us. Moaning, she places her palm on my chest and closes her eyes, letting her body guide her.

She looks stunning when she's wanton. Her cheeks are flushed, and her hair is a mess from when I had her on her back. Her breasts are full, swaying slightly with each roll of her hips.

"Is this the position you envisioned for me?" she asks coyly, the heaviness of our previous conversation completely gone from her tone.

A sharp intake of breath pulls between my teeth as she lifts up slightly, so the head of my cock pierces her entrance. I'll never get used to the magic of sliding into my wife. "I've envisioned you in every position, piccola ladra, but sì, this is one of my favorites for you."

"Then I better make sure I stay on top of my duties," she playfully quips, reaching between us to grab my cock as she slides down it.

We moan together when I'm fully inside her, my fingers gripping her hips so tightly, I know I am leaving indentations behind. For a moment, we stay together as one, our breaths mingling as she leans down close, but careful not to touch me. The moment is charged with electricity and anticipation, until finally, I can no longer take the desire that threatens to explode from me, and I tilt my head slightly, connecting our lips.

Then she begins to move.

Through the closed door of the Paladino mansion, I hear the echo of the doorbell throughout their foyer, followed by heavy footsteps. Vinnie shifts on her feet next to me as the sound of the lock disengages, and the door opens, revealing an old man in a crisp black suit. He wears a scowl and looks about as friendly as Lurch from the Addams Family.

There's a familiarness about him that I cannot place, and I wonder if this is the same butler from the first and only time I stepped foot on the Paladino's property.

Saying nothing, his eyes drift from me to Vinnie before he rudely steps aside and lets us enter the home.

"Hi, Capaul," Vinnie greets, though the man doesn't deserve a breath of her air, let alone the kindness of her words.

"Miss Paladino."

It's on the tip of my tongue to correct him, which my wife must sense because she squeezes my hand and says, "Let's go find my parents."

The fact that they did not greet their daughter in the foyer when she arrived immediately irritates me.

"Hello?" Vinnie calls, leading me further into the home. She peeks into the first room and practically runs into Luciano, who is on his way out.

"I thought I heard your voice," he remarks, pulling her into a half-hug. Extending his hand, he acknowledges me. "Sly."

"Luciano."

"Where are Mother and Father?" Vinnie wonders aloud.

"Father is in his office, and I would assume Mother is up in their bedroom getting ready still. I haven't seen her yet."

"And Samuele?"

"Packing his room, I believe."

"He's moving?"

My eyes ping-pong between Vinnie and Luciano, taking in their conversation as my thumb brushes against the side of her hand.

"Yeah, finally. He used his trust fund to buy an apartment off East 85th."

"That's wonderful! It's time he gets out of here. And Joseph? Is he coming?" Vinnie's voice wavers slightly when she speaks her brother's name.

Curious, I train my gaze on Luciano.

"According to Father, his presence is mandatory, so I would assume yes."

"Lovely." Vinnie's voice is strained as she says the two-syllable word.

"It will be fine, amore mio," I interject. I'm not worried about coming face to face with her brother, and she shouldn't be either.

"Vinnie. Sly." Maurizio's voice comes from behind us, and we both turn simultaneously. Vinnie's father looks as though he's seen better days. Dark rings sit beneath his eyes, and his hair is disheveled, as though he's been running his fingers through it repeatedly.

The sight of her father visibly reflects in Vinnie. Her shoulders fall as she takes him in, and I can't help but notice how she almost shrinks into herself a little. It diminishes her glow.

Seeing her turn timid in his presence ignites a fury deep inside me, and an overwhelming protectiveness rears its head.

"Maurizio," I say his name in a clipped, neutral tone.

Our frigid greeting is cut short when a door slams behind us and in walks Joseph, looking even worse than his father. His white button-down is wrinkled and slightly untucked, and there's a sway to his stance, which worries me. Is he inebriated? I don't want him anywhere near Vincenza, if that's the case. Joseph is a loose cannon to begin with. I can only imagine his demeanor when he's under the influence.

"You look awful," Maurizio spits, turning his attention to his middle son. His gaze narrows, and the disapproval is clear on his features.

"Pot meet kettle, Father." Joseph doesn't slur his words, but he is definitely under the influence of something. There's a glassy, far-off look in his eyes, and it causes me to shift my body in front of Vincenza's.

The movement catches his attention, and his reaction is instantaneous.

Clenching his fists by his sides, he stalks closer. Pushing Vincenza completely behind me, I ready myself mentally and physically for this altercation.

I had expected it. I just assumed it would have taken place after a *very* tense dinner.

"You have some nerve showing your face here, you piece of shit," he spits with a malice so intense it's practically tangible.

"I have every right to be here, Joseph. I'm your sister's husband." I smile at him, knowing the fury I've enraged.

"She's no sister of mine. Not anymore. You killed my best friend. Both of you did, as far as I'm concerned." Looking around my body, he stares at his father. "You're really just going to let him into our home? Like he didn't embarrass this family, murder Vinnie's fiancé, and drag the Paladino name through the mud?"

"Let's discuss this in another room, rather than the hallway," Maurizio suggests, and next to him, Luciano stifles a laugh.

"No, we can fucking talk about this right here, right now. I want him out of this house. *Now*," Joseph demands, and I do everything I can not to laugh in his face right here. Behind me, Vincenza stays quiet, which I am grateful for.

The audacity of this man is beyond belief.

"He is your sister's husband," Maurizio defends in a low tone, which surprises me, but I sense he has been waiting for this quarrel with his son as well.

"He killed August."

Before Maurizio can say another word, Luciano jumps into the argument. "He was beating our sister, which I have no doubts you knew about, so don't bother lying about it now."

A sneer highlights Joseph's features, and he rolls his eyes. "I'm sure that's what she told you to justify her affair with a *Lucchetti*. Are we all just ignoring the fact that she married the enemy?"

"Are *you* just going to ignore the fact that I told you I know you knew your *best friend* was physically harming our sister, and you did nothing to stop it? If anything, you willingly put her in danger by pushing for him to pursue her." Luciano steps toward his brother, and I recognize the signs of anger reaching a boiling point, and though I've never seen Luciano fully enraged, I suspect I'm about to.

Keeping my mouth closed, I decide to watch how this plays out. The men of the Paladino family going head-to-head is fascinating.

"What is it exactly you want me to say? Show me proof, and maybe I'll believe you then." There's a mocking tone in Joseph's voice, and instinctively I move to take a step forward when Vinnie's soft hand wraps around my wrist, stopping me.

"All because you want Father's business," Luciano

tsks, and all the air expels from Vincenza's lungs in a sharp breath. "You practically forced our sister into the arms of an abusive monster, all while manipulating Father into thinking it was a good idea. Does he know you two were threatening her, too? By having someone she loved followed so you could blackmail her into compliance?"

A growl rumbles in my throat, and I can't stay silent any longer. "All for a signature."

I want to wrap my hands around Joseph's neck and squeeze until the light fades from his eyes and his body crumples to the floor.

"Marry the girl, steal her business. Or so you thought," Luciano continues, prolonging every word to match up with the slow, deliberate steps he's taking toward his brother. "Because you're too much of a self-centered, egotistical narcissist to see what was literally right in front of you, *Joey*." Less than an inch from his face, Luciano whispers, loudly enough for us all to hear. "The businesses were *always* going to be yours."

Finally, Maurizio explodes. "I can't believe you'd let him hurt your sister and manipulate me to go along with it all so you could have the businesses! You're not the man I thought you were, Joseph, and it's clear you have no idea how succession works. Have all these years of training been no indication that you were the one to inherit them all when I retire? Yet, despite it all, this is how you treat your own sister? Your flesh and blood."

"YOU WERE NEVER GOING TO GIVE THEM TO ME!" Joseph screams, becoming unhinged.

Reaching over to the vase on the credenza next to him, he picks it up and slams it to the floor. "It has always been Sunshine this, and Sunshine that. Since the moment she was born I was tossed to the side."

"How can you even say that?" Vinnie squeaks from behind me, stepping around so she can look at her brother as she speaks to him. Instinct nags at me to pull her back behind the shelter of my body, but I know she has things she needs to speak about, too.

"BECAUSE IT'S TRUE."

"You've been Father's right-hand man with his businesses for years. I don't understand how you could ever think that when it came time, he would give them to me."

"I'm not going to stand here and argue with a whore who spread her legs for the first man who glanced in her direction and pretended to be a knight in shining armor."

"You watch your fucking mouth," I snarl, stepping closer.

"Oh, now he speaks. C'mon, Lucchetti. You've been awfully quiet tonight. Did my slut sister tell you to not talk to me?"

The disgusting words have barely had a moment to slide off his tongue before I have Joseph up against the wall with one of my arms pressed against his windpipe, and the muzzle of my gun pressed at the base of his chin.

"Whoa, easy there, Lucchetti," Luciano says, at the same time Vinnie cries, "Sly."

But I'm staring into the lifeless eyes of the Paladino brother at my mercy. "If you keep referring to my wife with degrading, disgusting names, I will end you, just like I ended the pathetic excuse of a man who dared lay a hand on her. I have no problem putting you in an early grave, Joseph. In fact, it would bring me great pleasure to do so."

Putting more pressure on his windpipe, I hold him in that uncomfortable position for a few seconds before releasing him suddenly and stepping back. I tuck my gun back into its holster under my shirt.

Seething, Joseph rubs his neck and looks at his father. "You're just going to allow this to happen? For him to treat me like *I'm* a criminal?"

Maurizio's eyes grow colder, but he says nothing. The room stays silent for several tense moments before Joseph sweeps his arm across the top of the credenza, sending photo frames, another vase, and a small stack of decorative books crashing to the floor.

Pointing a finger at me, he yells, "You'll fucking regret this, Lucchetti. That's a threat *and* a promise." Then he turns on his heel and stalks out of the home, sending the door slamming behind him.

Warm arms wrap around my waist as Vinnie burrows into my side, her body shaking slightly from what I hope is adrenaline and not fear. "I'm not afraid of him, piccola ladra," I say softly, for her ears only as I pull her closer.

"I am," she whispers back sadly.

"Sunshine, perhaps you can go check on your

mother while I speak with Luciano and Sly. She's upstairs in our bedroom," Maurizio suggests, though it is less of a suggestion and more of a gentle dismissal.

"I'll see her when she decides to join us, Father."

A smile pulls at my lips, proud of how she has seemingly turned a corner with her father and is more comfortable with speaking her mind.

"Anything you would like to speak to me about, I am comfortable with my wife hearing, Maurizio."

"It's about the St. Jeans pressing charges."

"All the more reason why she should hear the facts."

Maurizio looks unhappy, but nods curtly and walks to another room, followed by Luciano, and seconds later, myself and Vincenza.

We enter a small den, which I assume is a place where Maurizio retreats privately, based on the furnishings. Two leather loveseats face each other with a chestnut-colored coffee table between them, topped with a crystal cigar ashtray and a pile of business magazines. Frames line the walls with newspaper clippings, magazine articles, and photographs of Maurizio with various businessmen, highlighting his career.

Maurizio clears his throat as we all sit. "My contacts at the NYPD have done all they can to make this go away for you, Sly, but it's not foolproof. The St. Jeans haven't been quiet about their feelings on you being a free man, but luckily, they don't have the same sway Luciano and I do with the police department, or the court system for that matter."

"I dug up some information on August's father, and

let's just say the apple doesn't fall far from the tree," Luciano adds. "Back in twenty-sixteen, the St. Jeans had a woman institutionalized after she came forward to Mrs. St. Jean with allegations of being physically and sexually abused by August's father. I paid them a visit last week and let them know that unless they'd like the story resurfaced and investigated, they needed to lay this to rest just as they will their son."

"Thanks to Luciano learning that information, I was able to bring it to my contact at the department and file a couple of backdated domestic violence reports against August on Vinnie's behalf. It is now in writing that he was physically harming her," Maurizio concludes.

"Thank you, Father," Vinnie says to him with tears in her eyes. I squeeze her knee affectionately.

"How has the story not been in the news?" I ask, wondering how my name has not been dragged through the papers and gossip columns. "Surely not everyone is upholding their NDA, and August was a prominent figure in the community, as much as it pains me to say that."

Luciano smiles widely, scoffing. "You underestimate me. In addition to the NDA, I also paid off a few reporters, who ran with a story about the wedding being called off last minute and the couple needing time to grieve the loss of their relationship in private."

"There's no way that is going to work."

"It has so far. Eventually, we'll have to schedule an interview for Vinnie with the press so she can talk about how devastated she was that August never showed up to the altar and spin a story about how an old flame from the past reignited as she was picking up the pieces of her broken heart from her runaway husband."

"Schedule it," Vinnie asserts. "I'll speak with whoever, whenever. Get me in front of a camera."

"Relax, Sunshine. Everything will come together as it should." Maurizio smiles at her, but I can tell my wife is annoyed with her father's sudden change in demeanor. The way he's using her nickname again isn't lost on me.

"How do you feel about all of this, Maurizio?" I ask suddenly, interrupting the conversation. Something about his behavior in this moment isn't sitting well with me. "One minute, you're sitting in the church watching your daughter about to exchange vows with a man you thought was good, and the next, she's married to a man from a family you've hated for decades."

"What are you trying to say?" he asks, his eyes narrowed.

"It just seems odd that you haven't put up more of a fight."

"Would you like me to? I could sit here and scream at you both for blindsiding me. I could protest and tell both you and my daughter that you do not have my blessing and that I don't agree with this marriage. Would it change anything?"

"Absolutely not," Vinnie says, taking my hand. I can't help the smile that instantly appears on my face, or the way pride blooms in my chest. "I will *always* choose him."

Maurizio looks horror-stricken for a moment before realizing his composure has slipped. His features contort into a wide mix of emotions before he finally says something, casting his eyes downward at his hands. "August slipped under my radar, Vinnie, and for that, I apologize. I had no suspicion of what he was doing to you until the rehearsal dinner, and even then, I turned an eye, blaming it on a pre-wedding squabble. I let you down."

"You weren't the only one," she says softly, almost under her breath. My bride looks like she's on the verge of tears, so I pull the conversation away from her.

"And you, Luciano? Why your change of heart?"

His eyes meet mine, and his head tilts slightly, almost as if he's asking a silent question rather than asking one aloud. "Like you, I'm just another body stuck on the sidelines of the feud. I couldn't care less about your last name. All I want is for my sister to be happy, and evidently, she's found happiness within you."

"I appreciate that."

"How about you, Father?" Vinnie asks, and I swear to the Lord Almighty I have never been as proud of her as I am tonight, having the fearlessness to finally speak out against her father. Her newfound strength is not only sexy, but courageous, and I admire her for it. "Will you be able to move past the last name, and the things Sly's uncle did in the past?"

Awkwardly, Maurizio clears his throat. "I can't

make any promises on how long it may take for me to accept this, but I will try with time."

"That's all I'm asking for," she notes. Standing, she gives my hand a gentle tug, and I do the same. "I think Sly and I will head out for the night. Thank you for the invitation to dinner, but I'm exhausted and want to go home."

"Are you sure? Dinner should be ready by now." Maurizio comes to his feet, glancing down at the time-piece on his wrist.

She looks over at me, and I nod.

"I'm sure," she states with conviction. "Please tell Mother—well, you know what? Don't tell Mother anything, since she couldn't even be bothered to come downstairs."

"Vinnie," Maurizio scolds, but she ignores him and rounds the coffee table to hug her brother.

I watch with a smile as he embraces her fully, just as a brother should. The strength he radiates pushes into her, and it brings me peace knowing she had a protector in him throughout her adolescence. I have no doubts that he was the one to keep her safe.

Being the bigger man, I outstretch my hand in Maurizio's direction. "Thank you for having us this evening. I appreciate all the help you've extended to keep me out of jail, as well as the papers."

"You're welcome." He grips my hand, and we shake. It's brief, but there is a large part of me that hopes this is just the beginning of what could be some sort of cordial relationship between us.

Once Vinnie and I are outside of her childhood home, I wrap my arm around her as we walk down the road to where I've parked. Vinnie had suggested we have Ross drive us, but I hate the idea of being driven around when my Rolls Royce SUV sits unused in the parking garage.

Plus, I don't entirely trust Ross after he double-crossed her the day she flew home from Ridgewood. She insists it was mostly August, but I feel as though the driver could have refused to bring him, seeing as though he is on the Paladino payroll.

As we round the corner, my SUV comes into view. "I love you, piccola ladra. You know that, sì?"

"I do. And I love you," she tells me, looking up at me as we walk, smiling.

"I'm very proud of the way you spoke up to your father tonight. It was admirable, and sexy as hell."

"Oh, yeah?"

Chuckling, I lean down and kiss her as I withdraw the key fob and unlock the vehicle. "Yeah, it was. And I can think of many, many things I want to do to you to prove just how sexy I think you are."

I open the door for her, and she climbs into the passenger side, batting her gorgeous, gray-blue eyes in my direction as she settles into the seat. "I can't wait to hear them."

*And I can't wait to show you, over, and over, and over again, amore mio.*

# Chapter 27

## *Sly*



The message comes through as I am standing in the corner market that recently opened down the street from my apartment building, The Kenna, picking up a floral arrangement to bring home to Vinnie.

Almost a week has passed since we've sat down with each other's parents, and now it's time to blend our friends, hosting them for dinner in the home we've decided to share together.

As much as Vincenza adores her penthouse, we've come to the conclusion that it makes more sense for us to call my apartment home, especially since Cecilia still lives in hers.

My phone vibrates with another incoming message as I pick up a bouquet of roses and eucalyptus, bringing them to my nose to smell, before I look at the screen and read the messages that begin to flood our group chat.

LUCIANO

She's a nightmare. -10/10 would I recommend chasing after Raina.

SULLY

Not her. The other hot friend.

Cecilia?

LUCIANO

She's a little old for you. And by old I mean mature, with a good head on her shoulders.

SULLY

And fine as hell.

Sighing deeply, I type out my response.

Don't even think about it, Sullivan. Vinnie's friends are off-limits.

There isn't even time to pull my gaze from the phone when a response vibrates through, so I stand there and engage for a moment.

SULLY

You ruin all my fun.

NIXON

What time are we supposed to be at your place?

Six.

SULLY

Aren't you crashing in his guest room?

NIXON

Yeah, but I make myself scarce.

LUCIANO

How's the apartment search going?

NIXON

Not too bad. New York's just fuckin' expensive.

And California isn't?

NIXON

Ridgewood ain't.

SULLY

You better not be thinking about leaving us. You just joined the gang.

Speaking of gang, is Enzo ignoring us?

NIXON

I'm not leaving, don't worry. Although, I might need a new place to crash so I don't have to keep hearing Sly's headboard pounding against the wall every night.

LUCIANO

[Earmuffs emoji]

Chuckling, I step up to the register and pay for the flowers I'm holding. The young woman attempts to make idle conversation, asking me questions about who the flowers are for and whether I come to the market often—as though it's been open for longer than two weeks. I humor her, speaking kindly as she finishes my transaction and blushes under the breadcrumbs of attention I'm giving her.

Thanking her, I reach into my pocket to pull out my now ringing phone. Vinnie's name and photo of her laying in our bed in Italy flashes across the screen.

"Hello, amore mio," I greet, stepping out of the store.

"Hi," she replies, and I can practically hear her smile. "I just wanted to let you know that I'm at my apartment now packing up the last few boxes, then I have to run to my office for an hour or so."

"Not a problem. I'll set up the dining table for tonight while I wait for you to return home. Do you need me to go get the boxes?"

"No, Ross said he'd take care of it for me. Thank you though. If you want, I can swing by Di Mercutio and pick up the food on my way home?"

"It will be too early, amore mio. I'll run out for it later, or send Sullivan. Lord knows he needs something productive to do."

"Sounds perfect. I'll see you soon."

"Ti amo, piccola ladra. Be safe."

"I will. I love you too."

Glancing down at my watch, I notice it's only twelve-thirty, and decide to take a detour to stop by my clinic that's sat vacant since I left all those months ago.

So often, I think about re-opening my doors. Helping people is my passion, but I worry now, with Vincenza by my side, and the threat of a murder charge against me, that an illegal practice would not be the best idea.

With Vinnie's encouragement, I have been applying to residency programs, and have already been accepted at my father's hospital. Still, I am not sure that path feels entirely right, but I am choosing to explore it, if not for myself, then for Mamma, and for the family I dream of having with my wife.

Unlocking the door, I let myself in and set the flowers down on a chair while I flip the light switch. The fluorescents come to life, illuminating the space I cherish so wholly. The air is stagnant, the scent of lingering sanitizer and latex from the box of open gloves on the counter.

Breathing deeply, I look around the room and try to daydream about myself continuing here, but the vision doesn't come. It feels as though this door has already closed, and it is at that moment that I realize it may truly be time for me to move on from this chapter of my life.

Perhaps residency *is* the right path.

Taking the chair next to where I placed the flowers, I slump into it and pull up the email app on my phone, finding the notice I received yesterday from Manhattan Presbyterian, the hospital my father works at. The word *accepted* sits in the first sentence, in bold lettering, congratulating me on being selected to join their residency.

Yesterday, that word felt like a weight on my shoulders, but now, as I look around the empty clinic I helped so many patients at, it almost feels like a beacon, lighting the way of the path I'm supposed to follow now.

Still, it's difficult to determine which decision is right for me, and right now is not the time. Not with guests arriving this evening, and without speaking to my wife. So I darken the screen and push the phone back into my pocket, promising myself that I will circle back to the email later.

Leaning my head back against the wall behind me, I allow myself a few minutes to close my eyes and simply sit in the space that has brought me great happiness to think about the man I am, and the man I hope to become in the future.

# Chapter 28

## *Vinnie*

After hanging up with Sly, I'm about to toss the phone on my bed to continue packing my closet, when it begins to ring.

Seeing that it's Luciano, I answer it quickly, propping the device between my shoulder and ear. "Hey!"

"Hey. I just wanted to give you the heads-up that Sullivan Rochester may end up hitting on Cecilia at some point tonight, and I know she's been going through a lot on her end, so I figured I'd warn you. You can do what you want with that information."

"Oh goodness. Okay, thanks. I'll let her know to ignore his advances. She's been in such a bad headspace lately, though. Maybe his humor will cheer her up."

Cecilia has been exploring her options on becoming a mom and it hasn't been an easy road so far. If it's not the adoption agencies or the sperm banks giving her hoops to jump through, it's her own guilt eating at her for finally deciding to do this alone.

"Maybe," Luciano agrees. Through the phone, papers rustle as he multitasks at work.

"Have you spoken to Joseph since he stormed out last week?"

"Not one word. I guess he hasn't been showing up to work this week either. No one's heard from him."

Feeling dizzy, I sit down on the edge of my bed. I want to give my brother the benefit of the doubt, but a nagging feeling in my stomach rolls around like a marble. "Maybe he's grieving."

"Mr. Paladino, you have a call on line two," my brother's secretary pages through his phone's speaker system, and he groans.

"I have to go. I'll see you tonight, although I'm still not sure how I ended up in this odd friend group situation."

Laughing, I tell him, "That's what happens when you decide to help the good guys."

"Hmm, I'll have to consider that for next time. Didn't realize helping my sister not marry a psycho would result in me having the merry band of misfits blowing up my phone's messages twenty-four-seven."

His description of their group chat makes me laugh harder. "I'll see you tonight."

"See ya," he says, and then hangs up the phone.

Before I set my phone down on my bureau, I send a quick message to Ross, letting him know I'll be ready in five to go to the office, then I walk into the bathroom to see if I've left anything behind. Butterflies swirl in my stomach as I glance at the trash can, suppressing a small smile before I move back into my bedroom and set the last remaining bit of clothing into the open box.

I give a final glance to the room around me, feeling bittersweet about this transition. Tears start to line my bottom lashes and I quickly wipe them away, standing to go grab my purse. As I leave the room, I flip the switch down and shut the door behind me.

Where one door closes, another one opens, and this time the door opening is to my happily ever after.

When the elevator doors open to the parking garage, I'm not surprised to find the black town car waiting for me. What is unusual, though, is that Ross isn't standing there to greet me, but instead, the back passenger door is wide open.

Walking around to the rear, I check the license plate —it *is* my car. I'm about to walk to the driver's side to look through the window when it rolls down and Ross' hand pops out and waves.

*Maybe he's on the phone.*

Feeling better, I go back to the passenger side and climb in, pulling the door closed behind me. Immediately, the car begins to move and I settle into the seat and think about the things I need to accomplish while at work.

We're pulling onto the street before my seatbelt is even clicked into place.

Traffic is heavy, so I pull my purse into my lap to

grab my phone so I can call Cecilia and warn her about what Luciano said, only to come up empty. Thinking back, I realize I sat my phone on the bureau and never grabbed it on my way out.

We're only a few blocks away—I'll just ask Ross to turn around. Reaching to lower the partition, my heart clenches when it doesn't move.

I try again, and when the button does nothing, my heart drops. Blowing out an unsteady breath, I think about how Ross wasn't waiting for me outside of the car like he usually does, and how I didn't actually see him— just his hand—as he waved through the window.

"Ross!" I yell, unbuckling my seatbelt to move closer to the partition. "Ross! Lower the partition, please!"

I can't hear anything in the front, and I realize he probably can't hear me either. Father does value privacy, and obviously wasn't kidding when he said the back of the town cars are soundproof.

Still, I beat my fist against it, thinking if he can't hear me, maybe he'll see the movement. I hit the barrier repeatedly until my hand begins to

hurt, before forcing myself to stop. Scooting backward, I get back in my seat and try the button one more time, and the panic sets in when the button continues to do nothing.

Looking out the window, I realize we're going in the opposite direction of my office building, and there's no longer any doubt in my mind that something isn't right.

Dread builds inside me as I watch the street pass by, driving further from where we should be going. I white-knuckle my purse and the second the car rolls to a stop at a red light, I pull open the door of the car, ready to dive out if I have to.

But it doesn't budge.

"Shit!" I yell, realizing the child safety locks have been flipped.

Then the tears come.

Slow, steady streams roll down my cheeks. All I can do is watch out the window and try to figure out where we may be going, who might be driving, and why. I pray to God that it *is* Ross, and that he noticed something wrong and is taking me somewhere safe, but my instincts tell me otherwise.

And I'm a sitting duck. No cell phone, no way to escape the car unless I fling myself from the window.

My tears fall harder as I think of Sly, and how he has no idea anything is wrong. I told him I'd be home around three-thirty, but that's still hours away. Until then, no one will know I'm gone.

A sob racks through me, and I lean my face into my hands, trying to calm myself so I can think logically, but it's no use.

We drive for maybe another fifteen minutes before the car comes to an abrupt stop. As it turns off, my heart threatens to explode from my chest with fear of the unknown. Questions race through my mind as bile makes its way up my throat. I press my hands on my stomach and pray for the strength of whatever's to come.

I can't even bring myself to look out the window, too scared to take my eyes off the partition.

When it begins to roll down, I hold my breath.

All the air leaves my lungs in a strong *whoosh* as Ross comes into view, along with my brother in the passenger seat. His body is angled toward him, and a chill runs down my spine. "Joseph?"

"Hiya, sis. Beautiful day for a drive, isn't it? Thanks for the lift, Ross."

"Vinnie, I'm so sor—" but he never finishes his sentence. A gunshot pierces through him and I scream, watching as his lifeless head bounces against the glass window. I keep screaming, unable to stop, and unable to tear my eyes from my driver's body.

"SHUT UP," Joseph yells, turning his head to stare at me. I only do when he turns the gun to me and cocks it. "Get out of the car," he demands, then laughs. It sounds foreign and not at all like his normal laugh. "Oh wait, you can't. I guess I have to pretend to be your new chauffeur and open the door for you."

His door slams shut behind him and not even a second later, mine yanks open and his hand reaches in, grabbing onto my arm tightly as he pulls me out. Stumbling, I hardly catch myself from crashing to the ground, but my brother acts like he doesn't notice.

The air smells heavily of saltwater and metal, and as I look around, I realize we're at the docks.

"Stop crying," he orders through clenched teeth, but I couldn't stop if I tried. I'm too scared.

With the gun in one hand, he grips my bicep and

roughly leads me to a warehouse a few yards away, only stopping long enough to stow his weapon in the back of his pants to unlock the door.

I didn't even know he owned a gun, but I shouldn't be surprised, given the nature of Father's business.

When we enter the warehouse, I'm immediately hit with the scent of old, rotting fish, and a strong wave of nausea rolls through my stomach.

I can barely keep up with my brother as he pulls me over to a metal chair and shoves me into it. I never see him procure any rope, but the next thing I know, my wrists are tied to the chair behind my back.

"Why are you doing this?" I ask through a fresh wave of tears.

"You fucking know why," he seethes, raking his hand through his hair as he paces in front of me.

Instinctually, I pull against the ropes to check their strength, and feel a tinge of defeat when they don't budge.

"You killed Ross," I press, even though I know I shouldn't. I'm in danger—he's proven that, but still, my heart is cracking in two for the man in front of me. My brother, who isn't even a shell of himself at this point. Whispering, I ask, "How could you kill him, Joey?"

"DON'T FUCKING CALL ME JOEY!" he screams, moving at me so quickly I flinch and slam my eyes shut, reading myself for the blow.

But it doesn't come.

When I open my eyes, he's squatting down in front of me, his eyes cold and vacant. "This will go one of two ways, baby sister. Either you're leaving here alive and your precious *husband* will be dead, or vice versa. Either way, someone is going to pay for August's death. A Lucchetti did this, and I intend on getting retribution in the form of an eye for an eye. Sucks that you share the last name now. It might be your blood that runs, *sis*."

"You wouldn't," I cry through a strangled breath.

"Oh, I would," he remarks, then gives me his back and walks away, his boisterous laugh echoing mechanically off the walls of the empty warehouse.

# Chapter 29

## *Sly*

It's four o'clock by the time I finish tidying the apartment and preparing for our guests this evening, when I realize Vinnie hasn't arrived yet.

Walking into our bedroom, I pick up my phone from the nightstand and check it, seeing no missed calls or messages from anyone. It's not unusual for Vinnie to work later than she initially predicts, but it is strange that she hasn't updated me.

Perhaps a meeting ran late.

When the doorbell rings just a few moments later, I stalk over to answer it, annoyance peppering my bloodstream.

"Hey," Sully says as he waltzes past me, entering my home with a bottle of champagne in one hand and a bouquet of roses and hydrangeas in the other.

"You're entirely too early."

He shrugs. "Figured you could use some help. Put me in, coach."

"Shouldn't you be at work?"

"Work is overrated." He grins. "Plus, it's a Friday afternoon and I'm not needed. So I left." He takes it upon himself to move into my kitchen, setting the champagne down and pulling open a cabinet to find a vase. "The house seems quiet. No, Vinnie or Nixon?"

"Not yet." I run my fingers over my brows. "Actually, Vinnie is late. I was about to call her."

Clicking her contact, I bring my phone to my ear and listen to the continuous ring until it goes to her voicemail.

The gurgle of my espresso machine turning on echoes through the kitchen as I flip my phone to the side to turn it off silent then set it down.

"Coffee?" Sully asks, making himself at home by pulling out a mug for himself.

"No."

There's a tingle at the base of my neck, like the hairs are standing on edge. Worry plagues me since Vincenza didn't answer her phone. Picking mine up again, I debate on calling her office, while wondering if I'm overreacting.

It's only thirty minutes past when she said she'd be home.

Staring at the darkened screen, I waver between whether I should bother her just to ease my mind, or give her more time.

Ultimately, I decided to wait a little longer before trying to reach her at work. It is entirely possible that she entered into a meeting, and it's just gone over.

Turning my attention back to Sully, I find him watching me as I silently stew.

"No answer?" he asks curiously.

"No. She said she would be home at three-thirty."

He checks the Rolex on his wrist. "It's only a little after four. Was she at work?"

"Sì."

"Maybe she's playing catch up." He takes a long sip of the latte he made. "You did whisk her away unexpectedly for two weeks."

"You're right," I say, determined to believe that justification, even if it doesn't feel right. Looking down at my phone again, I click the side button to illuminate the screen, checking the time again.

"So," Sully starts, and I can tell he is about to change the subject. Leaning on the counter with both elbows, he gives me a megawatt smile. "Tell me about Vinnie's hot older friend."

Instantly, my blood boils. "No."

He looks offended by my instant irritation. "Wow, someone's touchy today."

"If the only descriptors you can think to speak of are her age and her attractiveness, then I fail to see the point in continuing the conversation."

He huffs an exasperated breath. "They're the *only* things I know about her. Currently. But I want to know more."

"She is too mature for you, Sullivan." I look down at my phone again. Only a minute has passed.

"How is that fair?"

"It's accurate," I snap. "Cecilia longs for a family—for a husband and a child. *Children.* She is older and wiser than you, and knows exactly what she wants for her life. Can you say the same?"

Running a hand through his haphazardly styled dirty-blond hair, he casts his eyes downward. "I don't know what I want."

It's the most honest thing I've ever heard him say, and if I'm being truthful, it breaks my heart a little to hear. "And there's nothing wrong with that. One day, you will. Until then, you are simply you, mio amico."

Without responding, he turns to the sink to clean his mug, but I can tell my words have gotten under his skin. An apology is on the tip of my tongue, but I decide against it. He needs to take a serious evaluation of his life, and perhaps this will be a nudge in the right direction.

Feeling as though I'm going crazy, I pick up my phone and try calling Vincenza again. The ring echoes in my ear as I silently pray for her to answer. When she doesn't, worry dips in my stomach.

*"Hi! You've reached Vinnie, I'm sorry I missed your call—"*

Hanging up, I immediately dial her office. When it goes to the after hours recording, I nearly hurl my phone across the room as the nagging feeling in my gut intensifies.

Sully looks at me with expectant eyes, so I tell him, "She's not answering her cell phone, and her office went to voicemail."

"She's probably on her way over. Relax, buddy. She's not even an hour late."

"It's just not like her to not communicate." And it's not. We speak frequently throughout the day, whether it be quick phone conversations or messages exchanged. In fact, I can't recall a time she hasn't answered my call.

Until now.

"Maybe she ran into a friend, or is picking up a surprise for you? You guys are romantic like that."

It could be, but still, I'm not convinced, and I can't ignore the concern I feel. Scrolling through my contacts, I find Luciano's number and get him on the phone.

"When was the last time you spoke with your sister?" I ask the moment he answers.

"Hello to you too, Lucchetti. I talked to V earlier today. Why?"

"How long ago?" I demand.

Through the phone, I hear a drawer close—or maybe a door. "Maybe three hours ago? Give or take. I warned her about your friend and his possible advances toward Cecilia tonight."

"Where was she when you spoke? Still at her apartment?"

"I'm not sure. She didn't say. Why? What's going on?" His voice is calm, but I sense he hears my panic, as his tone has changed, taking on a certain professionalism, as though he's speaking to me like a client.

"When was the last time you spoke with your brother?"

"Sly, what is going on?" he demands, wanting answers.

"Vinnie told me she would be home around three-thirty. It's almost four-thirty, and she is not answering her phone. Her office phone has been switched to voice-mail. She always communicates with me, and she's never more than a few minutes late." I drop my voice, pinching my finger and thumb to the bridge of my nose. "Something feels off. I can sense it, Luciano. When was the last time you spoke to Joseph?" My voice cracks slightly at the mention of his name.

"I haven't seen or heard from him since last weekend at my parents. I'm coming over. Stay there." He hangs up, and as I pull the phone from my ear, I see a message banner appear. Clicking it, I'm brought to the group message.

SULLY

Vinnie's late coming home and Sly's worried. Anyone passing by her office on their way here?

NIXON

I'm not, but I could swing by.

ENZO

I'm already on this side of the park. I was planning on showing up early.

SULLY

Nixon, if you could.

NIXON

Sure thing, just drop me the address as a pin.

SULLY

You've got it.

"Grazie," I say to Sully. "Luciano is on his way, too. I'm going to ride over to her apartment and see if she's there. Will you stay here and let him in?"

"Yeah, of course. Do you want to call her friends? See if they've seen her?"

"Good thought," I say, pulling up Raina's contact information.

She answers on the second ring.

"Hey, Sly," she greets, confusion thick in her voice. I've never called her before, so I'm sure this comes as a surprise.

Rather than engage in small talk, I simply get to the point. "Is Vinnie with you?"

"No, she isn't…"

Shaking my head at Sully, I race to the front door, first stopping to grab my gun and my helmet from the coat closet. "Okay, grazie," I tell her, and hang up the phone.

It is rude, but the only thing I can think of is getting to Vinnie's apartment.

"Sly, take a breath," Sully says as I race around, grabbing my things. "I'm sure she's fine."

"My gut tells me otherwise," I snap, pulling my

helmet on. I'm out the door before I can hear a response.

Not bothering with the elevator, I race down the stairwell and out into the parking garage of my building, and hop onto my Superleggera. The faster I arrive at her apartment, the faster I have peace of mind.

Or so I pray.

"Hello?" I say as I enter with the key Vinnie gave me, not wanting to startle her if she's here, or Cecilia, for that matter. "Anyone home?"

The only thing that greets me is silence.

Swallowing around the lump in my throat, I close the door behind me and go straight to Vinnie's room.

"Vincenza?"

But the room is dark. Turning the light on, as I push the door open further I see various boxes scattered throughout the space, all filled to the brim with her things. The only hint of her she's left behind is the bare furniture and her scent lingering in the air.

Pulling my phone from my pocket, I call her again.

This time, when it rings, the sound fills the room. My brows furrow as I look around, and I find her phone on the dresser by the door. Ending my call, her screen illuminates with dozens of missed calls and text messages as I pick it up and begin to scroll.

Fear strikes me then, as messages from her assistant grow more concerned by her not arriving to work, wondering if she forgot about her meeting, and if she's okay.

There's an unread message from Raina, which I don't read, and all of my missed calls.

Continuing to look through my wife's missed messages for any indication of where she may be, I use my phone to get her brother back on the line.

"I'm almost at your place," Luciano barks, answering my call.

"I'm not there. I'm at Vincenza's apartment."

"Is she there?"

"No, but her phone is."

"That doesn't make sense."

"No, it doesn't."

"What time did you say you spoke with her?"

Wandering into her bathroom, I look around for—well, anything.

"It was probably around a quarter to one or so."

"Was she still at home?"

"She didn't say. What are you thinking? Say what's on your mind."

"Something doesn't feel right," I tell him as my eyes scan every inch of the space, wishing the writing would be on the wall.

But it's not.

"I can't put my finger on it, Luciano. But something is very wrong. This isn't like her."

I'm about to leave the room when my gaze catches on the trash can. More specifically, it catches on a white and blue stick sitting on top. All at once, my entire world comes toppling down around me. I vaguely hear Luciano speaking, but his words don't register as more than gargled tones. My vision fills with darkness as the room spins, and an overwhelming sense of terror sends a shock wave through my bloodstream, freezing the warmth inside me.

Bending, I pick up the plastic and stare at it.

"We need to find her," I tell Luciano, my voice low and unsteady. I then realize I'm shaking. "We need to find her immediately."

"We will—"

"No, we need to find her now. Get your father on the phone, the polizia. I don't care who you call, but we need to find my wife, *now*."

"I'll call him. Come back to your place, alright? I'll have an update when you're back."

"Sì," is all I say before I hang up on him.

Closing my eyes, I expel another deep breath, willing myself not to cry. There is no time to get emotional—no time to waste.

I have to find her.

I have to find *them*.

# Chapter 30

## *Vinnie*

My eyes are dry, but they still burn from the tears I want to shed but can't. I've been crying since I realized what was happening, back before I watched my brother kill Ross.

When he dragged me into this warehouse and left me alone on this cold, hard chair, the only thing I could do *was* cry.

A chill racks through my body as a breeze pulls through a shattered window high above me. The sun set a while ago and the air is now cold without the warmth of the rays beating down on the metal frame of the building.

Joseph hasn't come back, but I know he's watching me. I can feel his eyes through the window of the office behind me, but I refuse to give him the satisfaction of looking over my shoulder to confirm my suspicions. So I look straight ahead and try to think of things that make me happy.

The things I have to live for.

Most importantly, I think of Sly, and there's no doubt in my mind that he knows something is terribly wrong.

Will he find me?

*Yes. It's not a matter of if, but when,* I remind myself.

My stomach rumbles, flipping slowly with a faint nausea lacing through me, and I wish I could rub it, if only to ease some of the discomfort.

It's only been hours since I found out the reason I've been feeling so off lately, and the cause of my ever persistent nausea. I should have realized sooner and taken a test, but I've been so wrapped up in my husband that I chalked everything up to being completely thrown off my normal day-to-day routine.

That, and travel. Jet lag does strange things to the body. But when it didn't go away, I grew suspicious. There's a reason why contraception was invented.

The moment I took the test, the word *pregnant* appeared within seconds. It took everything I had to not immediately call Sly and tell him.

I was supposed to tell him tonight.

A sob catches in my throat, but the tears still won't fall.

"Pathetic," Joseph's voice sneers from behind me. I hadn't heard him approach. I was too caught up in my thoughts. "You just never stop crying, do you?"

"It's not every day your big brother kidnaps you," I croak, my throat feeling dry now, too.

"I'm a little disappointed your husband hasn't

shown up to find you yet. I thought he would have figured out where you are by now."

"How would he know to come look here?" I prod to keep him talking. If he's talking, maybe he won't hurt me.

"He strikes me as the type of man who's in constant contact with his family, including his piece of shit cousin. The same cousin who dug into my personal business and followed me out here one day. Did I ever tell you that story? Don't worry–I roughed him up. Still, though, it should have been easy for them to put two-and-two together. Maybe I gave Sly too much credit."

"Why are you telling me this, Joseph?"

"Because it won't matter, anyway. You see, if this plays out like I hope it does, then by the time you have the ability to speak with anyone of importance—like say, the police—you'll be too deep in your grief over your dead husband to realize that I've been gone for hours. You'll never see me again, dear baby sister."

"Why don't you just let me go? You've made your point. *You* have the power here—you successfully took me, and Sly can't find me. We all can see that you've shown your dominance."

"It has nothing to do with dominance."

"Then what does—"

"THAT YOU DON'T ALWAYS WIN, VINNIE."

Lowering my gaze to my lap, I realize how deeply rooted his hatred for me is. It doesn't matter if I live or die, or if Sly lives or dies. Either I've lost someone I love, or the ones I love lose me. Either way, Joseph will always see me as the woman who ruined his life. In his mind, I've won, regardless of the outcome. There is no winning for him.

There's just an end.

Looking up at him, our gaze connects, and the amount of malice reflected in his eyes takes my breath away, shattering my heart in the process. He truly hates me. I can see it as clear as day on his face as he sneers at me, looking like he'd love to end me right here and now.

But that wouldn't give him the satisfaction he's hoping for. He wants the audience. The hurt.

He wants someone else to feel the pain he's feeling.

Tapping his pointer finger against his watch, he smirks, acting as though this is all just fun for him, while my fight-or-flight instincts start to kick in.

My heart hammers in my chest, but I hold my chin up, staring at him with an unwavering stare as he tells me, "Tick-tock, Vinnie. If Sly doesn't show up within the next three hours, I'll make sure he does."

# Chapter 31

## *Sly*

The amount of people in my home while my wife is missing is a problem. Instead of continuing to look for her, everyone is crowded around my kitchen, yelling at each other while I stand against the wall, watching it in what seems to be slow motion.

It's been four hours since Vinnie was due to arrive home. Four hours of my heart feeling like it's been ripped from my body, and like my lungs are being squeezed with an iron fist.

And to learn that it's not just my wife missing, but our child she carries, too? It feels as though the rug has been swept from beneath me—like the world is playing a cruel, cruel joke.

I spent hours riding around the city on my Ducati, swerving in and out of traffic as I looked everywhere I could think she might be.

Raina searched the stores she enjoys shopping at.

Cecilia searched all of Central Park on foot.

Sully and Nixon went to the grocery store where Sully ran into her, then back to her apartment to see if she turned up there.

Luciano and Enzo went their separate ways, not elaborating on where exactly they searched, but I trust Luciano went to the places he thought he may find his sister. Lorenzo, I can't be too sure he even looked for her, but his presence counts for something.

Wasting no time, Luciano looped his father in, and Maurizio pulled together his security team to start their search. And *still*, there has been no sign of her anywhere.

But I know who is behind this. I know it as certain as I know the sky is blue, and the grass is green.

"Think, Luciano. He's your brother. Where could he have taken her?" Raina snaps, glaring at him from across the island. She is confident Joseph's behind this, too.

He glares back, holding her eye contact as they play a silent battle of the wills. She swipes at a tear that falls, then crosses her arms over her chest, never looking away.

I know she feels guilty. She and Vinnie track each other through their cell phones, and Raina immediately thought of that, only seconds later to realize *I* have her cell phone. Watching the hope drain from her face was just another sucker punch to my gut.

"Have they checked his apartment? The office building he works out of?" Cecilia asks no one in particular.

"Of course they've checked those places. My father and his men went there first," Luciano counters. "His car was at his apartment, too, which is unsettling."

"Could he have hijacked Ross's car?" Cecilia questions, the fear evident in her voice. Sully shifts closer to her but keeps his hands to himself.

"It seems like the most logical of explanations," Nixon chimes in. "Have you tried calling him?"

"I did earlier, it just rang."

"Try again," Sully urges.

The sound of everyone's voices is like nails on a chalkboard as I rack my brain about where they could be.

I'm also battling with myself silently. The monster within is clawing his way out—the only thing I can think of aside from bringing Vinnie home safely is killing Joseph for what he's putting my wife through.

I'm on the verge of snapping.

My cousin catches my eye from where he sits at my kitchen island, wiping the condensation off a bottle of water with his thumb. He hasn't said much this entire time, and I briefly wonder how he's feeling. What he's thinking.

It's no secret he's struggling to accept my marriage to Vinnie because of who she is, but I know my cousin as well, and with the Lucchettis, family is family. Because of that, I can see the confliction on his features each time I look at him. And I understand it, truly I do.

Her father killed his father.

Separating years of hate won't happen overnight,

especially when Enzo and Joseph have had many altercations. The time Enzo and his friend showed up at my clinic after his friend was shot, enters into my mind, and I'm transported into the memory.

*What happened?" I asked again, walking to my cabinet to grab supplies.*

*"Intel gone wrong," Enzo said, his tone clipped.*

*"Intel on what?"*

*"Just a business situation," he snapped, and I take note of his annoyance.*

*"Don't be so casual about it, man," Nathaniel interjected. "Fuckin' Paladino assholes shot at us!"*

*My head snapped over to Enzo. "Paladino? Enzo, what are you doing starting a war with the Paladinos?"*

*"I'm not starting anything, cousin. I'm just gathering information. Seeing what they're up to."*

*"If Papà finds out——"*

*"He won't."*

*"But he will, and when he does——"*

*"He won't find out, Sly. I have it handled."*

*"They shot at you."*

*"It's fine, we were just spotted this time and——"*

*"IT COULD BE YOU ON MY TABLE RIGHT NOW," I screamed, losing all control, my sense of level-headedness completely gone. "Or worse, Lorenzo. You could be dead. And for what? Information?"*

*"I'm going to bring them down, Sly. If it's the last thing I do, the Paladinos will get what's coming to them. Maurizio will pay for what he did to my father."*

The memory swirls away, and realization dawns on me. Stepping forward, I stand beside Luciano.

"Lorenzo, do you recall the time your friend was shot after you went looking for information on the Paladinos?"

He looks at me, his eyes narrowing slightly as he recalls the memory himself. "Yeah."

"Where were you when that happened?"

"At the Paladino's warehouse down by the docks."

Turning to Luciano, I bark, "Get your father on the phone."

He glances at me, then pulls his phone from the pocket of his coat. Maurizio answers on the first ring, his voice radiating through the phone's speaker. "Did you find her?"

"I should ask you that question, Father, you're the one out there looking."

"Call your contact at the NYPD, Maurizio," I demand over Luciano. "I think I know where she is, and unless you want me to have the death of your son on my hands, I suggest you have them meet us there."

"We don't know he took—"

"Yes, I do," I say with pure confidence. "They're at the docks. They have to be."

Luciano and I make eye contact, and he nods before taking his father off speakerphone. "We'll meet you there."

I'm already halfway to the door when Raina yells, "Wait up!"

"No," I say over my shoulder. "Joseph is dangerous. You're staying here."

"You can't expect me to just wait here—she's my best friend!"

"And she's my wife!" I say firmly, turning on my heel to face her as I swipe my keys from the entryway table. "What kind of husband would I be—*man* would I be—if I allowed my wife's best friend to be put in harm's way? Stay here, Raina. Stay with Cecilia. Sully, Enzo, and Nix will wait with you."

"Like Hell I will," Nixon grumbles, striding through my living room. "Let's go, I'm driving."

"This is bullshit," Raina complains again. I'm about to retort when Luciano steps close to her, engulfing her with his size.

His voice is low when he says, "Vinnie will be happy to know you're here, safe. For once in your life, don't be a pain in the ass, Raina. Stay for her."

Quickly, she wipes away another tear, and I can't help but notice the way Luciano's fingers stretch out by his side, as though he wants to reach up and wipe them for her.

Then he turns and stalks toward where Nixon and I stand. "Let's go find my sister."

As we approach the building Luciano points out as the one belonging to his father, Nixon cuts the lights, drenching my SUV in total darkness as we park several yards away. "We should go the rest of the way on foot, so we have the element of surprise."

"Has your father responded about whether la polizia is on their way?" I ask, looking at the building to see if there is any movement.

"He says they're five minutes out."

"And where is he?" I ask, noticing a shadow through a closed window shade directly ahead. Reaching forward, my hand clasps the handle of the passenger door, my instincts kicking over into high gear to go investigate, just as a small knock comes from the window.

Turning, I see Maurizio standing there, along with the butler—who is also his head of security—Capaul, and another man I don't recognize.

Pushing open the door, they step back to give it space, and I get out. "He's in there," I tell them with urgency. "I saw his shadow."

"We still don't know it's Joseph," Maurizio states. "The police are on their way, let's let them handle this.

"The way you handled Joseph at the dinner? You barely said a word when he began yelling with great hostility, and now that he's taken Vinnie, you want to *wait?*"

"It seems a little peculiar that you're so keen on proving that it's my son in there. Maybe I should be wondering why that is." The accusation in his tone enrages me, and it takes everything I have to not lose all control.

My hands ball into fists by my side, and I slam the

car door shut. "If you are so uncertain of my intentions, then explain to me why someone with the Lucchetti name would go to such lengths to protect a *Paladino*. The moment Vincenza entered my life, she became my priority, and I will not stand here while you accuse me of having ill-intentions." I push past him with a rough bump of my shoulder.

Behind me, the sound of two car doors closing reverberates through the night, and gravel crunches beneath the footsteps that follow.

"Then wait for the police and let them handle it," Maurizio hisses as he stumbles behind me.

"I'm not wasting another second, Maurizio. My wife is inside there—your *daughter*. Don't you value her safety?"

"Of course I do," he snaps.

"Then act like it," I snarl, quickening my pace. My eyes are trained on the window of the warehouse, watching for any more movement. I'd be shocked if Joseph can't hear us coming with how loud this argument has become.

"Don't be reckless. Those are my children in there," Maurizio says with exasperation.

"*Now* you believe it's Joseph? Which is it, Maurizio? Did he take her, or did he not?" I argue, my voice in a whisper as we get closer to the window I saw movement in.

"Shh," Nixon commands, pressing his body against the side of the building. His gun is in his hand, ready for anything.

The blinds of the window are open enough to see through them, which I am grateful for. Carefully, I peer through the small opening, and rather than seeing the shadow that was moving around just moments ago, I look through the window on the opposite side of the room that shows through to the warehouse.

Immediately, I see the back of Vincenza, seated just a few feet from the glass, her body slumped forward slightly as she sits in a metal chair with her hands tied behind it.

I don't think when I see her, the feeling of desperation seizes my body, and rather than force myself to keep calm, I find myself crying out her name.

# Chapter 32

## *Vinnie*

"*Vinnie!*"

The sound of my name lulls me from the dream-state sleep I'm in, and I sit up, inhaling a breath.

*Am I imagining things?*

Looking around, I see nothing but darkness and the faint glow of what I assume is a lamp in the office that Joseph is in. He hasn't come back since telling me Sly had three hours to get here, and in that time, I've fallen in and out of sleep—or maybe consciousness.

I'm so exhausted, it feels like I can't keep my eyes open for another minute. When I'm sure I dreamt of Sly's voice calling my name, I close them and immediately drift back to sleep.

# Chapter 33

*Sly*

Nixon's hand slaps over my mouth the moment her name falls from my tongue, pulling me out of the way of the window. Caught off guard, my body slams into his.

"You idiot," he reprimands gruffly as the door to the office swings open.

Joseph strolls through it with his hands in his pockets and a smug look on his face as looks around at us. "It's about time you showed up."

Nixon releases me, training his weapon on Joseph, so I have time to remove mine from its holster.

"Joseph," Maurizio says in disbelief. "Tell me it isn't true. Tell me Vinnie isn't here."

Rolling his eyes, he ignores his father, still focusing his attention on me. "You took entirely too long and my patience has worn thin. I'll tell you the same thing I told her. One of you isn't leaving here alive, and since you brought every single person you know, it looks like several people won't be leaving here. It's a shame you'll have so many deaths on your hands, Lucchetti. But your family has always only thought about themselves."

Sirens cut through the quiet night air and Joseph's eyes turn dark, zeroing in on me as he realizes this is all about to be over.

Faster than I would have ever given him credit for, he withdraws a handgun and fires a shot in Nixon's direction, only narrowly missing him. Fast on his feet, Nixon sends a shot of his own and hits Joseph in exactly where he intended—his shin.

Joseph's howls pierce the air as he drops his gun and doubles over in pain. "You motherfucker!"

At the same moment, Vinnie screams, and my heart nearly explodes when I hear her, relief washing over me that she's conscious. As I rush into the building, I see Luciano walk over to his brother and kick the gun further away from him.

Pulling open the door to where Vinnie's being held, I don't stop moving until I reach her. Dropping to my knees, I work as quickly as I can to untie the ropes that hold her.

Tires squeal outside, followed by doors opening and shouts of, "Hands where I can see them!" and, "Put your hands in the air!" as the police officers navigate the chaos in front of them.

As quickly as I possibly can, I work through the knots around Vincenza's wrists.

"I'm here, amore mio. Tell me you're okay. Please tell me you're unharmed."

"I'm okay," she croaks, her voice scratchy and strained. "Thirsty, and exhausted, but I'm okay."

"He didn't hurt you?" I question, frantically working to loosen the ropes. Freeing one of her hands, I start on the other.

"No. But…but he killed Ross."

My heart sinks. "Did you have to witness it?"

"Yes."

"I'm so sorry, *piccola ladra*." Anger spikes through my blood, furious that she watched her brother take her driver's life.

*Two* deaths she's had to witness in the last month. One by me, the other by her brother. That's two too many, and I feel immense guilt for my part in the devastating memory she has to live with.

She chokes back a sob.

I wish I could rub her back and settle her, but I know I must continue on the ropes holding her in place, so instead, I soften my voice and try to comfort her with words. "It's okay, Vinnie. You are so strong, *piccola ladra*. You will get past this. Let it out."

And she does, shaking her head as she hangs her head and cries. But her cries quickly turn to hyperventilation, and suddenly she's gasping for air. The strangled sound of her breaths nearly shatters me.

The second her wrist is free, I rush around, pulling her from the chair and into my arms.

"Shhh," I soothe, holding her tight with one arm as my other hand strokes her hair. She trembles against me, her body vibrating with adrenaline and unshed emotion from the last several hours.

She bawls in my arms until her tears turn silent, and her body begins to relax. She's exhausted, and I can feel her physical strength diminish as she lets me care for her. As I hold her, I look past her and watch the scene outside unfold.

The officers have their guns drawn and pointed at Joseph as he tries to negotiate his way out of the situation he's put himself in. Unfortunately, their guns are pointed at Nixon as well, but I am not worried about him. There are enough witnesses around to ensure he is not taken away in cuffs.

From my peripheral, I see Maurizio speaking to a man wearing smart pants and a dress shirt. Their discussion looks like it is getting heated. Maurizio's arms fly up into the air while he speaks, and the man looks irritated. Closest to us, an officer clears the office space. His eyes dart around the room while he keeps an eye on me and Vinnie.

"Carpenter, call for transport," an officer outside yells to the man Maurizio is speaking to. "He's been shot in the leg."

"Hey!" another officer yells over the commotion. "We have another body over here!"

La polizia begins to spring into action, pulling out radios and barking orders to each other.

"We need medics in here, too," I yell over Vinnie's head, letting them know I want her evaluated.

"I don't need an ambulance," she insists, but I don't

answer. Instead, while everyone is distracted and frantic, I catch movement from the corner of my eye and everything happens in a blur.

Somehow, Joseph has managed to reach his firearm, and despite the many officers that surround him, he aims it directly at me and Vincenza, and fires the gun.

# Chapter 34

## *Vinnie*

The wind is knocked from my lungs as I land roughly on top of Sly's body, the reverberation of the gunshot ringing through my ears. I'm disoriented, but jump when another *pop pop* radiates through the air.

Sly groans beneath me, having taken the brunt of the fall.

"Are you o—" I start to ask, but the bloodcurdling sounds of my father screaming my brother's name stops me mid-sentence.

Ripping my eyes from Sly, I scurry to my feet, swaying slightly from the pounding in my head.

Through the open doors, Joseph's lifeless body lies on the ground as blood begins to pool around him. His head is turned toward me, eyes still open. My father stands over him, horror-stricken, repeating "no" over and over.

Unable to control it, I double over in pain. Physical pain from the nausea that immediately rolls through my stomach, and the overwhelming grief that slams into me, realizing my brother is gone.

I scream, an agonizing, soul-wrenching scream.

For him.

For myself.

For the relationship with my brother that started off perfect and ended with such hatred from him, I refused to accept it.

"Vinnie," Sly's voice cuts through the noise. Grabbing my shoulders, he rights me, then places his hands on either side of my face. "Breathe, amore mio," he says frantically, searching my eyes wildly, then skimming down my body. "Are you hurt? Were you hit?"

"No," I sob, at the same time, he yells, "WE NEED A MEDIC IN HERE!"

"I'm okay, Sly. I wasn't hit. I'm okay," I say through tears.

"You're okay?" he asks again, tears streaming down his face.

"I'm okay," I repeat, trying to catch my breath as sobs rack through my body.

Sinking to his knees, he squeezes my midsection tight, crying against my stomach before he presses soft kisses to it.

My breath catches in my throat.

"Grazie Dio," he cries, hugging me close. "Te amo, piccola ladra. So much it hurts."

My fingers weave through his hair, and I bend, kissing the top of his head. "I love you."

"LET ME THROUGH, MY DAUGHTER IS IN

THERE," my father yells and comes rushing through the doors, Luciano right behind him.

Our gaze meets and I watch as his face morphs into varying emotions as he takes in the sight of me and Sly—him on his knees, pressing his lips to my stomach. I wonder if he's putting the pieces together.

My brother stands behind him, a relieved smile on his face as he sees that we're okay. I return it with a weak smile of my own until I look back at my father and see his relief has turned into pain as a guttural groan pushes past his lips.

Just when I thought I couldn't break any more than I already have, my father's hand moves to rest over his heart, his fingertips digging into the fabric of his shirt as his face contorts into agony.

Then he collapses.

# Chapter 35

## *Sly*

"Mrs. Lucchetti, please try to relax," Vinnie's nurse begs after she tries to get out of her hospital bed for the second time. "Your body has been through a lot today. Dehydration. A rough fall. Please, let us run our tests."

"I'm fine," she reiterates, being stubborn. I know she is desperate to check on her father.

"Piccola ladra, please, if not for yourself, for the baby," I sigh, leaning forward in the chair next to her bed so I can reach to hold her hand.

Her eyes soften, and she touches her stomach.

"I'd like to get OB down here to do a transvaginal ultrasound, but right now, your vitals are looking good. You might need another bag of fluids, though, so please, Mrs. Lucchetti, relax for a bit, and I'll be back to check on you shortly." The nurse gives me a pointed look, then grabs her patient chart and walks out of the room.

"I know it's the last thing you want, amore mio, but please try to rest. It's the middle of the night, and the exhaustion is evident on your face. You need to sleep."

"I'm sorry I couldn't tell you about the baby before you figured it out on your own," she sighs, changing the subject as she settles into her pillow. Standing, I grab the extra blanket by her feet and open it, draping it further up her body so she can get comfortable. "I had just found out. I took a test right after we got off the phone. I've felt so off lately, and thought, why not? I had planned to tell you the second everyone left after dinner." She looks down at her lap, sadness overcoming her. "But dinner never happened."

Creasing her brow, she looks up at me again. "Have you checked in with Cecilia and Raina? I need to call them." She pats around the bed for her phone, and I settle my hand on hers, stopping her.

"Luciano called. They are relieved, piccola ladra, and they'll be by to see you tomorrow."

"I'm not staying here," she begins to argue, but I shake my head.

"You are if the doctor orders it. Please, Vincenza, just let them care for you. Let us both get peace of mind. As soon as you have the approval from your doctor, we will be out of here."

I can tell she is not happy with my request, but after a moment, she says, "Okay," and squeezes my hand. "I know it's late, but please, can you see if there's any update on my father?"

"Of course, piccola ladra. Let me see what I can

find out." Rising from my seat, I kiss her forehead. "Get some sleep," I tell her, before walking into the hallway.

The door closes quietly behind me, and for a moment, I lean against it, closing my eyes as my chest rises and falls.

I could have lost her today. Her, and our child I now know she is growing.

A shaky breath expels from my lungs, and I rub my eyes. Stress sits heavy in my chest, the ever-present feeling that refuses to leave my body, and likely won't until I get Vinnie home safely.

The hall of the hospital is bright despite the early morning hour, and I realize I have no idea where they took Maurizio. Retrieving my phone from my pocket, I call Luciano.

His phone rings continuously, and I'm about to hang up when he finally answers. "Hello?"

"You sound exhausted, amico."

"You could say that."

"Vinnie has requested an update," I tell him as I walk further from her door toward the elevator. "What floor are you on?"

"Christ. There's no update that I want to give to my sister right now. We're on the third floor. In the waiting room."

"I'm on my way."

Hanging up, I press the elevator call button and step into it when the doors open moments later. The ride from the fourth floor down to the third is short, and when I step into the hallway, I follow the signs to the waiting room.

Upon opening the doors, I am immediately engulfed with the sadness around me.

Luciano sits next to his mother, his arm around her shoulders as she sleeps, her head leaning on him. Two dried rivers of black mascara track down her cheeks from the tears she's shed, and there is still a tremor to her breathing, even in slumber.

Beside her, Vinnie's youngest brother, Samuele, is asleep with his head propped in his hand. He looks uncomfortable, yet somehow content.

But Luciano is wide awake, his eyes bloodshot and dry, as he stares at me from across the room.

"Can't sleep?" I ask quietly, taking the chair across from him.

"My brother is dead. My sister was kidnapped by said dead brother, and my father is undergoing surgery that he may or may not make it out of. So no, I can't sleep."

"Your sister is doing well. She's stronger than you think she is."

"I know exactly how strong she is," he counters. "She's a Paladino."

Smirking, I shake my head. "She's a Lucchetti now, but I suppose that just means strength runs through her both in blood and in name."

Luciano nods his head in agreement, a far off look in his eye.

The room grows quiet, with only the low voices

coming from an infomercial on the TV that hangs in the corner.

"What is the update on your father?" I ask. "You said he is in surgery?"

"He was coherent in the ambulance, and when they brought him into the emergency room, but about thirty minutes later, he began having shortness of breath, grew ghastly pale, and then he completely lost consciousness. The doctor made it into the room just as he began to crash and rushed him back for emergency surgery. They didn't elaborate—I still don't fully understand what is happening. I'm a lawyer, not a doctor."

But *I* am, and going back for emergency surgery after a heart attack is not nothing. It typically indicates a blockage of some sort. Or worse.

I do not wish to worry him further, so I don't press the topic more. "Can I get you anything? Would you like a coffee?"

He shakes his head. "No, I'm probably going to try and get some sleep in this horribly uncomfortable chair. How's V?"

"They're running some tests and will observe her for several hours, but she is okay. I hope she is asleep now. Exhaustion and dehydration are the biggest causes of concern."

"Good."

Standing, I walk to him and squeeze his shoulder. "If you need me, just call. I am one floor above you."

"Thanks. Tell my sister to rest."

"Trust me, mio amico. I'm trying."

He laughs, but the sound is distant and small.

My heart feels heavy as I leave the waiting room, knowing that I must be the one to tell Vincenza that her father is undergoing heart surgery. I can only hope that when I return to her room, she is asleep, and the update can wait until tomorrow.

Perhaps by morning, there will be better news.

# Chapter 36

## *Vinnie*

It's around seven in the morning when a knock sounds on the door to my hospital room and a young female doctor walks in, pushing an ultrasound machine.

"Good morning, Mrs. Lucchetti," she greets, coming to my bedside.

My eyes burn as I push myself up in the bed. "Good morning."

Sly hands me a bottle of water, which I drink gratefully before coughing gently to relieve some of the tightness in my throat.

"My name is Dr. Douglas," she says with a smile, holding the ultrasound probe in her gloved hand. "I'm going to do a transvaginal ultrasound and see if we can find a heartbeat. Your chart says you're not sure how far along you are—is that accurate?"

"Yes, I only found out yesterday with a home test, so

I'm not sure how far along I am." I glance at Sly, who is grinning at me.

"What was the date of your last period?"

Pursing my lips, I try to think back. It's been a while since I've truly had one.

"There's been a lot going on lately…I'm not sure, actually." My hand flutters down to my stomach, and I shake my head.

"That's okay," the doctor tells me. "We'll see how big the baby measures and approximate a due date based on that. Typically, I bring my patients up to OB for this, but for your comfort, we can do it here. Is this dad? Would you like him to stay?"

"Yes," I tell her immediately, and Sly laces his fingers through mine, coming to stand by my head.

"Excellent. If you could lie back and put your feet flat on the bed, please."

Adjusting, I scoot myself down and bend my legs, tenting the blanket as I do. The doctor adds lubricant to the ultrasound probe and lifts the blanket at my legs.

"This will be cold and you might feel some pressure, but it shouldn't hurt." She places her gloved hand on my thigh, then gently inserts the probe. Immediately, a gentle whoosh and a steady beat fill the air. The doctor smiles. "Your baby has a strong heartbeat already, Mr. and Mrs. Lucchetti."

Tears fill my eyes and I look up at Sly, the joy evident in his features.

"Of course they do," he says, swiping beneath his lashes at a tear. "Look at who their mother is."

"Vinnie!" Raina cries as she comes flying into my hospital room, a bouquet of flowers bigger than she is in her hands. She pushes them into Sly's chest, letting them go before he has a grasp on them, forcing him to catch them midair as they start to fall.

Cecilia comes into the room behind her, clutching a brown paper restaurant bag to her chest.

Crashing into me, Raina sits next to me on my bed, wrapping her arms around my body. "I've never been so scared in my entire life. Are you okay? Let me look at you." Her hands fluff my hair then run down my arms, as if checking that I'm in one piece.

Laughing, I tell her, "I'm fine. More than fine, really." There's a huge smile on my face, the ultrasound photos of the baby sitting beneath my thigh as I anxiously hold in the information that I'm dying to tell her and Cecilia.

But there's also a twinge of guilt in my chest, being so happy under these circumstances.

I'm not far along—about eight to ten weeks—which puts the date of conception when I went to Ridgewood while Sly was in the hospital.

I began to bawl when I pieced together the timeline, realizing that August could have killed our child when he abused me the day I returned, but my body protected it.

"We brought breakfast," Lia says, setting the bag on

the floor next to Sly's chair. "Thought you might want some comfort food."

"Bagel sandwiches?"

"Of course," she says with a grin.

Sly walks over to the counter to put the bouquet down, then returns and opens the bag, distributing the sandwiches to each of us. The scent of bacon, eggs, and buttery bagels drifts into the air and my stomach rolls, both in hunger and what I now realize is morning sickness.

"Grazie, Cecilia," he says, keeping a hold of a fourth sandwich. It brings another dopey smile to my face to know that my friends thought of him, too. Closing the distance between us, he leans down and kisses my forehead. "I'm going to give you guys some privacy and go check on your brother for an update. I'll be back. Te amo, piccola ladra."

"Thank you." I grab ahold of his hand, holding it until he steps back so far, I'm forced to let go. "Love you, too."

"You guys are sickening," Raina declares with a hint of playful mockery.

"I take that as a compliment," I brag.

"How are you doing, Vinnie? We've been so worried. We wanted to come last night, but Luciano insisted we wait. I barely slept."

"I'm so sorry I didn't reach out myself. I was in and out of sleep so much last night. I'm exhausted, but things could be worse, so I'm choosing to be grateful and stay positive. The only thing I really would love is an update on my father. The last I heard, he was in surgery, so I'm sure he's out and resting by now."

"Has your mother been by to see you?" Raina asks.

"Sly said she stopped by around six this morning, but I was still asleep, so he sent her away."

"That woman infuriates me," Lia grumbles, shaking her head.

I place my hand over hers. "I know. I've been learning to let it go."

Still holding the breakfast sandwich, I set it down behind me and grab each of my friend's hands. "I have something to tell you guys, and I was going to wait, but I don't think I can hold it in any longer."

Raina adjusts how she's seated, bringing her leg beneath her as she shifts her body toward me. Excitement bubbles through me as I let go of her hand and reach for the pictures I'm hiding, but then a small wave of sadness and guilt hits me.

This is all Cecilia has ever wanted.

*Am I a bad friend if I share news with her right now, knowing what she's going through?*

Looking down at my lap, I wonder if I actually should keep this to myself for a while longer. I don't want to hurt her.

As if she can sense what I'm about to say, she squeezes my hand and smiles. When our eyes meet, she gives me a nod, as if she knows what I'm about to say, and I can see the mix of emotions on her face.

A tear falls from my eye, and I release my hold on

the ultrasound photos, leaving them under my leg as I wipe it away.

"I'm pregnant," I tell them, never pulling my gaze from Lia's. Holding my breath, I wait to see the anger wash over her face, suddenly feeling sad about my news instead of joyous.

Raina squeals, "Oh my God, oh my God, oh my God! Vinnie!"

Tears form in Cecilia's eyes, and silently she puts her arms around my neck and pulls me to her. I start to fully cry alongside her, and we hold each other tightly. "I'm so happy for you, and proud of you, Vinnie. You're going to make the most amazing mother."

"I'm so sorry," I choke in a whisper, squeezing my eyes shut.

Roughly, she pushes me back, holding on to my shoulders. Looking me straight in the eye, she sternly says, "Don't you dare be sorry. This is your journey, and I am absolutely thrilled for you. Do you hear me? I want nothing but happiness for you. You're my best friend, and I love you so much. I can't wait to be an auntie."

"Really?" I weep.

"*Really*," she confirms, pulling me back in for a hug.

"Okay, my turn to hug my baby mama," Raina complains, and the three of us laugh together as she tosses her arms around me and Lia.

"I love you guys so much," I tell them, meaning it with every fiber of my soul.

Pressing a big kiss to my cheek, Raina quips, "Why

don't you put your money where your mouth is then, and name the baby after us? Raina and Cecilia are beautiful names. Just sayin'."

I shake my head, rolling my eyes as I pull the ultrasound photos from beneath my leg and hand them to her, and Cecilia goes to stand next to Raina to look at them.

"Definitely a Raina Cecilia in her belly, don't you agree?" Raina asks with all seriousness, looking up at Lia.

"I'm thinking more of a Cecilia Raina, but we can negotiate with her parents about it later."

"And if it's a boy?" I counter.

"It's not," Cecilia says with conviction. "That's our niece in there."

Thirty minutes later, Raina and Cecilia leave, shooed out by my doctor so they could do one final evaluation. I lay back in my bed, closing my eyes once I'm alone, exhausted and in desperate need of a nap. A daytime soap opera offers mindless chatter in the background— a subtle comfort so I don't feel alone.

I hate that I feel jumpy now, startled by every small sound I hear. Joseph stole my peace of mind, and as much as I'm grieving the loss of my brother, I also can't help but feel an overwhelming amount of anger toward him, too. Even in death, the fear left by my brother and August haunts me.

My heart skips when a light knock on the door sounds, and in walk Sly, followed by Luciano.

"You don't have to knock, Sly," I tell him as he comes to kiss me. I tilt my head up, wishing for more than the peck he gives me.

"I didn't want to startle you, amore mio."

Sly walks over to the counter where he left the bouquet Raina brought earlier, and starts busying himself with it, which I find a little strange, but then I turn my focus toward my brother, who's standing at the foot of my bed with his hands in his pockets.

"Hey, Luce," I greet with a smile. "How's Father?"

The color drains from his face and he takes the seat across from me, leaning forward on his elbows.

As I watch him, my heart begins to beat erratically, and my nerves kick in.

My brother scrubs his face with both hands, avoiding eye contact as he looks down at the floor.

He looks wrecked. Dark circles are under his eyes. His hair is a mess. There's wrinkles all over his shirt, and I know he's spent the night sleeping in a chair. It makes me wonder if Mother and Samuele did too, or if they went home to their beds while Father underwent surgery.

My stomach falls.

A dark cloud hovers over Luciano, and he scrubs his face again, the agony rolling off him in waves.

Whatever he's about to say is going to alter this family forever, and I'm not sure I'm ready to hear it.

Swallowing around the lump in my throat, my voice is small when I say his name again. "Luce?"

He looks up at me, his eyes red and raw, with a fresh lining of tears on his bottom lashes. He blows out a shuddering breath, and with a slight tremble in his chin, he says, "He's gone, V. Father is gone."

# Chapter 37

## *Sly*

The sun begins its descent as Mamma and I walk through Central Park after dinner at a nearby French bistro. With Papà working at the hospital and my brothers preoccupied, I thought it would be nice to treat Mamma to dinner and the quality time I know she has been wishing for.

Vinnie is spending the evening at her parents' house, helping her mother with funeral arrangements.

Next week, we will bury her brother, and then her father.

Maurizio's unexpected death was the one that left the Paladino family in shambles. One minute he was alert and speaking with Luciano, and the next he was gone.

Complications from his surgery.

It has been a grief-filled few days, but spending tonight with Mamma has been a welcomed and much needed distraction.

Reaching for her hand, I place it in the crook of my bent arm, leading her through the park as we stroll silently. Mamma loves Central Park, and tonight is an especially beautiful night to take a walk. The weather is perfect with the heat of the sun contrasting against the early September breeze that floats through the trees.

"Figliolo, possiamo sederci un momento?" *Son, could we sit for a moment?* Mamma asks, locating an empty bench up ahead.

"Ovviamente," *Of course,* I tell her as she steers us in the direction of it.

As we sit, the bench gives us a lovely view of open grass where children play while their parents watch. It is a humbling sight to see families enjoy a beautiful evening together. I ache to tell Mamma about Vincenza's pregnancy, but the announcement needs to come from both of us, so I bite my tongue for now.

Mamma breaks our comfortable silence. "Sono orgoglioso di te, Sylvester." *I'm proud of you, Sylvester.*

"Per cosa, Mamma?" *For what, Mamma?*

"Per sapere cosa vuoi nella vita e coglierlo. Il tuo matrimonio. La tua nuova posizione di residenza che hai accettato. Siamo molto orgogliosi dell'uomo che sei diventato." *For knowing what you want in life, and seizing it. Your marriage. Your new residency position you have accepted. We are very proud of the man you have become.*

She reaches over, taking my hand in hers. Her skin looks frail against my own, reminding me she is aging, and it breaks my heart. The pain Vinnie is harboring from the death of her father is something I very well could feel within the next decade or two, though I hope it will be much later.

Mamma has always been my rock, and here, beside her on this bench, I feel more like a boy again. Feeling compelled to confide in her, I say, "L'unica cosa di cui sono certo è la donna che ho sposato." *The only thing I'm certain of is the woman I married.*

She smiles, patting my hand. "E ne hai scelto uno buono. Lei è il tuo opposto, eppure la tua coppia perfetta. Gentile, ma forte. Tu e lei farete cose meravigliose nella vita." *And you picked a good one. She is your opposite, yet your perfect match. Gentle, yet strong. You and her will do wonderful things in life.*

"Non la merito." *I don't deserve her.*

"Certo che lo fai. Sei una persona meravigliosa. Non dubito che sarai un marito meraviglioso per lei e, un giorno, un padre straordinario per i tuoi figli." *Of course you do. You are a wonderful person. I do not doubt you will be a wonderful husband to her, and someday, an amazing father to your children.*

Mamma gestures to the families playing in the park. "Aspetto con ansia il giorno in cui mi renderai nonna. Qualche progetto per il futuro?" *I look forward to the day you make me a grandmother. Any plans for the future?*

Hesitantly, I tell her, "Vincenza ne ha passate tante, Mamma." *Vincenza has been through a lot, Mamma.*

"Sì, l'ha fatto. Ma lei guarirà, figlio mio. Ed è molto fortunata ad averti al suo fianco mentre affronta le sfide." *Yes, she has. But she will heal, my son. And she is very lucky to have you by her side while she navigates the challenges.*

"Non ti dà fastidio che sia una Paladino?" *It does not bother you that she's a Paladino?*

"Cosa c'è in un nome, Sylvester?" She shakes her head, her brow furrowing with confusion. "Toglilo e lei è solo una donna. Una donna bella, compassionevole e straordinaria che non vedo l'ora di conoscere meglio." *What's in a name, Sylvester? Take it away, and she is just a woman. A beautiful, compassionate, extraordinary woman who I am looking forward to getting to know better.*

"E Papà? Si sente lo stesso?" *And Papà? Does he feel the same?*

"Tuo padre è uno degli uomini migliori che conosca. Non la vede come nient'altro che la sua nuova nuora." *Your father is one of the best men I know. He does not view her as anything other than his new daughter-in-law.*

Her words are comforting, but there is still a weight on my soul—one person whose approval I secretly seek, who will devastate me if I never obtain it.

"E se Lorenzo non la accettasse mai? Il risentimento che nutre per il nome Paladino è più profondo delle ferite esterne. Temo che non riuscirà mai a superare i suoi legami familiari, anche ora che Maurizio se n'è andato." *What if Lorenzo never accepts her? The resentment he holds for the Paladino name is deeper than external wounds. I fear he will never see past her family ties, even now that Maurizio has passed.*

"Se tuo cugino non riesce a vedere oltre, allora è per lui con cui convivere. Non influisce su di te o sul tuo rapporto con tua moglie, né dovrebbe. Il legame che condividete tu e Lorenzo è speciale, ma non viene prima della santità del vostro matrimonio. La ami, vero?" *If your cousin cannot see past it, then that is for him to live with. It does not affect you or your relationship with your wife, nor should it. The bond you and Lorenzo share is special, but it does not come before the sanctity of your matrimony. You love her, do you not?*

Nodding my head, I answer from the depths of my heart. "Certo che lo faccio. Lei è una parte di me, mamma. Più vitale degli organi del mio corpo o dell'aria che respiro. Il mio amore per lei è infinito. Senza di lei, non ci sono io. Non più." *Of course I do. She is a part of me, Mamma. More vital than the organs in my body or the air I breathe. My love for her is infinite. Without her, there is no me. Not anymore.*

"Allora è tutto ciò di cui hai bisogno, Sylvester. Insieme, sarete voi contro il mondo per sempre." *Then that is all you need, Sylvester. Together, it will be you against the world forever.*

Her words have a sense of finality to them, but I still ask, "Lo credi davvero?" *You truly believe that?*

She laughs, her smile wide as she shakes her head like I know nothing at all. "Sì, perché l'ho vissuto, figliolo. Che tu ci creda o no, il matrimonio tra me e tuo padre non è sempre stato quello che è oggi. Abbiamo superato molti ostacoli e superato molte tempeste. Infatti tuo nonno ha quasi smesso di parlarmi quando ho incontrato il tuo Papà per la prima volta. Non sentiva di essere abbastanza bravo per me." *Yes, because I've lived it, son. Believe it or not, me and your father's marriage hasn't always been what it is today. We have lived through many *obstacles and weathered many storms. In fact, your grandfather almost stopped speaking to me when I first met your Papà. He did not feel he was good enough for me.*

And perhaps I do not know anything, because her story surprises me. I have never known anything other than love between my parents. Never witnessed a true fight between them, other than the occasional argument. Their example of love, devotion, and marriage is something I have watched wholeheartedly throughout my adolescence, hoping one day to use it as an example. So to hear there is another side to their story, is a shock to the perfect image they've always portrayed.

"Perché non me lo hai mai detto?" I ask. *Why have you never told me this?*

"Perché dovrei? Il mio lavoro è proteggerti. Racconterai ai tuoi futuri figli quello che ha appena passato Vincenza?" *Why would I? It's my job to protect you. Will you tell your future children about what Vincenza just went through?*

"Ovviamente no!" *Of course not!*

She looks at me with an expression that speaks for her. Still, she says, "Proprio per questo non ho detto a te o ai tuoi fratelli che io e tuo padre abbiamo quasi chiuso la storia prima ancora che iniziasse." *Precisely why I did not tell you or your brothers that your father and I almost called it quits before it even began.*

"Quello che è successo?" *What happened?*

"Questa è una storia per un altro giorno, figlio mio. Vieni, si sta facendo tardi, il sole è quasi tramontato. È ora che mi porti a casa così potrai tornare da tua moglie." *That's a story for another day, my son. Come, it is getting late—the sun is almost down. It is time for you to take me home so you can return to your wife.*

Standing, I help Mamma to her feet, placing my hand on the middle of her back to guide her through the park and to where we left my SUV. Warmth floods my heart as we enjoy small talk and the rest of the beautiful sunset, strolling slowly together.

When I open the passenger door, I kiss the side of her head before helping her to get in. "Grazie per avermi accompagnato a cena, mamma." *Thank you for accompanying me to dinner, Mamma.*

Reaching up, she touches her palm to my cheek, looking at me with the same love pouring from her that I was lucky enough to grow up with. "Certo, Sylvester. Sarai sempre il mio ragazzino." *Of course, Sylvester. You will always be my little boy.*

# Chapter 38

## *Vinnie*

Grief is a fickle thing. One moment, you can be going about your day as normal, and the next you're breaking down in the middle of a busy sidewalk, so inundated with sadness it physically hurts to move.

My grief is like driftwood riding on an ocean wave—calm and steady, floating beneath the bright sun, until the tide picks up and suddenly the driftwood is pulled beneath a wave by force, unable to fight its way back to the surface until the water mollifies.

Throughout my days, I'm strong for my mother. I take on the planning of the funerals because she's so consumed by her grief she can barely make it out of bed in the morning.

Every day passes like it's been a thousand years, and I'm forced to hold it together for the sake of my family, until the night falls and I'm back home in Sly's arms, where I can finally crumble.

My husband is my solace. Patient and kind, he holds

me tightly in our bed, stroking my hair while he allows me to completely shatter, knowing it's what I need to heal.

He feeds me. Makes sure I'm staying hydrated. Even bathes me when I'm too weak to do it myself.

I don't know what I'd do without him.

I don't know what I did to *deserve* him.

"Tell me what you need, piccola ladra," he says, kissing my temple as the family limo pulls in front of the gravesite for my father's funeral.

We buried my brother three days ago in a burial much smaller than the one planned for my father.

Looking out the window, there are a hundred or so chairs facing an open hole in the ground, and my father's closed coffin held up by supports.

Almost every chair is filled, except for the front row, which has been saved for us.

Across the limo, mother sobs quietly into Luciano's jacket as he holds her, and Samuele stares down at his lap, like he did the entire ride over.

"I don't know what I need," I tell Sly, answering his question. Sadness sits heavy in my chest and I know for the time being, there is no remedy.

The driver opens the door, and my husband slides out first, holding his hand to help me. I take it, and pull myself out, the skirt of my black dress billowing down to my knees as I stand. Lowering my sunglasses, I allow Sly to guide me over to the chairs as the rest of my family gets out of the limo.

An endless sea of black apparel and gloomy faces

watches us all closely as we take our seats in the front row and wait for the eulogist to begin. Lacing my arm around Sly's, he places his hand on my thigh, stroking it with his thumb. It brings me comfort and allows me to push back the tears I'm holding in.

"Ladies and gentlemen," the eulogist greets. "It is with great sorrow that we gather here today to honor and remember a life who was not only impactful to his family, but to his community. Maurizio Paladino touched the lives of many, and to know him was to respect and appreciate the great gifts he gave to those whose lives he entered. I'd like to call upon his brother, Marcel, to speak a few words."

My mother grabs my hand from my lap, pulling it into hers.

As my uncle begins to speak about my father, I close my eyes and let myself drift to the recesses of my mind in an effort to push past my grief. I think of my child-hood and the happy memories with my father, seeing them flash through my mind like a movie in slow motion. The memories progress from my childhood to my adulthood, the recent years flashing through my mind more prominently—even the less than desirable moments. Then my thoughts drift to Sly, the baby, and the family we're creating.

I lose all perception of how much time has passed, and before I know it, everyone is standing in prepara-tion to say goodbye to my father for the last time.

One by one, guests step forward to pay their respects, placing a rose on top of his casket or simply touching the side of it. They give us their condolences, and many hug my mother, praising her strength, and my father's life and accomplishments.

I don't hear a word that is said, but beside me, Sly thanks each person who steps forward to speak to us.

The only thing I'm feeling is numb when it's finally just my family left at the gravesite.

My mother's tears have intensified, and this time, it's Samuele who comforts her, sitting with her, rubbing her back.

"Are we ready?" a man asks, approaching with another. He gestures to the coffin.

Luciano nods, his voice strained when he answers, "Yes."

Sly and I walk to the side of the grave, standing with my brother as we watch the men lower my father in the ground.

Birds chirp around us, and a light breeze blows, reminding me that love still continues, even when it feels like it's standing still.

I wish I had more time. I'm not ready to say goodbye.

Tears line my lashes, spilling over silently. Sly wraps his arm around my shoulders, rubbing the top of my arm, trying to bring me a sense of comfort.

But I realize at this moment, through all of his flaws, all I really want is one more hug from my father.

"I can't believe this is it," Luciano comments, his jaw clenched. I can see him forcing the emotions back, refusing to let them show. "I wasn't prepared to say goodbye so soon."

"Neither was I."

When the coffin is completely lowered, the men give us privacy. The five of us just stare at the top of the mahogany box my father rests in, and I can't help but wonder if I should have brought roses to place on top of it as well.

"I'm going to wait in the car with Mom," Samuele tells us, guiding her past the grave. She glances in and stifles another sob, leaning into him for support.

"Be there soon," Luciano confirms. Walking over to the mound of dirt next to the grave, he picks up a handful, then walks back over to stand beside me. "Until we meet again, Father. I'll miss you," he speaks quietly, then he lets the dirt fall from his hand and onto the casket.

Swallowing around the lump in my throat, I go pick up my own handful of dirt and hold it above where my father rests. Everything I want to say to him escapes me, so I simply whisper, "I love you, Daddy." Then I let the dirt fall as I cry.

Lifting my sunglasses, I wipe the tears before resting them on top of my head.

Luciano stares blankly at where the dirt just landed, not looking at me as he says the thing that's been haunting the back of my mind for the last several days. "Father is gone now, Vinnie, and so is Joseph. I've made it very clear I want nothing to do with the businesses, which means they fall to you. What are you going to do with them?"

Sly reaches down and laces his fingers through mine, and I recognize it as a sign of solidarity. Whatever decision I make, he supports me.

I've been thinking about this moment all week, knowing the decision would have to be voiced. It's weighed heavily on me, but I know in my heart it's the right choice, and the only one I can imagine making.

A small smile upturns the corner of my lips as a sense of peace washes over me—perhaps, after everything that's happened, Father would support this decision too.

The only thing the businesses have done in my life has been to destroy one of the relationships I valued most.

Looking at Luciano, I utter the two words that my intuition has been screaming at me for days, feeling ready to close the door on this chapter of our lives.

"Dismantle them."

"My bounty is as boundless as the sea,
My love as deep; the more I give to thee,
The more I have, for both are infinite."

*Act 2, Scene 2 - Romeo & Juliet*
*William Shakespeare*

# Epilogue

## Sly

*Two Years Later*

"Dada! Duckie!" Emilia squeals as she chases after a plump white duck who's trying to find its way back to the pond.

Deep brown ringlets bounce as she toddles her way down the path of Shakespeare's Garden in Central Park. The garden is in full bloom, and though it once held a memory of intense pain, it now is being replaced with happiness.

Long ago, I watched a family enjoy the grounds as my heart shattered. Now, being here with my family, it feels like it is coming full circle as Vincenza and I follow behind our daughter, hand in hand, enjoying the first warm day this spring.

Life with Emilia has been utterly blissful. Since the moment she entered the world and opened her bright blue eyes, I was forever changed. I've marveled at the joy of watching her grow and explore, all the while falling deeper in love with Vinnie as I've witnessed her settle into motherhood.

"Do you think it's time to give Emilia a sibling?" I ask, sweeping my hand beneath Vinnie's hair and gently rubbing the back of her neck.

"She's not even two!" She laughs, shimmying out of my hold. "I didn't realize barefoot and pregnant was something you'd be so fond of, Mr. Lucchetti."

"I didn't realize how sexy motherhood would be on you, Mrs. Lucchetti." I grab her wrist and pull her to me. Nuzzling my nose against her cheek, I growl, "I will happily put as many babies inside of you as you will allow me to, piccola ladra."

"Two will be plenty," she quips, pushing out of my hold so she can keep a better eye on Emilia.

"When?"

She smiles coyly, shaking her head. "You really want another baby so soon?"

"What's not to want? Emilia is perfect. Just like you."

Sighing, she leans into me, and presses up on her tiptoes to kiss my lips. "Always charming me, aren't you?"

"I promised you I'd never stop."

"Dada!" Emilia squeals again, pulling my attention from her mother. Scooping her into my arms, I pepper kisses all over her face while she wiggles against my grasp. "Down, peas!"

Laughing, I set her down, and she begins chasing

another duck that's just emerged from behind a lavender bush.

"So, baby number two…" Vinnie begins, lacing her fingers through mine again. I quirk a brow, her tone of voice makes my heart skip a beat, and when I look down at her, she's biting her lip.

"Should we start practicing this evening, piccola ladra?"

"There's no need to practice. You're already a professional and have succeeded." She giggles, and the sound, along with her words, are like music to my ears.

"You're pregnant?" I ask, excitement pouring out of me as I stare at her wide-eyed.

"I'm pregnant!"

Beyond thrilled, I pick her up and spin her around as she laughs. When she's firmly on her feet again, I grab her face in my hands and kiss her, absolutely speechless by the excitement I'm feeling.

She's made me a father again.

Just as I deepen the kiss, the piercing sound of Emilia's cries emit through the air and Vinnie and I pull apart. Immediately, she springs into action, racing the short distance to where Emilia lies on the ground, crying after falling down.

Vincenza lowers herself to tend to her, running her fingers along her slightly bloody knee, and I watch her in awe.

My heart inflates as I admire the woman before me, kneeling in the dirt to wipe our daughter's scrape, and I thank God, as I do daily, for the woman he made specifically for me to love.

My life could have been drastically different had we never met. From the age of nine, she captivated me, and though we both resisted, fate had a plan much bigger than either of us.

Vincenza completes me, and I cherish every day we spend together, looking forward to our future together as we grow old.

And when the time comes for us to pass on, I hope I am the first to go.

Because a world without her is not a world worth living in, and I can say with utmost certainty that my final breath on this Earth will be her name.

# CAN'T GET ENOUGH OF THE BOY BANTER?

*Download the Sins of Bliss Bonus Chapter!*

# Acknowledgments

I can't believe the time has already come to say goodbye to Sly and Vinnie. A huge chunk of my heart and soul went into this duet and I hope you loved it as much as I did. This cast of characters will always hold a special place in my heart.

I'd like to extend a million thank you's to my amazing editor, Virginia Tesi Carey, for putting up with me even though the manuscript was delivered to her a month late. I appreciate you more than words can describe! Thank you to Barbara Hoover for ensuring my Italian translations of the beautiful language are accurate throughout both Sins of Sorrow and Sins of Bliss.

Another very special thank you goes out Ellyn Leuelling for not only stepping in as my proofreader, but for pushing me to say "hold my latte" and inspiring me to write the Biblioteca Capitolare spicy scene.

Thank you so much to my amazing alpha readers (DeLynda, Cassie, and Amanda) and my team of beta's (Megan, Kendra, and Manda), my PA, Cassie, and the dedicated readers on my street team, ARC team, and influencer team!

I love and appreciate you all so much.

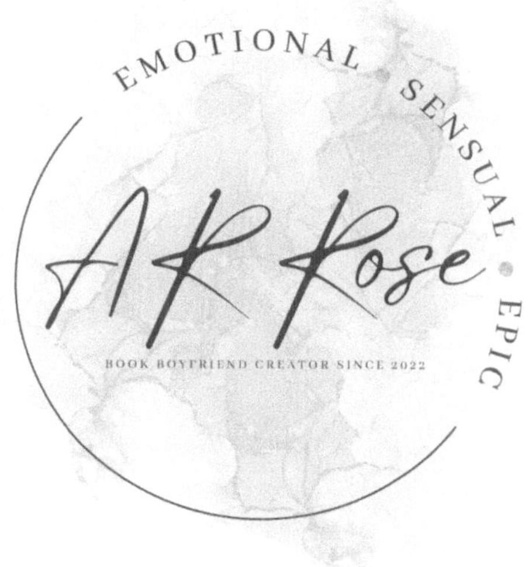



A.R. Rose's greatest job in life is being a mom to her two boys. She is a born and raised California native who loves to hang out at home with her kids and her dog.

A.R. realized her passion for writing in the third grade, although it wasn't until early 2022 when she began to pursue it. Now, if she skips a day of writing, she feels as though her day is incomplete.

On any given day, you will find A.R. toting around her laptop and her Kindle, with a coffee in hand, daydreaming about the characters and worlds she's building. She is grateful to have the opportunity to bring her stories to life and is excited about her journey as a romance writer.

# CONNECT

**Join A.R. Rose's newsletter for info & updates**

https://www.authorarrose.com/email-subscribe

**Website**

www.authorarrose.com

**Reading Group**

https://www.facebook.com/groups/authorarrose

**Facebook**

https://www.facebook.com/authorarrose

**TikTok**

https://www.tiktok.com/@authorarrose

**Instagram**

https://www.instagram.com/authorarrose

Ready to go to Ridgewood?

Continue reading for a standalone romance that
will keep you hooked page after page!

# WRECK
# ME

## A.R. ROSE

💋 Rich Girl Poor Boy
💋 Strangers to Lovers
💋 Emotional Scars / Keeping a Secret
💋 Small Town
💋 Insta-lust/love

# Chapter One

## *Isla*

"I'm so sorry, Miss, but I can't let you check out a library book when you have a dollar twenty-three balance due on your account. The system won't allow me to override it."

"I… but, I somehow left my wallet at home…" I frantically murmured to the older gentleman behind the checkout counter as I sifted through my Louis Vuitton bag. A fierce heat coated my cheeks as the embarrassment set in and sweat pooled at my hairline. The eyes of several other library patrons watching—*judging*—my every move grew heavy on my back. I bit my tongue to keep the tears that flooded my eyes from spilling over.

If my father could see me now, he'd be staring at me with a smug grin on his face, readying himself to gloat to whoever would listen, saying I'd come crawling back to my trust fund any day now. Since the moment I had left the house with my luggage in tow and hopped into my Mercedes S Class—which, unfortunately, he had paid for—I had been the object of his ridicule.

Actually, let's back up.

Since before I was born, I had been the object of his ridicule. His lack of confidence in me was not something he was interested in hiding.

It had been a long couple of years at college, and despite being excruciatingly tired of ramen noodles made on a stove that only worked half the time, I had refused to ask for any more help than the agreed-upon amount my mother sent me monthly. We bickered for weeks about how much I should receive and, ultimately; I had won. I would receive monthly deposits to keep my modest one-bedroom apartment's rent paid and the utilities on. My parents also covered my car insurance and cell phone bills, so my primary responsibilities were food, gas, and anything extra I wanted to buy.

Fourteen hundred dollars.

Some months I had extra to spend, and other months, such as this, my empty wallet was "accidentally" left at home in fear I would spend my last few dollars on something stupid.

*Poor little broke rich girl.*

God, I still sounded like a snob.

The clearing of a throat snapped me back to reality. "I understand, Miss, I do, but perhaps you can come back later when—"

"Excuse me, sir? I can cover the balance for her." A man who looked just slightly older than me stepped forward from his place in line with a five-dollar bill in his outstretched hand.

Words escaped me as I stared at this stranger who had just become my library knight in shining armor.

Short chestnut locks fell in front of his deep brown eyes while the rest hung haphazardly, looking like it desperately needed to be brushed. His light gray t-shirt clung to the muscles that were so clearly hidden beneath, looked worn and had pinholes scattered near the collar and hemline. My eyes traveled further to take in the rest of his appearance, and it conflicted me with what to think. He didn't look dirty, per se, but he looked unkempt. It was hard to tell if he was poor or if he just didn't care.

*And I was judging.* I was judging the man who had stepped up to pay my dollar twenty-three balance so I could check out a freaking library book.

Sometimes I really hated the way my parents conditioned me to think.

My mouth hung agape when he turned around and I finally got a good look at his face, not just his profile. His eyes were so dark, they were nearing black. I bit my lip to keep from salivating over his sharp features and the sexy slight bump in his nose as if he had gotten into one too many fistfights. He was everything I dared to dream about, and everything my father would hate. The sort of bad boy slash grungy 'I don't give a damn' vibe he emulated made my heart skip a beat.

Trying my best to hide my idiotic smile, I could barely register a coherent thought as he paid the balance. The *beep* of the machine processing my book's check out emitted into the air. My smile faded, bursting the lust-filled bubble I was caught in, as he thrust my now checked-out book into my hands and rushed past me to dart out the door.

"I—uh," I stuttered, my brain catching up to his hasty departure, before I flew toward the door after him. I had to at least thank him, right?

The cool, early-fall air assaulted my senses as I stepped out onto the library's stoop. My library knight had just barely made it to the street corner when I screamed out, "Wait! Stop! Please."

To my surprise, he heard me and stopped immediately, but didn't turn around. I moved as quickly as my Jimmy Choo's would get me to him and nearly collided into his back, my body gaining more momentum than I had expected. With his back still to me, I could see the movement of his chest rising and falling by the way his shoulders slightly rocked, as though he was angry and trying to rein in his temper. Still, he didn't turn around.

"I—uh," I stuttered again, finding it hard to formulate the words. "I wanted to say thank you. For paying my balance at the library. I left my wallet at home," I lied, but I didn't feel the need to explain the truth. "It must have fallen out of my purse when I sat it down on my entryway table. I should have double checked when I got home earlier, but I was so excited the text had come through from the library saying the book I put on hold was ready. So I just grabbed everything and ran out the door. I didn't realize my last book was overdue and I would have a balance on my—"

"Do you always ramble when you try to thank someone for a deed that doesn't deserve praise?" he questioned, his voice dry and petulant. Slowly, he turned his body so he could see me, pinning me in his gaze.

I stared at him with what I could only imagine was a shocked expression. People, especially men, weren't typically curt with me. My entire life, I'd been treated like a porcelain doll, spoken to like a child, as though I couldn't understand. Raised in a family where children were to be 'seen, not heard', and unfortunately it was something I had grown accustomed to.

The candidness was refreshing.

"Excuse me?" I questioned back, wondering if I had, in fact, heard him correctly.

This time, he turned to face me completely, and I sucked in a breath, overwhelmed by his very presence. "I paid your balance. It's not a big deal," he told me with a hint of irritation in his voice.

The entire world faded to black around me. The only thing I could see was him, and the only sound I could hear was the pounding of my heart. "It is a big deal," I whispered, unable to look away from him. His eyes dipped down to my lips before snapping back to mine.

I was dying to reach out and touch him—his face, his arm, whatever I could.

*What was it about him that made me feel like this?*

His eyebrow shot up, and he assessed me through narrowing eyes. "It's really not. Like I said, it was a dollar."

"Dollar twenty-three," I corrected, as he turned away again. Without thinking, I reached out, wanting to stop him from leaving. My fingertips brushed against his, and he instantly yanked his hand back like I had electrocuted him. He took a step away from me, his brows scrunched together in a glare. It still looked like he was about to flee, and the air constricted in my lungs. "I'm sorry. I don't know why I did that."

He grunted, not giving me any more of his time, before he turned on his heel and walked away.

"Wait!" I shouted desperately, following him. "Please, wait a second. What's your name?"

His head shook slightly, but he didn't stop again or give me the decency to turn around as he spoke. "You're better off not knowing, Starlight."

*Starlight? What did that mean?*

"What kind of answer is that? I want to know." My tone was demanding, prissy. It was the tone I often used when I wanted to get my way—an art I had perfected.

He ignored me and kept going.

"I'm Isla, Isla Donohue," I called after him, but his pace didn't waver as he kept walking down the busy sidewalk. I, however, stopped walking and watched him weave through the bodies, never once turning to look back at me. My shoulders sagged and the feeling of defeat washed over me.

I hated not knowing if I would ever see him again.
My library knight in shining armor.

# Chapter Two

## *Caleb*

Two paper bags stacked full of groceries threatened to fall from my arms as I struggled to unlock the front door of the piece of shit decrepit house I shared with my equally shitty old man.

Almost twenty-two years old and I was still living with my deadbeat dad, who still hadn't learned when to put down the bottle.

Shoving the door closed with the heel of my worn sneaker, it slammed and shook the entire frame of the small two-bedroom, one-bath roof over our head.

As usual, dad was passed out on his old as fuck, blueish-gray recliner wearing only boxers and a stained wife-beater that barely covered his giant beer belly. His mouth hung open as he snored, with a bottle of Jack about to fall out of his grasp.

"Fucking cliché," I murmured to myself as I readjusted the grocery bags and stomped into the kitchen.

Setting them down on the kitchen counter, I started pulling the contents out of the bags to put them away.

I needed to get the hell out of this house, out of Ridgewood all together. This city had nothing to offer me—it never had. Nothing more than crushed dreams and a broken family. Can you even call it a family, though, when it's just you and your alcoholic Pops?

Back in high school, I had dreamt of going off to college, living in a dorm, and partying my way through the semesters, just like the rest of my friends. But lady luck had different plans when I received acceptance letters to every single school I applied to, just no scholarships. Guys like me couldn't afford college, let alone an Ivy, without a scholarship.

So, unlike my friends, I stayed behind, stuck in Ridgewood pushing through community college. Eventually, I transferred to Ridgewood University to finish the last portion of my bachelor's degree in science. I made it through the years by applying for every grant and private scholarship I could get my hands on and financing student loans for the rest. It wasn't ideal, but I needed to take things one step at a time. Step one was getting the degree. I needed that stupid piece of paper to get a move on with my life, and I wouldn't stop until I had it. My degree would get me one step closer to being a forensic analyst. Later I'd figure out how to pay for it.

My curiosity about science began when I was young and wanted to play mad scientist by mixing random things together. But after years of watching true crime shows after my dad had passed out, drunk off his ass, I developed a new curiosity about things like blood spatter and evidence—crime scenes in general.

After many discussions with my high school science teacher on the topics, he encouraged me to pursue a career as a forensic analyst or something similar. I had no idea what it was, but after spending some time researching, it seemed like a solid option. And working for the police department would just be icing on the cake, knowing I'd have a job that'd pay me decently and give me something I hadn't had in years: health insurance.

Yes, I had officially hit the point in my life where I was looking forward to having health insurance. My current job at the Pack N Mail gave me some money in my pocket and kept me fed, but the owner didn't offer health insurance for part-time employees, which I had to be, thanks to my grueling school schedule. I had been maxing out my units to try to finish sooner—shave off a semester or more—eager to find a department that'd hire me on and allow me to gain experience in the field.

The closer I got to finishing, the more I daydreamed about which police departments I would apply to. With every hopeful glance at the map, my eyes wandering over different cities and states, the pit in my stomach grew. I would never leave Ridgewood. How could I?

It was because of my dad's addiction to alcohol that I stayed. If I left Ridgewood, my old man would drink himself to death. He already basically did, killing off a bottle almost daily. Passing out, breaking shit. He was a messy drunk, and there were times I had to clean up his vomit and piss, too.

I hated it. But what kind of son would I be if I left town knowing it would ultimately mean my father would probably die?

I resented the life I lived and frequently wondered what type of life I might have if my mother had stayed.

The preemptive guilt of abandoning my dad had me in a chokehold. I was stuck. He needed me around to babysit him. Do welfare checks and shit.

Life had me by the balls and was laughing in my face, shitting on me every chance it got. It was as though I had a neon sign on me flashing "BAD LUCK STRIKE HERE", because it was literally one thing after another.

That's how it'd been all week long. My car's dash had more lights on it than a Christmas tree, and a new light indicating another problem just popped up. My boss cut my hours this week because she had incorrectly scheduled another employee and had to make up their hours. And if that wasn't enough, I completely fucked off and forgot about a huge test I needed to study for in advanced chem and probably fucking failed it.

Just when I thought I was really down on my luck, sitting at the library working on my anatomy homework, I saw *her*, and I suddenly felt like the luckiest bastard alive.

Isla Donohue. *Isla.*

Even her name was as mystical as she was. I had never seen such a strikingly beautiful woman until I saw her in the library, gnawing on the end of her pen, deep in concentration. Her stack of textbooks told me she was in college, thank fuck, because it was practically love at first sight and if she had been underage, I would have died. From the looks of it, she was taking business classes, which baffled me since the clothing she wore screamed *money*. I would guess she didn't need to work a day in her life, but despite the shiny exterior, something told me she was more than what meets the eye.

For nearly two weeks, I felt like a stalker as I sat at a table directly on the· other side of the shelves from where she sat, my position giving me the perfect vantage point to peer at her through the books.

Like. A. Fucking. Creeper.

Yet I couldn't stop myself from taking the same table every single day hoping when she came in, she'd find *her* table, too.

And she always did, like the good girl she was.

My intention was always to watch from afar and silently worship the ground she walked on, but when she forgot her wallet and couldn't check out her book, I could hear the wobble in her voice—practically see the quiver of her lip. She was embarrassed, and I wanted nothing more than to shield her from the embarrassment. Reflex kicked in and before I could stop myself, I had already made myself known.

The moment I opened my mouth was the moment I knew I had sucked myself into her orbit. Stepping out from a few people behind her in line, I offered to pay her balance, and I handed the guy a five. Once I could see the transaction was finished, I practically threw her book at her and bolted out the door as quickly as I could. The book I had wanted to check out was left abandoned on a shelf by the exit.

Maybe it'd be there waiting next time. Or maybe I'd forget the title and it wouldn't even matter anymore.

I *had* to run. She was too pretty, too perfect. Too out of my league.

The world crashed down around me when she caught up with me, calling out for me to stop. To talk to her.

And then she touched me… I almost fucking lost it right then and there. The raw fucking need I felt to pull her body flush with mine and kiss the shit out of her—like I said, I nearly lost it.

Even her name was beautiful—one that'd haunt me in my dreams.

*Isla Donohue.*

The unmistakable sound of glass shattering pulled me from my dream and I groaned, rubbing my fists into my eyes to wake up. The red glare from the alarm clock on my bedside table read it was nearing three in the morning, and I cursed my father for whatever drunken stupor he had found himself in this time.

Tossing the comforter off my naked body, I stepped onto the cool tile and made my way to my dresser to grab a pair of sweatpants. My cock was half-mast from a hot dream when I woke, but now hung completely flaccid as I raked a hand down my face and made my way into the pitch-black hallway.

As I entered the living room, I could see my father's legs perched on the couch while his upper body laid on the end table, illuminated by the moonlight coming through the broken curtains. A smashed bottle of vodka was on the floor below him, while a broken lamp hung between his grasp, dangling less than an inch from the shards of glass below it.

"The fuck, old man?" I growled into the room, knowing my words were to no one—he was out cold.

Taking my time, I walked into the kitchen and grabbed the broom and dustpan, carrying it back with me to my bedroom so I could slip on a pair of flip-flops I owned for situations like these.

Once back to where my father laid snoring, I removed the broken lamp from his hold and unplugged it, setting it down on the floor behind me before I cleaned up the glass. I didn't bother trying to wake him up or move him, but I would clean up the glass fragments so he wouldn't get hurt when he inevitably fell off the table and couch.

He needed help. Over the years, I had tried everything, but we couldn't afford rehab centers, and the resources the city offered were worthless. He tried and failed more times than I could count. His sponsor quit on him, my mother left him, and I... Well, I'm still here, but evidently am not enough of a reason for him to get sober.